"EVERYTHING ELSE SEEMS TO HAVE CHANGED, BUT NOT YOU. YOU STILL LOOK JUST LIKE YOU DID BACK IN HIGH SCHOOL."

"Do I?" He laughed. "Then that brings to light one more change right there—that you need glasses." Rohn grinned as she rolled her eyes at his teasing.

For the first time during the encounter, the smile she flashed him seemed genuine and not forced. "I don't need glasses. It's true."

"Well, you don't look the same."

She lifted her brow high. "Well, it has been twenty-five years."

She'd taken the comment as an insult, but she was wrong. He hadn't meant it as such. Rohn was at the age he knew experience created beauty, not youth.

"I meant, you look even better than you did back then."

MIDNIGHT
Wrangler

CAT JOHNSON

ZEBRA BOOKS
KENSINGTON PUBLISHING CORP.
http://www.kensingtonbooks.com

ZEBRA BOOKS are published by

Kensington Publishing Corp.
119 West 40th Street
New York, NY 10018

All Kensington titles, imprints and distributed lines are available at special quantity discounts for bulk purchases for sales promotion, premiums, fund-raising, educational or institutional use.

Special book excerpts or customized printings can also be created to fit specific needs. For details, write or phone the office of the Kensington Sales Manager. Attn.: Sales Department. Kensington Publishing Corp., 119 West 40th Street, New York, NY 10018. Phone: 1-800-221-2647.

Zebra and the Z logo Reg. U.S. Pat. & TM Off.

First Printing: December 2015
ISBN-13: 978-1-4201-3623-4
ISBN-10: 1-4201-3623-2

eISBN-13: 978-1-4201-3624-1
eISBN-10: 1-4201-3624-0

10 9 8 7 6 5 4 3 2 1

Printed in the United States of America

For all the cheerleaders who keep me writing,
be they near or far, online or in real life.

For the real Rohn and Colton,
the Alaskan cowboys I met in Vegas,
who gave me both inspiration and the use of their names.

For all my Oklahoma peeps,
who always make this New Yorker wish I was
there with them eating barbecue.

For Eliza Gayle, my word sprint partner,
who kept me in line when my chronic procrastination
threatened to take over.

Chapter One

Some days, no matter what a man did, nothing seemed to go right. Today at the Double L Ranch was one of those days.

Rohn Lerner let out a sigh tinged with frustration as he found his three ranch hands shooting the breeze by the barn instead of tackling all the chores that needed to get done.

"Hey!" He strode toward the group.

"Hey, boss." Tyler tipped his chin in Rohn's direction. "What's up?"

Tyler was usually the ringleader of the lazy hands so his *what's up* particularly rubbed Rohn the wrong way today. They'd know what was up if they weren't so busy jabbering.

Rohn came to a stop as he reached the three young men. "The bull pushed over the water trough again."

Tyler glanced at the field where the bull was currently penned without water. He scrunched up his face and looked back to Rohn. "Yeah, I saw that before."

Rohn's eyes widened at the revelation. "Then why aren't you over there refilling it?"

These boys had been working for Rohn for enough years that they should know what to do without him having to tell them.

Colton knocked his hat back a notch. "We're fixin' to get to it, Rohn. Relax."

"You're fixin' to get to it?" Being told to relax by an employee half his age made Rohn's blood pressure rise. "And when would that be, this *getting to it?*"

"We were going to head over right after lunch." Justin, a couple years older and apparently wiser than the other two, stepped in with his attempt to soothe the situation.

"That bull is worth his weight in cash, so how about if he gets his water before y'all get your lunch?" Rohn would really like to know when the youth of this country had been taught that it was all right to talk back to their boss. Probably about the same time they'd convinced themselves it was all right to put off doing important tasks until later.

Justin gave a nod. "A'ight, Rohn. Sorry, but you know in this kinda weather the hose bakes in the sun and we have to drain the hot water outta it before we can fill the tanks. I just figured since we were going to scrub and refill all the buckets after lunch anyway, we'd take care of it then instead of wasting the water draining it twice."

They had been through some pretty bad droughts lately in this part of the country, and wildfires were always an issue in Oklahoma. Justin's point about saving water was a valid one, but Rohn was in no mood to concede that.

He cocked one brow. "Then maybe you outta finish all the watering now and then take a late lunch."

Tyler blew out a breath. "Somebody's cranky today."

"Today?" Colton frowned beneath the brim of his cowboy hat. "Try every damn day lately."

"Yeah?" Rohn lifted his brows high and hooked a thumb toward the drive. "There's the way out. Y'all feel free to hit the road and look for another job whenever you want."

Colton snickered. "Yeah. All right."

It was Rohn's own damn fault. He'd always been more of a friend to these kids than a boss. He'd joke around and act like a buddy, but in his current mood that last threat hadn't been completely in jest.

Tyler turned to Colton and Justin. "Can you two go on over, right that trough and start on the water? I'll meet you out there in a bit and we'll figure out how to make it stay upright for good this time."

Colton's mouth dropped open. "Since when do you get to tell Justin and me what to do?"

"Since I wanna talk to Rohn alone for a minute." Tyler crossed his arms over his chest, not backing down.

"Come on, Colt. Let's go." Justin tipped his head toward the field.

Colton continued to sputter. "But why should we?"

"So we can talk crap about Ty behind his back, that's why." With a grin, Justin winked at Tyler and pivoted on the heel of one boot toward the pasture. Colton shot Tyler a parting glance that expressed exactly what he thought about the situation, but followed Justin.

Once they were gone, Tyler turned to Rohn. A crease furrowed the forehead above his dark brows. "You a'ight? You need to talk?"

Rohn let out a snort. "What, are you a therapist now?"

"No, I'm your friend. And it wasn't too long ago you pulled me aside to talk privately when I was wrestling with some shit of my own. Remember?"

That all had been barely a couple of months ago. Back when Rohn had been dumb or desperate enough to listen to Colton and ask his widowed neighbor Janie out on a date. Rohn remembered that dinner with Janie, as well as the exact moment he'd figured out that the woman already had feelings for Tyler.

That's what Rohn got for taking relationship advice from a twentysomething-year-old cowboy with little experience and no serious girlfriend that he knew of.

Meanwhile, being twenty-four and dense as a lump of coal, Tyler had been too young and stupid to realize how Janie felt until Rohn had explained it to him.

Nope. Rohn hadn't forgotten any of it. "Yeah, I remember. Except what you were wrestling with was that a beautiful, smart, intelligent woman was in love with you. So, I'm sure that *shit* wasn't all that difficult for you to get over."

Tyler tipped his head. "I was miserable for a while, just the same, and you stepped in and straightened me out."

"Somebody had to." Proven by the fact that since that conversation, as far as Rohn could see, the couple was not only together, but looking pretty serious. If he wasn't mistaken, Tyler was all but living at Janie's. "So are you officially moved in to her place yet, or just staying over there every night?"

Tyler opened his eyes wide. "Wait a minute. Is that what this crap mood of yours is about? You're upset I'm with Janie?"

"No, I'm not upset you're with Janie." Rohn shook his head, sorry he'd said anything at all. "As long as you're treating her right, I'm happy for her and for you. That's not it at all."

"Then what is it?" Beneath the brim of his hat, Tyler drew his brows low.

"Nothing." His love life, or lack of one, was one thing Rohn didn't want to discuss with a cocky twenty-four-year-old who had everything in the world at his fingertips and his whole future ahead of him.

"Rohn, come on. Just spill it." Tyler crossed his arms and leaned back against the fence, as if he was willing to wait as long as it took.

Damn persistent kid. Rohn silently mouthed a cuss, but finally gave in. "I guess I'm just kinda lonely sometimes, okay?"

Tyler threw his hands in the air. "That's why I've been telling you to come out with us. You ain't meeting any girls here at the ranch."

"And I told you I don't want to meet *girls* and I'm not going to find a woman of any substance at the bars where you yahoos hang out."

"Then set up one of those online dating accounts. They have them for older folks now."

"Older folks?" Rohn let out a snort as that hit him hard, like a punch to the gut. "Great. Thanks a lot."

How the hell old did these kids think he was,

anyway? Rohn had quite a few years left before he turned fifty. Enough years he felt justified still holding on tight to his claim of being in his early forties. Okay, maybe he was inching closer to his *mid*forties, but still.

"I'm not trying to insult you, Rohn. I'm just trying to give you some options."

"Well, no offense, Tyler, and thanks for trying, but I don't like your options."

The kid had work to do still, and lunch to eat, but he didn't seem to be in any hurry to get going. Tyler stayed put, eyeing Rohn. "You know, if it's just sex you're missing, there are girls you can call for that. . . ."

"Jesus, Tyler. Please stop talking." Rohn scrubbed his hands over his face, ignoring the dust and dirt he'd probably smeared all over himself.

"I'm serious. You can probably ask for any age woman you want, too, if you don't want a girl who's too young."

Letting out a laugh at the ridiculousness of this surreal conversation, Rohn still couldn't help but ask, "How the hell would you know about any of that?"

Rohn had no doubt this former playboy had never had to hire a professional in that area. Before settling into a relationship with Janie, Tyler was the type of guy who would never have come home from a rodeo or a night out on the town without a willing recipient of his affections in his passenger seat.

Sure, over the years Tyler had probably spent a small fortune buying drinks for women before he got a little loving in return, but to outright pay a prostitute for sex? No way. Rohn couldn't see it happening. Not for Tyler and definitely not for himself.

"I planned my brother's bachelor party. The place

I hired the stripper from also offers girls who provide *other services,* if you know what I mean. I have the phone number—" Tyler reached to pull his cell phone out of his jeans pocket.

Rohn threw up one hand to stop him. "No. Enough. I don't want the number. Not now. Not ever. Okay?"

The dead last thing Rohn needed was Tyler putting some stupid idea into his head about paying a woman to have sex with him. Worse, as the years of celibacy since his wife Lila's death started to add up to be more than he could count on one hand, the idea didn't seem as horrifying to him as it should.

He'd been lucky enough to love two women in his life. Bonnie Martin for that single magical perfect summer after high school. And Lila, who'd been his wife and best friend for the fifteen years they were married.

Rohn knew finding love again, a third time and at his age, was a long shot. But that didn't mean he was willing to explore the alternative Tyler had suggested.

"Okay, but if you change your mind . . ." Tyler let the suggestion hang in the air.

This conversation had gone on for too long already, and all it had done was make Rohn more agitated. He'd gone from cranky to being both appalled and needy. As crazy as it seemed, talking about strippers and hookers had woken up his long suppressed sex drive.

With his luck, he'd probably call for a woman to come over and get robbed by some con artist posing as a hooker. Or he'd end up sending her home after one look because she'd be young enough to have been his daughter. Even though Rohn was childless, he knew the girl would be some man's little girl, and Rohn would never be able to get that out of his head.

He glanced up and found Tyler still watching, waiting for him to say something, he supposed. "Ty, I won't change my mind."

"A'ight." Tyler gave a single nod. "You know I could ask Janie if she's friends with any nice, single women from her church."

"No. I do not want your girlfriend fixing me up." Rohn stared at the sky in frustration. This situation was getting worse by the minute. "Please, Tyler. Promise me you won't say anything to Janie."

"Fine. I won't say anything. I just hate seeing you like this, Rohn. I care about you. You're like a second father to me."

If that didn't make him feel old, nothing would. Though Rohn couldn't argue. Biologically, he was plenty old enough to be Tyler's father, but it wasn't exactly a comfort to hear the kid voice that reality.

On top of that, it reminded Rohn of the void in his life. The realization that his greatest disappointment, aside from the devastation of Lila dying way too young, had been never having a son of his own. A boy to teach, and then work side by side with. To pass the ranch on to when he was too old to work it himself. Someone to leave it to after his time on this good earth was done.

But that couldn't be changed and there was no use dwelling on it. Rohn brought his gaze back to Tyler.

"Don't worry about me. I'm fine." Rohn tried to

sound convincing as he said it. He wasn't sure he succeeded.

Finally, Tyler nodded. He hooked a thumb toward the house. "I gotta run inside for a sec. Then I'll go see if the boys and me can't figure out how to stop that water tub from tipping so easily. I'm thinking maybe a brace made out of some two-by-fours will keep the big guy from flipping it."

"A'ight. Thanks. That'd be a big help." Rohn watched the younger man head for the house, probably to hit the bathroom given the amount of coffee the kid drank.

Turning in the opposite direction, Rohn headed for the barn. The boys had a bad habit of tossing paperwork to the side when a delivery came or the blacksmith handed them a bill. Rohn needed to routinely hunt for invoices and packing slips before he could work on the bookkeeping.

A few minutes later, found paperwork in hand, Rohn emerged from the barn and out into the glare of the noonday summer sun.

He noticed Tyler was back outside and working. His ranch hands appeared to be having a meeting of the minds about the water tub situation. Tyler, Justin, and Colton surrounded the trough as the bull watched them from across the pasture.

Hoping they could handle things on their own now that they were finally focused on the problem and not on him, Rohn went inside the house. He had work of his own to take care of.

Chapter Two

Bonnie Martin plucked the weeds from between the flowers she'd planted on either side of the front door. The wide brim of her straw hat shaded her face, but the Phoenix sun beat on the exposed skin of her arms.

Swiping the beads of perspiration off her brow with the back of one hand, she couldn't help but think maybe she should just let the weeds take over. They seemed to thrive in the Arizona heat, while the flowers and humans both struggled.

"Bonnie! Where are you?"

With a groan, she straightened up and stood, brushing her hands together. "I'm out front."

Her mother came to the glass front door. The older woman had Bonnie's same coloring—fair complexion that roasted in the sun, pale blond hair, and blue eyes, though her mother's hair had turned gray now, and she stayed inside the A/C most days. They probably should be living up north, yet here they were in the 120-degree heat. Of course, this being

Arizona, it was a dry kind of heat . . . or so the natives liked to tell people.

Stepping out of the air-conditioned house to stand on the stoop, her mother let the storm door slam shut behind her. "I just got a phone call."

That didn't seem like cause for an announcement. "Okay."

"It was from Colleen." Her mother said it as if that name should mean something.

Bonnie's brow furrowed. "Colleen?"

"Colleen and Andrew. Our old neighbors from Oklahoma." Her mother's mention of Oklahoma caused the usual tightness in Bonnie's chest, even twenty-five years after they'd left there.

Some memories never faded. The memory of the two men she'd left in Oklahoma—the one she loved and the one she loathed—hadn't.

Bonnie swallowed away the dryness in her throat. She climbed the two stairs and reached past her mother for the doorknob. "I need a drink of water."

Her mother followed her through to the kitchen in the back of the modest two-bedroom house. "Bonnie, Colleen said your father's in the hospital. He's dying. He doesn't have long—days maybe, if even that much. He asked her to call. He wants to see you."

Yanking open the door of the fridge, Bonnie reached for a bottle of water. She twisted off the cap and took a sip, surprised she could swallow given how tight her throat felt. She let the cold wetness slide down her parched throat before she could even begin to address her mother's shocking revelation regarding the man she'd long ago put out of her life.

"My father has been dead to me since the summer I turned eighteen." Bonnie realized she was grinding her back teeth and consciously forced herself to relax the tight clench of her jaw.

One mention of that man, of that time in her life, and it all came flooding back. The heartache. The pain. The hell that no teenager should ever have to suffer at all, never mind at the hands of a father.

And it had all been over one careless mistake. A moment of stupidity that had altered lives forever. Bonnie had lived with the weight of that knowledge on her shoulders for so long she barely remembered a time before the guilt and the shame had settled inside her and become her constant companions.

"Of course you don't have to go see him, but do you want to just call and talk to Colleen—"

"No." Bonnie spun to face her mother. "You go if you feel you have to. I don't. I don't owe that man anything."

"He didn't ask for me. He asked for you." Her mother laid a hand on her arm. "Bonnie, I think he wants to apologize."

"The time for that has long passed." She put the cap back on the bottle. "I've got to finish weeding."

Her heart pounding with emotion she'd kept buried for over two decades, Bonnie headed for the front door. The summer heat outside would be welcome given the icy chill the memories had sent down her spine.

There was no way she could step foot in Oklahoma. Not as long as that man still lived and breathed.

There was another reason for her not wanting to go back to that town ever again. The boy whose heart she'd broken, the boy who'd made it impossible for her to ever love again.

Sweet Rohn. He'd probably moved by now. To another town, if not a different state. Then again, not much changed in Bonnie's hometown. People were born, lived, and died there. Generation after generation.

He'd probably married long ago. Not that it mattered. He could never be hers again.

Still, the curiosity pricked at her. The weeds and the heat did little to distract her from wondering, was Rohn still there in the town where she'd left him?

Did she dare look?

And if she found him there, then what?

Before she could stop herself, Bonnie had gone inside, sequestered herself away in the A/C of her bedroom, and had the laptop open. She opened a new browser window and found herself entering his name into the search field.

It popped up, multiple results on the first page, every one indicating he was still there.

She didn't want to know more. Didn't want to see pictures of him, or a wife, or even children. Selfish, yes, but self-preservation had become her priority long ago. Bonnie clicked the window closed and opened a new one. She was already down the rabbit hole. She might as well go farther.

Bonnie typed in her father's name and the address of the house she'd grown up in. The listing came up but nothing else. Nothing personal.

She didn't know what she'd thought she'd find. Something to redeem him perhaps. Some community service award. Anything. He always had kept to himself, so she supposed she shouldn't be surprised.

Sighing, she closed that page, too, then flipped the lid completely closed on the laptop. Nothing good would be found by pawing through the past.

The house phone rang as Bonnie was standing up from the desk chair. She ignored it, knowing her mother would answer. It would be one of her mother's friends anyway. It almost always was.

Besides, Bonnie needed to shower. Working out in the heat had made her hot and sticky. Not to mention dusty.

She'd just grabbed a fresh T-shirt and shorts to put on after her shower when she turned to find her mother standing in the doorway, the phone in her hand.

"Bonnie."

"What's wrong?" It didn't take more than a look at her mother's face to know that something was.

"It's your father."

"I told you. I'm not going—"

"He's passed on."

Bonnie's mouth opened, but it took her a few seconds to gather herself enough to speak. "Oh."

Apparently, the prognosis that her father would last a few days had turned out to be less than accurate. No surprise.

The man always had been obstinate and spiteful. She wouldn't put it past him to have held on longer just to show the doctors they were wrong. But in the end, the throat cancer won out and God help her, Bonnie felt relief at the news.

The relief she felt was followed quickly by guilt. He had been her father, even if he'd been a bad one. And any death, even that of a man she'd hated for years, was cause for sorrow.

"I'm sorry, Mom." In spite of it all, her mother had loved the man once.

Her mother nodded, swallowing hard before she drew in a deep breath.

"Uh, so I'm going to shower." Bonnie moved toward the doorway, and finally, her surprised-looking mother moved out of the way to let her pass through.

Bonnie couldn't escape the situation that easily or for very long.

Her mother spent the following hour on the phone making calls to Oklahoma. Making final arrangements, Bonnie supposed.

She didn't know much about that since her mother had also handled things when her grandmother had passed. Of course, everything had happened right there in Phoenix where her grandmother and they lived. The service, the burial. Bonnie hadn't considered how difficult, how complicated, things could get from a distance.

Again, Bonnie felt the guilt, this time for letting her mother bear the burden of the planning.

So she stayed with her mom, bringing her iced tea as she took notes and made calls. Making dinner and setting the table for them while the phone calls continued.

From what she gathered, her father would be cremated and the ashes would be buried in the family plot in Oklahoma.

Her mother put down the receiver just as Bonnie was bringing the salad bowls to the table. "So, apparently he had a will."

Bonnie cocked one brow at her mother's comment.

"That could be the only smart thing the man ever did."

Her mother's exhale showed she was being patient with Bonnie. Even after all the shit he'd put them both through, the woman still refused to talk trash about him. Now he was dead, so of course, she wouldn't start.

Finally, Bonnie gave in when she saw her mother was waiting for her to listen. "Okay, so what about this will?"

"That last call was the executor of the estate. He'd like you to come to Oklahoma."

"Me? Why?"

"I'm guessing because you're the heir named in the will."

"He left the farm to me and not you?" Bonnie shook her head, confused. "Why?"

"We were divorced. I'm no longer his wife and haven't been for a very long time. But you'll always be his daughter. And he loved you." The calm understanding in her tone as her mother reasoned it out angered Bonnie.

"No, he didn't." Bonnie's control broke. "How can you not hate him for what he did?"

"Hate does no one any good. He's gone. Don't waste your energy on bad feelings any longer."

"I've got plenty of energy for that." Anger fueled her until her pulse raced fast and furious.

"Hate will poison you, Bonnie."

"Save the sermons for church, Mother." Bonnie was lashing out at her mother when it was really her father she was angry at.

Apparently, the woman was a saint. She'd forgiven

her ex-husband and she seemed to ignore Bonnie's insults now.

Wearing an expression of indulgence, one of a mother humoring her child, the older woman drew in a breath. "What should I tell the lawyer? I have to call him back."

"Tell him to do whatever he wants with the house. Sell it. Burn it. I don't care." The vision of her child-hood home going up in flames caused a kaleido-scope of emotions within her. There had been some good memories made there once upon a time. Sadly, the bad memories would always overshadow the good for Bonnie.

Her mind spun with alternatives. Could she hire a handyman to clean out the place and then contract with a real estate agent to sell it? Could all that be ac-complished without her ever setting foot back in Oklahoma?

"Neither the farm nor the house is the lawyer's re-sponsibility, Bonnie. It's yours now. Like it or not, you need to handle it." Gone was the indulgent, understanding mother. In her place was a firm, no-nonsense woman.

Bonnie couldn't deny that she spoke the truth. This mess was hers now. Her father's final blow from the grave.

"All right. Tell the lawyer I'll be there by the end of the week." It would cost a fortune to book a flight on such short notice and she wasn't going to drop that kind of money on a trip she didn't want to make in the first place. She'd have to drive.

What was that old saying? All roads lead back home. That's where she'd be going, at least for long enough to put some demons to rest. She'd do that as soon as her car could get her there.

Maybe all those hours in the car with nothing to do but remember the past were her penance for what had happened that summer twenty-five years ago.

Hours and hours, alone, reliving her mistakes, her heartbreak, and memories of her first love.

Her sweet Rohn.

June 1990

Bonnie evaluated her reflection in the mirror above the dresser of the bedroom.

Her senior prom was something she'd dreamed about for all four years of high school. The one thing she'd never imagined over all those years of ripping pictures of dresses and hairstyles out of magazines was that she'd be attending alone.

That was fine. She'd have fun anyway, all on her own. There were a few girls, and guys, too, from her class who were going solo. Okay, maybe not many, but at last three, counting her.

Bonnie sighed. She really was a loser. She couldn't even get somebody to ask her to prom. She probably should have sucked it up and asked someone herself, but the one guy she really liked, the one she would have wanted to attend with if she lived in a perfect world, didn't even know she existed.

Of course, Rohn Lerner wouldn't have said yes to her anyway, even if she had somehow gotten up the nerve to ask him.

From behind the door of her locker, she'd watched him walk the halls with the other guys on the football team, but he'd never noticed her. She'd spot his dark head above the other boys of the class, his broad chest and shoulders making them all look puny. Bonnie would sometimes stare at him, trying to catch his sky-blue gaze, but his eyes never met hers.

It was as if she were invisible.

She'd heard that Rohn was taking a cheerleader to the prom.

Of course. Why wouldn't he? He was the football team star. Lena Duncan was the head cheerleader. She was tall and shapely with dark brown hair and deep green eyes. It was a match made in heaven. With Lena standing next to Rohn in the photos, they'd be perfect together.

Bonnie was a head shorter than Lena and in comparison, felt as if she was built like a boy. Her mother always said she was going to have an athletic build, but Bonnie didn't want to be athletic. She wanted to be beautiful and sexy and everything Lena was and she wasn't.

Though she had to admit that tonight, all dressed up, she looked pretty. Maybe almost beautiful . . . if she didn't stand too close to Lena.

At least if Bonnie was attending prom alone, she'd look good doing it. The dress had cost all of her babysitting money, but it was worth it. Everyone else was wearing the supposed hot color of the 1990 prom season—blue. Everywhere there were yards of shiny taffeta in all shades of the color, ranging from dark blue to ice blue.

Bonnie had decided to break the mold. She'd found a dress she loved in a beautiful buttercup yellow chiffon. The hue might not be the height of fashion according to the magazines, but it made her blue eyes stand out. At least that's what the salesgirl had said at the store. Of course, the woman might just say that to all the girls trying on dresses for their prom.

Staring at the mirror now, Bonnie thought the color also complemented her blond hair, which she'd done up herself in a French braid. The bottom of the braid she'd secured with a matching yellow scrunchie she was lucky enough to find at the accessory store. And of course, she had shoes dyed to match the dress.

It had all been a lot of work, and money, but looking at her reflection, she knew the end result was worth it.

She picked up from the dresser the corsage she'd ordered for herself, and brought it to her nose. She breathed in the scent of the fragrant yellow freesia that surrounded the single white rose. The yellow blooms were interspersed with stems of both light and dark blue flowers. Delphinium. That's what the florist had said the pretty flowers were called.

That was her only concession to the blue fashion trend, and only because the contrast of the blue and the yellow really did look beautiful surrounding the tight white rosebud in the center.

She slipped the elastic band over her left hand and felt the weight of the flowers. It was probably a good thing she didn't have a date. Any dancing might have the corsage flying off her wrist.

Leaning a bit closer to the mirror, Bonnie checked her makeup. She had put just a bit of blue eyeliner along the inner rim of her lower eyelid and had put some blue eye shadow in the outside corners of her upper lids. Her pink blush had just a tinge of shimmer to add some sparkle to her face. A bit of mascara and pink lipstick completed her look.

That was it then. She was dressed and as ready as she was going to get. She turned to find her mother standing in the doorway, smiling. "You look absolutely beautiful, sweetie."

Bonnie smoothed the skirt of the dress with one palm. "You really think so?"

"Yes. You're going to be the prettiest girl there."

She doubted that. That honor would no doubt belong to Marie Jorgensen, who'd already been voted prom queen by the senior class. "Thanks, Mom."

"Are you ready to go?"

"Yup." Bonnie grabbed her purse, also yellow to match the dress, and turned toward the door.

"I want to take a picture before we leave."

"Okay."

"Go and show your father how nice you look while I grab my camera. He's in the dining room reading the newspaper."

"Okay. Then we have to leave. I don't want to be late." Not that it mattered, she guessed. It wasn't as if anyone was waiting for her.

"You won't be late. Don't worry." She shot Bonnie a smile before disappearing into the bedroom.

Bonnie continued down the hallway to the dining room. She found her father sitting at the table reading, the ever-present cup he used to spit his chewing tobacco into set near his elbow.

She stood in the doorway and smoothed the chiffon of her long skirt. "Hey, Dad. I'm leaving for the prom."

He glanced at her over the top of the paper and

drew his brows down in a frown. "How much did that thing you're wearing cost me?"

Her mouth fell open, about to protest that she'd paid for it herself, when her mother came into the room. "Bonnie saved up her money from her baby-sitting jobs and bought it herself."

Her father scowled. "Waste of money, if you ask me. When will she ever wear something like that again?"

"It doesn't matter. It's the prom." Bonnie's mother laid a hand on her shoulder. "Doesn't she look nice?"

He looked her over, from the top of her head all the way down to her kitten-heeled shoes and back up again. "She's wearing too much makeup. It makes her look like a streetwalker."

With that he raised the paper, and Bonnie was very happy to be dismissed. She hadn't expected much from her father. She should be happy she'd gotten away with just that little bit of criticism and not more.

"Come on, Mom. Let's go."

"I want to take your picture first."

"Can we please take it outside? Okay?"

"That's a good idea, sweetie. Then I won't need to use the flash. Stand by the tree next to the driveway. That might be a pretty shot."

How could her mother not see that Bonnie couldn't get away from this house fast enough?

Bonnie nodded and moved in a daze to the front door. She only had to endure two quick pictures, then they could leave.

"I'm just dropping Bonnie off at the school, then I'll be home and we can eat."

"Don't drag your feet getting home. I'm hungry." The sound of her father's voice followed them out the front door. It grated on Bonnie's already jagged nerves as she felt her shoulders tighten.

She forced a smile long enough for her mother to snap her pictures. Then, thankfully, her mom was happy and Bonnie was allowed to get into the car, where she slumped in the passenger seat.

Surrounded by the pouf of the dress she'd loved above all else, right up until the moment her father had deflated her happiness bubble, Bonnie watched the scenery pass by.

Every mile took her farther from home, even if it was just for a little while. That was good enough for her.

Blue and white helium balloons tied to the fence at the entrance had Bonnie's heart quickening. It was going to be a great night, even if she didn't have a date. And unlike her father, she didn't care how much the dress had cost. It made her feel beautiful and that made it worth more than all the money in the world.

Chapter Three

Summer, 2015 (Present Day)

In his office, Rohn took a seat at the desk. The old rolling desk chair creaked under his weight. Hell, it could just as well be his bones creaking, given the way he felt lately.

He was bone-deep weary, but he had to cut the guys' checks. He paid them every two weeks and today was both a payday and a Friday—double cause for celebration for the young and wild cowboys of Oklahoma.

The single guys would likely cash their checks and go out on the town, throwing money around buying ladies drinks and hoping to get lucky. Tyler, now that he'd settled down, might use his money to take Janie out to dinner. Though more than likely, knowing the kid and how he loved to tinker, he'd spend a good chunk of his pay on parts for the old truck he insisted on restoring and driving rather than buying a new one.

The day of the week didn't matter to Rohn. Why

should it when one day was just like the next? He'd sit in his house alone and hope there was something on television that didn't make him want to blow his brains out.

Rallying his energy after that depressing thought, Rohn leaned forward and reached for the pen. That's when he spotted the small yellow sticky note stuck to the cover of the checkbook. He slid his reading glasses onto his nose and grabbed the note.

In what had to be Tyler's handwriting was the word *GIRLS* and a phone number. He mumbled a cuss that didn't nearly cover all he was feeling when he realized what it was—the phone number for Tyler's hookers.

The number was the local exchange from the next county, just a short drive away. Scowling that he'd even thought that, he tossed the paper into his drawer and slammed it closed.

Shaking his head at Tyler's attempt to be helpful, Rohn cussed one more time as he realized he should tear the thing up and throw it away, not keep it in his desk where anyone could find it, Or, God forbid, he could be tempted to call it in a moment of weakness and extreme loneliness.

He reached into the drawer, grabbed the little square of paper, and wadded it up into a tiny ball before tossing it into the trash beneath his desk.

That done, he still couldn't wrestle his mind back onto the payroll. Giving up for now, Rohn pushed the button to turn on the computer. Of course he'd never consider Tyler's crazy idea to hire a woman to have sex with him, but damn he needed to do something about his lack of companionship, because one more long, lonely winter on this ranch might drive him insane. Like shoot-the-television-with-a-shotgun kind of insane.

When the old desktop computer finished chugging along and finally showed him the screen he needed, he punched the only name he could think of into the search bar—*Matchmaker*—because he kept seeing their damn commercials every night on television.

Desperate times called for desperate measures. That was probably exactly what he was going to find at this site—desperate women. Christ, he didn't want to do this, but he'd be damned if he went to Tyler and Janie asking if they could set him up on a blind date with one of Janie's single female friends.

Never in a million years when he took those wedding vows with Lila twenty years ago did he imagine he'd be back here now. Alone. Lonely. Thrust into the dating world.

An old framed picture of Lila from when she'd been young sat next to the computer, taken in the days before cell phone cameras and digital photography.

Rohn drew in a deep breath and shook his head. "Ah, Lila. Why'd you leave me so soon?"

Then again, Lila hadn't been the first to leave him. His girlfriend from high school had, too. Bonnie with eyes so blue they put the Oklahoma sky to shame.

College had taken his Bonnie Blue away. Cancer took his wife, Lila. Maybe Rohn was just destined to be alone.

He glanced at the screen, amused that Matchmaker's proven dating system guaranteed a perfect match for him and wanted to prove it with a free thirty-day trial.

Would Lila have approved of this online dating crap? She'd be far less disappointed in him for this, than if he'd taken Tyler's suggestion and called a hooker. Of that, he was sure.

Either way, at this point Lila's blessing was beyond his ability to get. She'd moved on to a better place, and until it was his time to join her, he had to move on with his life.

He swallowed the dryness in his throat and clicked on the field for New Accounts, knowing with every fiber of his being he was going to regret it.

Two questions into filling out his profile, when the philosophical shit they asked began to make his brain hurt, Rohn abandoned the form and turned back to the checkbook on the desk.

It was saying something that the paperwork he usually avoided was preferable to setting up his online dating account. One big old warning sign, that was, and a smart man would heed it.

Rohn would decide if he was a smart man later, after he wrote the checks and got some dinner in his belly.

Maybe he'd throw a nice thick steak on the grill. He couldn't fill the void in his life with a female, but it was simple enough to fill the hole in his gut with some tasty meat. And a beer wouldn't hurt.

Of course, one beer would lead to more, and that might not be a bad thing because the sudden resurgence of memories long buried was just going to depress Rohn more than he already was.

Memories of Bonnie Blue in her pretty yellow prom dress.

June 1990

Rohn slumped against the wall between his buddies Pete and Brian. Collectively they watched their dates gyrating to the beat of the music.

As the disco ball spun above their heads, showering everything in the gym with shards of light like so many pieces of shattered mirror, he was simply grateful to be standing on the sidelines with his buddies. Lena, his date, was more than happy to dance with her friends rather than him.

If Rohn was going to dance at all, it certainly wasn't going to be some Milli Vanilli song.

"What the hell is with all these huge bows on the girls' asses?" Pete frowned as he watched the same scene as Rohn.

"I know, right?" Brian let out a snort. "Like Mary Beth's ass isn't big enough already, she feels she has to go and decorate it with that big butt-bow?"

Rohn laughed. It was a sad day when the first string of the football team had to resort to talking about dresses, but Pete's observation was true. There was no getting away from the gigantic bows tonight.

Even Rohn's date, Lena, was sporting the big butt-bow. You couldn't miss the damn thing, it was so big and shiny. Though the whole dress was shiny. When she'd walked beneath one of the spotlights the DJ had set up, Rohn had been nearly blinded by the reflection off the dark blue satin.

He'd told Lena that her dress was nice, even if he

really wasn't feeling it. He figured it was his job as her prom date to say shit like that.

If he was nice enough to Lena, who knew what could happen? Maybe he'd even lose his virginity for real tonight. That would be one burden lifted off his shoulders since he'd been lying to the other guys on the team for a couple of years now by saying he'd already done it.

He'd even made up a whole scenario about how he and his father had been away for the weekend at a stock auction and rodeo. About how he'd met a barrel racer a couple of years older than he and how they'd done it in the field where she had her horse tied up when his father was asleep in the trailer.

Rohn had been very proud of himself for crafting that particular lie. It was completely untraceable and pretty damn believable, if you asked him.

He glanced around the space. The school's activity center was barely recognizable with the overhead lights off. The colored spotlights flashing in time with the beat of the music were the only illumination. It made it hard to see, and to walk. Rohn had been bumping into people all night.

Too dark to see or not, he was thirsty, which meant he'd have to take the hike to the snack table and buy something to drink.

"I'm gonna go grab a Coke. Tell Lena where I went if she asks."

"A'ight." Pete nodded, his eyes still on the gyrating girls in front of them.

Rohn didn't know what his friend was so busy staring at. It wasn't like he could see their asses wiggling behind the butt-bows, anyway.

His suit had to be the most uncomfortable thing

he'd ever worn. It was bad enough he'd had to rent one at all, but then Lena had insisted he buy a blue shirt and tie to match her dress. He looked like an idiot with a navy-blue shirt that matched the color of his tie exactly.

Who did that? Not that he knew about fashion, but wasn't the tie supposed to stand out from the shirt? If not, why bother wearing the dang thing in the first place?

Maybe it was a good thing it was so dark. No one would see his stupid shirt and tie.

Out in the hallway the snack table was manned by students who he guessed must have volunteered to work there for the night. Or at least for a shift.

It was far quieter there and the lights were actually on in the hall where they'd set up the table. Rohn had to think they had the best seat in the house because being inside with the pounding bass and the spastic lighting was beginning to make him twitch.

He walked up to the table and waited his turn. When the kid in front of him had paid, Rohn took a step closer to the table. "Coke, please."

The girl seated behind the table looked up at him, her eyes, blue like the color of the cornflowers that grew along the highway, widened as if she knew him. "Hi."

"Hi." Rohn tried to place where he knew her. It was a fairly big school, and his was the largest year. That meant he hadn't been in classes with everyone in his grade. He asked, "You a senior?"

She nodded. "Yes. We have lunch during the same period."

Hmm, he would have thought he'd remember this

girl from the cafeteria. Her hair was as golden as a sunny field of wheat. She might possibly be the only girl there tonight with hair that wasn't twice the size that nature had intended. Hers was pulled back into an intricate braid. He liked it.

He tried to glance behind her without being too obvious. He suddenly needed to know if she was sporting the butt-bow like the rest of the clones on the dance floor or if, as he suspected, she really was unique. One of a kind.

"I like your dress." Unlike before when Lena had asked, he actually meant it.

"Thanks, Rohn." A blush crept across her cheeks, making her even prettier. But he was more intrigued that she knew his name when he had no clue what hers was.

"What's your name?"

"Bonnie."

Rohn tipped his head to the side. The name fit her perfectly. "Bonnie blue eyes, nice to meet you."

"Bonnie Martin, actually. And it's nice to meet you, too."

He was having fun talking to this girl, but he was still thirsty. "So, do you have any Coke left?"

Her eyes flew wide. "Oh. Sorry."

She got up from her chair and spun around to lift the lid of the cooler behind her. Just as he suspected, she was bow-free, and rather than the slippery fabric of his date's dress, hers was made from a pretty, flowing material that billowed like a cloud when she moved.

Bonnie turned back toward him and put the icy can down on the table. He waited for her to tell him how much it was. When she didn't, he asked, "How much?"

"Oh, um, seventy-five cents."

"Okay." He threw down a dollar. That sent her scrambling for change in the metal box in front of her. He would have told her to keep the change but she was so intent on taking out the quarter, he would have felt bad, ungrateful even, telling her she didn't have to bother.

The quarter held between her two fingers, she thrust her arm toward him. "Here you go."

He reached out his hand. As she pressed the coin into his open palm, the warm skin of her hand brushed against his. He stood, fascinated, staring at where her smaller hand touched his.

Rohn raised his gaze and met hers, amazed one more time at the clear blue color of them. Finally he cleared his throat. "Uh, thanks."

"You're welcome."

The song had ended and another one had begun. A slow one this time. Lena would most likely be looking for him to dance. Regretfully, he picked up the soda. "I guess I'd better be getting back inside."

"Oh. Okay. Have fun."

Something about the sadness in her eyes had him hesitating. "You ever get to leave this table? Or are you stuck here all night?"

She laughed. "No. We get to leave. I only volunteered for an hour shift and that ended a little while ago."

When she smiled, her whole face changed. It made him regret he couldn't ask her to slow dance.

How messed up would that be? Asking Lena to be his date and then asking the girl at the soda table to dance? Though to be fair, Rohn had only asked Lena because Pete had asked her best friend. He'd kind of been strong-armed into the whole thing.

"Well, you should go and enjoy yourself. That dress is too pretty to hide behind the table all night. You should take it out for a spin on the dance floor."

"Okay." She blushed and he smiled, finding he enjoyed getting a reaction out of this girl.

"Promise?" he asked, teasing her some more and loving how she had trouble holding his gaze now because of it.

"Yes. I promise."

"Good. See you later, Bonnie Blue." He winked.

After having had a lot better time at the snack table than he had the whole night, he left his new acquaintance with regret and headed back inside.

"What took you so long?" Pete frowned at him.

"It wasn't so long." Rohn shrugged. Popping the top, he looked around them. "Where are the girls?"

"Bathroom," Brian answered.

A flash of yellow by the door caught Rohn's attention. "Hey, either of you know anything about that girl standing alone by the door? The one in yellow. Her name's Bonnie Martin."

The two glanced her way. Brian nodded. "Yeah. She lives out by me."

"Really? She says she's a senior, but I wonder how come I never noticed her before."

"Because she's in the advanced classes, not in the dumb jock ones you're in. That's why," Pete teased. "I heard she got into Arizona State."

Rohn's brow furrowed. "Hey, I got into college, too."

"Yeah, NEO." Pete snorted.

"NEO's a good school." Rohn was heading to North Eastern Oklahoma A&M in the fall to study agriculture and hopefully play on the football team. It was a good school and he was proud to have gotten in, no matter what his friends said.

"Not as good as ASU where smart girl over there is going." Pete just liked to argue, about everything and anything. Rohn knew that from experience, but he was happy the conversation had swung back to the topic he was interested in. Bonnie.

He turned to Brian. "So she lives near you? Where?"

"Her dad owns the wheat fields you can see from the highway right before you make the turn for my road. In fact, I gotta stop by there this week. I heard he's looking to hire some help for the summer."

Wasn't that interesting? Rohn just happened to be looking for a summer job, and he couldn't think of a better place to look for it than at pretty Miss Bonnie's place.

Rohn would stop by the next day. Since tonight was going to be a late night, if he couldn't get there first thing in the morning then he'd go as early in the day as he could manage because he'd be damned if Brian got there first.

"Hold this. I'm gonna go take a piss." Rohn held the can out to Pete.

"Sure. But I'm warning you. I'm probably gonna drink it."

"Go ahead. I don't care." Leaving his friend and his Coke behind, Rohn spun toward the bathrooms.

A few steps into his journey the DJ decided to turn on the strobe light, making it nearly impossible to see, and even harder to walk.

Not getting the fascination with being blinded, Rohn mumbled under his breath. He pushed through the door to the hall and smacked directly into someone.

Someone dressed in yellow.

He reached out to steady the girl, who'd reached for the nearest wall as he knocked her off balance. "Bonnie. Sorry. You okay?"

"Yeah. Fine."

Rohn's hands were still wrapped around her forearms. More, he realized he didn't want to let go even though she was no longer in danger of falling over. He finally dropped his hold. "Um, so, you probably don't want to go in there right now. The lights are pretty crazy."

"Oh, okay."

He nodded, satisfied he'd offered proper warning. "I was just heading to the bathroom."

"Sorry. You go ahead." She turned to head down the hallway.

"Bonnie?"

"Yeah?"

"You look really pretty tonight." It was just a simple compliment, but it had Rohn's heart thundering as he said it.

She smiled at him, and he was lost. "Thanks."

Chapter Four

Bonnie parked in the driveway of the house she'd grown up in, and cut the engine, but didn't get out.

It wasn't exhaustion from the drive from Arizona to Oklahoma that kept her in her seat. She'd broken the more than twelve-hour trip in half by staying at a cheap hotel overnight. It was the memories of a past she'd worked to put behind her that had her frozen in place.

It hit her hard, the visceral reaction to seeing the place she'd hoped she'd never see again.

The minutes ticked by until the inside of the car began to get uncomfortably warm beneath the noon-day summer sun.

As an older couple came into view, Bonnie realized she'd sat there so long, the neighbors had come over to investigate.

Colleen, a bit grayer, a little plumper, but always smiling and looking happy, waved at her through the windshield.

Drawing in a bracing breath, Bonnie opened the car door and stretched one leg out, feeling her stiff muscles protest.

"Bonnie Martin. Good golly. Look at you, all grown up," the older woman exclaimed as she came forward.

Standing, Bonnie slammed the car door and moved to hug first Colleen, and then her husband. "Colleen, Andrew, thank you both for everything you've done. My mother and I appreciate it."

"No thanks necessary, Bonnie." Shaking his head, Andrew held up one hand to dismiss her gratitude. "We were happy to do it for Tom."

No one in town knew the truth about why she'd left town. Not even the closest neighbors. To them, her father was just good old Tom. Quiet but hard-working. A man who kept to himself mostly but who could be counted on to be there in an emergency.

When all hands were needed to fight the wildfire that threatened this side of town, he had been there alongside the volunteer firefighters all through the night battling the blaze. Bonnie was well aware of that, but it didn't make up for the rest in her mind.

No one knew what the man was truly like or what had happened that summer. All the neighborhood knew was that Bonnie graduated from high school and left for college. Sent off to her grandmother's home in Phoenix, where she chose to remain even after she got her degree from ASU.

Her mother had followed her there shortly after. The divorce papers came by messenger. Her father's signature on them was the final break she and her mother had needed to make a new life in Arizona.

When Bonnie landed a good job teaching in a

Phoenix school system after graduation, no one questioned that of course she'd stay in Arizona. No one knew then, and there was no reason for this smiling couple standing in front of her now to suspect that there was anything more to it than that.

"Of course, we'd be here to help your father." Colleen echoed Andrew's sentiment. "We've known your family for as long as we've been married."

"And that's a long time, I can tell you." Andrew grinned when Colleen backhanded him in the arm.

Bonnie forced a smile at their bantering. "Well, I appreciate it."

"We barely did anything. Really." Colleen shook her head. "Once he started feeling poorly, your dad sold off the lower field. And he didn't even try planting a crop this season. So really, all we did to help out was make sure he had someone to call if he needed anything. Sometimes he'd ask for a ride to the doctor if he were particularly bad that day. And I'd drop off a hot meal for him a couple of times a week."

Andrew nodded in agreement with his wife. "Truth is, I wish we could have done more for him, but he didn't accept help readily. But you know that, I'm sure."

"Yup." Bonnie nodded, hit with more guilt that the neighbors had stepped in out of the goodness of their hearts when his own daughter hadn't been there.

Did they think less of her because she hadn't come home to help out? Did she care if they did?

Surprisingly, yes, she did. She'd never been one to take it lightly if someone thought badly of her.

If they knew the truth, they'd understand, but the reality was Colleen and Andrew didn't know. No

living person save her mother did—and Bonnie
wasn't about to tell them.

Obviously her old neighbors had seen some good
in her father she didn't see herself. And maybe he
did have some good in him, buried beneath the bad.
Or maybe he had changed.

Bonnie didn't know and squashed the small urge
to care. She could show gratitude to Colleen and
Andrew just fine without knowing their motives.
Without looking past the goodness of their hearts.

Hell, maybe they had seen his faults and chosen to
overlook them. Folks forgave criminals serving life
sentences in prison for horrific crimes all the time.
Forgave them, blessed them. She'd seen it on television more than once.

Pushing aside the thought niggling on the edge of
her consciousness that she hadn't forgiven her father
and had no desire ever to do so, Bonnie said to her
neighbors, "You still helped out a lot, and that was
really nice of you."

"So what can we do to help you now?" Andrew
glanced around them, probably thinking what Bonnie
was—her father had become quite the hoarder over
the years.

That was evidenced by the piles of junk she saw.
Old appliances. Tools. Scrap wood and metal. If the
outside looked this bad, what would the inside look
like? She supposed she'd have to find out.

"Nothing. You've done enough already." When
they looked as if they would protest, Bonnie held up
one hand. "I honestly haven't even been inside yet.
But I'm sure it's nothing I can't handle. It looks like
I'll be occupied for quite a while just clearing this
place out before I can even think about what to do

next with it. And that's something I have to do on my own."

Sorting through the remains of her father's things would surely raise a lot of ghosts. Bonnie wanted to be alone when they descended upon her.

"I understand." Colleen dipped her head. "If you need any help—"

"Thank you." What Bonnie needed was to get away from the overwhelming kindness of these people. She needed to wrap her head around everything.

There was a lot to deal with. Her father leaving the whole place to her after she hadn't seen or talked to him for twenty-five years. Him being this *good man* the neighbors kept talking about and had been so close to. It was hard to reconcile that image with the memories she'd carried for so long of the man she knew.

The scene around her seemed to shift. The landscape tilted just a bit. Bonnie felt light-headed until she feared she'd fall down if she didn't sit down. She took a step to widen her stance so she'd be steadier on her feet.

Hoping the older couple hadn't seen, she hooked a thumb toward the house. "Um, I think I'm going to go inside and lie down. I'm a little tired from the trip."

Colleen's brow furrowed. "Of course you are. And here we are keeping you out here in the hot sun."

"It's okay. Really. It was good to talk to you."

"Do you want to come over to our place for dinner later?" Colleen asked. "There won't be any fresh food inside—"

"Thank you, but no." Bonnie cut off the invitation. The last thing she wanted to do was have dinner with them and spend the night talking more about her father but she hadn't meant to be rude. She had to scramble to cover and the first thing that popped into her head was a lie. "I've, uh, made plans to have dinner with some old friends . . . from high school. I promised them."

"Of course. You should catch up with your friends. Just know that the offer's open any time." Colleen smiled sweetly.

"Thank you." Even with as kind as these people were, Bonnie still prayed they'd go home. She couldn't hold it together much longer.

As wobbly and uncertain as she felt facing being back, she might as well have been that scared teen she'd long ago put behind her.

"Come on, Colleen. The girl drove a long way. She needs her rest." Andrew put an arm around his wife's shoulders and Bonnie got a look at what a healthy marriage should look like.

She needed the reminder. It was easy to forget since she couldn't remember a time when her parents' marriage hadn't been volatile, or kept peaceful only by her mother pandering to her father's every wish.

"I'll see you both soon. Thanks again." She waved and smiled and had already turned to head for the door when Colleen called to her by name. More than ready to be done with this conversation, Bonnie spun back. "Yeah?"

"We forgot to give you the key." Andrew held up a key as Bonnie let out a breath.

"Oh. Thanks." She felt the need to explain her foolishness. "The door was never locked when I lived here, so I didn't even think."

"Of course you didn't, darlin'." Colleen shook her

head. "You've got a lot on your mind right now. It's all right."

"We've got you covered." Andrew smiled and took the few steps forward to close the distance between them.

She took the key with yet another thanks and made a break for the house.

Her hands were shaking when she turned the lock and pushed the front door open. She'd thought she'd be relieved to be alone, but as she stepped inside and swung that thick wooden door closed between her and them, exactly how alone she was in this house struck her.

The sense of relief she'd expected to feel, the peace and quiet she'd expected to soothe her once she was finally left to herself, didn't come. The eerily quiet house held too many ghosts—memories she'd buried deep surfaced quick and brutal.

The atmosphere as well as the clutter smothered her until she couldn't breathe. She strode through the kitchen and toward the door at the back of the house. After wrestling with yet another lock, she threw it open, gasping in the fresh air and the scents of summer.

How was she going to spend a week here, or however long it would take to clean out the house, when she couldn't stand being inside for more than a minute?

How was she going to sleep in this house tonight when she knew the panic clawing her insides would grow worse after the sun went down and darkness brought with it more shadows and demons?

Drawing in a deep breath, she turned, but left the

back door propped wide. She had to be strong. She'd survived far worse than an empty house.

Methodically, she made her way through the dwelling, throwing open curtains and windows until every room had sunlight and a warm breeze streaming inside. Dust particles danced in the air and the house filled with the heat of outside. She switched the air-conditioning completely off and opted to let summer in. She didn't care if the house became sweltering. It was better than feeling trapped, unable to get out.

Even after all her efforts, Bonnie still felt unsteady. She needed food. It had been a long drive and she hadn't stopped to eat, opting to make do with a couple of granola bars and bottled water on the road.

The house needed much attention, but she needed some TLC herself. First things first. If she didn't keep herself strong, she'd never be able to face the task at hand.

Colleen had been right. There was nothing fresh to eat in the kitchen. She checked the fridge, not that she'd thought she'd find anything enticing in there.

Giving up on the kitchen, and its many memories, Bonnie decided she'd have to go into town.

At least that would kill two birds with one stone. She'd get out of the house and be able to grab something to eat at the same time. Then, fortified with a full belly, she'd come back and face the overwhelming task of cleaning up.

Still unsure of where she'd be able to find a room in this house not so filled with bad memories she'd be able to sleep in it, she left, leaving the front door open to let air in through the screen.

Let thieves come in and take everything. They'd save her the trouble of dispensing with a lifetime of clutter belonging to a man she hated with every fiber of her being.

Getting into the car, she glanced back at the house. Yes, there were bad memories here, but there were some really good ones, as well. Maybe once she'd eaten and had gotten a good night's sleep she'd be able to enjoy reliving them.

June 1990

"So tell me everything." Bonnie's mother, in her usual place at the kitchen stove, looked as excited to hear about the prom as Bonnie had been to actually go to it.

"There's not much to tell." Bonnie had slept kind of late this morning and then had to rush to get to her babysitting job on time, so this was the first opportunity her mother had had to pin her down for information.

"Oh, come on. It was prom. What were the other dresses like? Did someone ask you to dance?"

The biggest thing that stuck out in Bonnie's mind was Rohn talking to her—for quite a while, too. But she wasn't going to tell her mother about that even though she was still walking around on cloud nine.

A little bit of the fun had been sucked out of the night when she'd seen Rohn and his date together. The one thing that made her feel better about that whole thing was the fact he seemed to talk way more to his guy friends than to Lena.

Even better, Bonnie never saw Rohn dance with Lena. Not even once.

It was as if he'd rather be there alone than with his date. It might mean Bonnie was a bad person, but she liked that idea.

"There were lots of pretty dresses." But none she liked more than the one she'd chosen.

"Long or short?"

"All long, I think. Or at least three-quarter length. No short ones."

"And did you dance?" Her mother wasn't going to let that topic go. Too bad Bonnie didn't have any earth-shattering news in that department.

"Yes."

Her mother's eyes widened. "You did? With who?"

Bonnie laughed at her mother's reaction. "Melody. Us girls all danced together when they played good dance songs. The DJ played some really old stuff. You know, like from the seventies."

"Old. Like from the seventies. Lovely." Her mother rolled her eyes.

Bonnie smiled. "Sorry, Mom."

She dismissed the apology with the flick of one wrist. "So what else?"

"That's it." Bonnie shrugged. "I volunteered at the snack table for a shift and then hung out with Melody, mostly."

"Did you have fun?"

"I did." That was no lie.

Rohn had talked to her. That was more than had happened in four years of high school. It seemed he really enjoyed talking to her, too. Even if nothing else had happened of note at the prom, the conversations with Rohn were something she'd remember forever.

Her mother continued with whatever she was doing at the counter as she said, "So now there's just graduation and then you're done."

"Yup."

"Are you sad?"

"No." Except for her unrequited crush on a boy who hadn't known she existed until last night, high school hadn't been the most glowing time period in Bonnie's life.

Though she'd miss those lunches staring at the football players' table. She would definitely miss that.

"I dropped the film off today, so it won't be long before we'll have those pictures I took of you in your dress."

"Great." Pictures of her in her prom dress all alone were nothing to get too excited about.

"And I bought a new roll of film so I'm all prepared for the big day. I can't wait to see you in your cap and gown." Her mother seemed more enthusiastic about her graduation than Bonnie did.

"Yeah."

"Then after that, we can go shopping for what you'll need at college."

"I think I should wait for the list they send of what I'll need. Melody's older sister was a freshman last year and she got a list in the mail from her college."

"Okay, we can do that." Her mother paused in her preparations to turn to Bonnie. "It's so exciting, baby girl. You're embarking on a whole new chapter in your life. I think Arizona will be good for you."

"Yeah, I guess." Bonnie lifted one shoulder.

There was one problem with going away to Arizona for college, though. Rohn wouldn't be there.

When she'd applied and gotten accepted with a scholarship, Bonnie had thought that leaving this town behind for a couple of years might be a good thing. In Arizona, she could start fresh. Be who she wanted to be. Make a new start someplace where she wasn't already labeled and put away in the box of being the quiet only-child who didn't play any sports and never had friends over after school.

In Arizona, the potential was limitless. Bonnie could be the most popular girl in school. She could even have a whole bunch of boyfriends, if she wanted.

She might need some new clothes for that, though. She glanced down at the denim cutoffs and tank top she was wearing. The clothes she'd worn to classes in high school weren't much better—mainly jeans and T-shirts, cowboy boots or flip-flops.

Yeah, she definitely needed a wardrobe makeover for college. She'd better start looking around for more babysitting jobs and save up the cash to go shopping. Her father had thought the prom dress was a waste of money. He'd probably think new clothes for college would be, too, since she had plenty of things from high school that were still perfectly good.

Her mother moved to the stove to stir a pot on the burner. "We're having your favorite dinner in honor of your big night last night and your graduation this weekend."

"Spaghetti?"

"Yes, ma'am." Her mother smiled.

"You didn't have to do that just for me." Bonnie

knew her father really didn't like spaghetti, so they didn't eat it often. Her mom making it tonight was only asking for him to be cranky. "Did you make meatballs, too?"

"I did."

Bonnie had crossed her fingers the answer would be yes. "Good. Thanks."

That would help. His biggest complaint about spaghetti was that he worked too hard all day to feel satisfied with just a belly full of noodles. But with meatballs on the menu, he might not be so unhappy.

The front doorbell rang and interrupted Bonnie's thoughts on tonight's dinner menu.

"Can you get that, baby girl?"

"Sure, Mom."

She headed through the living room and pulled open the front door, only to have her mouth drop open. The absolute last person she'd ever expected to be at her house was standing in front of her.

Rohn Lerner was at her front door.

He smiled when he saw her. It started at his mouth with the lips she had dreamed so often of kissing, and moved up over his strong cheekbones, and reached all the way to his eyes that were such an incredibly deep blue she could lose herself staring into them forever.

"Hey, Bonnie."

"Rohn. Hi. Um, what are you doing here?" She would have slapped herself in the forehead for that stupid question, if the move wouldn't have made her look like even more of an idiot.

In her defense, Bonnie was tongue-tied on a good day. Rohn's appearance had taken her by complete surprise so she really had no hope of being capable of making smart, smooth conversation with him.

"I heard your father might be looking for some help around here for the summer. I've got experience. I've been taking odd jobs since the year I turned thirteen, so I'd be good at it, if he's still looking for help . . . Or did he hire somebody already?" He kept talking, probably because she was standing there slack-jawed with nothing to say and he felt like he had to fill the silence.

"Um, I don't know." That contribution to the discussion was no better than her prior effort. She hadn't even known her father was looking to hire someone.

Bonnie glanced over her shoulder toward the kitchen. Her father was still out working, but her mother was here. She should invite him in rather than let him stand outside the front door. It seemed basic manners eluded her in the face of such hotness.

"Do you wanna come inside?"

"Sure." He dipped his head.

Unlike at school, where he wore a baseball hat or nothing at all on his head, today he had on a straw cowboy hat. She liked it on him. Liked it a lot.

He stood there, eyebrows raised, and she realized he couldn't come in with her blocking the doorway. She jumped back, nearly tripping over her own feet in the process. He didn't comment or act like he'd noticed as he walked inside and looked around.

She'd never thought much about the house she lived in before, but with him inside she looked around herself trying to see it as he would. Trying to imagine what he was thinking.

It was small. But they were a small family. That didn't prevent her from wishing that they had nicer furniture, and a grander living room.

The property was plenty big, but those were fields for growing crops. It didn't count. Not like the sweeping, lush green lawns that stretched in front of the bigger houses on the fancy side of town.

She wondered where Rohn lived, and what kind of house he lived in.

He didn't seem to be too disappointed in her home. Hopefully, that meant he wasn't from a family with a big, fancy place. The kind with the sprinklers in the lawn and the garage big enough for three cars. Bonnie's family had no garage at all. They had a couple of sheds for equipment, though.

"Um, let me get my mom. My dad's still out working." She flung her hand in the general direction of the kitchen and was just turning to go when she realized it was rude to leave him standing in the living room all alone. "You can sit if you want."

"Nah, I'll come with you."

"Oh. Okay."

All right. Now Rohn Lerner, the love of her life, was going to be in her kitchen. She might never be able to walk through this house again without remembering him there.

"Mom, is Dad looking to hire help?" Bonnie asked as she cleared the kitchen doorway, Rohn on her heels.

She knew her father's back had been acting up a lot lately, making him extra cranky, but to actually hire someone meant he must be in a lot of pain.

Possibly enough pain he couldn't drive the tractor himself.

The doctor, once they'd finally convinced him to go to one, had said something about a disk in his spine or a pinched nerve. She wasn't sure of the details, but when the doctor mentioned possible surgery, her father wouldn't hear of it. He said it would heal on its own.

Maybe it would. Bonnie didn't know, but she certainly hoped it did since he wasn't pleasant to be around lately.

"Yes, he is." Her mother turned from the stove where she'd been browning the meatballs for the sauce and smiled. "Hello."

"Evening, ma'am. I'm Rohn Lerner." Rohn swept his hat from his head, holding it in front of him with one hand while he ran the other through his dark hair. "I was hoping I could speak to your husband about a summer position here."

"Sure. He hasn't come in yet, but I expect him shortly. Why don't you sit at the table and wait."

Bonnie's heart stuttered. Rohn was going to sit in her kitchen and wait. This was a good thing, but still her gut twisted with nerves. She'd have to be on her game, sound smart, and not make a fool of herself the whole time he was here.

"Yes, ma'am. Thank you." Rohn pulled out a chair and sat, while Bonnie wished she'd taken the time to glance in a mirror and see what she looked like before answering the door.

"Bonnie, pour the boy a sweet tea." There was an amused reprimand in her mother's tone.

"Okay." She should have thought of that herself.

She took down two glasses from the cabinet and turned toward the pitcher of tea that was always on the counter. Her mother made a fresh batch of sweet tea every evening before she went to bed, and by morning it was room temperature. Her father would drink it all day. By the time dinner was over, the pitcher would be almost empty again and ready for another batch to be made.

Bonnie poured two glasses and then turned to Rohn. "Ice?"

"Nah, that's fine."

She handed him the glass and then reached into the freezer to grab an ice cube for herself.

"So Rohn, are you in Bonnie's grade in school?"

"Yes, ma'am."

"So you were at the prom last night."

"I was."

"Was it fun? Tell me about it. Bonnie here is a little stingy with her details." Her mother sent her a look.

Bonnie stood with her glass in her hand and wanted to crawl under the table. The last thing she needed was her mother embarrassing her. She sat in a chair on the other side of the table from Rohn and took a sip of her tea for lack of anything better to do.

"Well, there's not much to tell. The girls all looked nice in their fancy dresses. The girls had on corsages, much like Bonnie's. There was music and dancing. Some guy got caught trying to smuggle some liquor inside and got thrown out. Not one of my friends, mind you. But I did know him."

"See, Bonnie? I knew there were more stories you weren't telling me."

Bonnie's face heated at the scrutiny. "I didn't know about the liquor thing, Mom."

"Nah, don't worry, ma'am. Bonnie wouldn't know this kid. He's a troublemaker and a joker. He was in my classes, not in hers with the smart kids."

And that in a nutshell was why Rohn would never like her, and would never have come here for anything more than a job. But he was here now and maybe that's all that mattered.

If only she wasn't behaving like such a dolt in front of him. She wished she could be cool and sexy like Lena the head cheerleader or Marie the prom queen. Instead, she answered the door in cutoffs and couldn't string more than half a dozen words together when talking to him.

She stifled a sigh, but didn't have long to wallow in her misery as the back door swung open.

"It's hot as blazes out there." Her father stopped dead in the doorway, his stare pinning Rohn where he sat at the kitchen table, before his focus moved to Bonnie, and then her mother at the counter.

"Honey, this is Rohn. He's a classmate of Bonnie's and heard you were looking to hire help."

"You tell him that?" her father asked Bonnie.

"No, sir. I didn't even know you were looking to hire anyone."

Rohn pushed his chair back and stood. Bonnie knew he was tall, but it wasn't until he moved to stand in front of her father that she realized how tall. He had about six inches over the older man.

Knowing her father, he'd really hate having a kid in high school dwarf him.

"Sir. My friend Brian lives not far from here. He told you you might be looking to hire and since I'm looking for a job myself, I thought I'd stop by and inquire."

Her father's gaze went from Rohn's face to the hand he extended. Bonnie held her breath, thinking for a moment that he wouldn't do Rohn the courtesy of shaking his hand. Finally, he reached out and pumped Rohn's hand once.

Rohn continued, "I've got experience. I've worked with combines and harvesters. I've done plenty of haying. I've worked with livestock, too. Horses and cows, if you've got any. If you take a chance on hiring me, I can guarantee you won't be sorry."

"So you know Bonnie from school?"

"We're in the same grade, but I'm sorry to say we've never been in any classes together."

"Why sorry?"

Rohn smiled. "Well, you see she's in the advanced classes and I'm sorry to tell you that I'm not. I hope you won't hold that against me when considering me for the job. I try keeping my grades up, but with football practice and chores, it's hard to find time to study."

The mention of football seemed to impress her father. He looked interested and less suspicious of Rohn for the first time since walking through the door. "You play football?"

"Yes, sir. I'm a linebacker. First string. I'm going to NEO in the fall to hopefully play on their team."

"Linebacker. That makes sense, a boy your size." Her father nodded. "I played a bit myself back in high school."

"What position?"

"Quarterback."

Rohn smiled. "That was going to be my guess. I bet you were real fast."

Bonnie's eyes widened as her father actually smiled, when she couldn't remember the last time she'd seen him do that. At least, not in the house with just them. Usually his smiles were reserved for when he was talking to his male friends after church.

"Yup. No one could catch me. I held the record for touchdowns." Her father tipped his head toward the table. "Let's sit down and talk about this job. Bonnie, pour me some sweet tea."

"Yes, sir." She'd barely left the seat to do as he'd asked when her father sat in her chair and pushed her glass of tea aside.

She'd be fine with his dismissal if it meant he hired Rohn for the summer. Her heart sped at the thought as she moved to the cabinet and took down another glass. She shot her mother a sideways glance to see her reaction to this odd situation.

Her mom smiled. "Looks like we might have some help around here. Nice-looking help, too."

Her mother had kept her voice low so only she could hear. Even so, Bonnie drew her brows low. "Mom. Shh."

She laughed. "Don't worry. They're too busy talking about football and crops to bother with us. Now go deliver that tea and then come back over here and help me make the salad for dinner."

Bonnie moved to the table and put the glass down in front of her father. She turned away again, but not before noticing they'd moved on to talking about what hours and days Rohn would be working.

When she returned to stand at the counter, her

mother asked, "Should we invite our new hired hand to dinner?"

Pulse racing at the thought, Bonnie considered that, and then shook her head. "No, I don't think so."

"Why not?"

Just because her father was on his best behavior now didn't mean it would last. Rohn seemed to be saying all the right things at the moment, but that didn't mean he wouldn't say something to get her father mad later. Better to be safe than sorry. End things on a high note.

Bonnie didn't want to tell her mother her fears, so she came up with what seemed like a plausible excuse. "His mother's probably expecting him for dinner at home. And I'm sure he'll want to tell them about his new job."

His new job at her father's farm. The realization hit her full force. Rohn Lerner would be working at her place nearly every day for a whole summer.

It was like a dream come true. She could only pray that things stayed just as good as they were right now.

Chapter Five

"Hey, boss man." Rod, owner of the lumberyard that had been in his family for two generations, shot Rohn a grin from behind the counter. "What're you doing here? I don't often see you in town running errands these days."

"I need some eight-foot fence posts and some two-by-sixes."

"Don't you got no kids on the payroll to do this kinda menial shit for ya now that you're a big successful rancher?" Rod had been around long enough to have seen Rohn go from a hired hand to a ranch owner in his own right.

Rohn smiled at the old man's teasing. "Yup, but I'm smart enough to know my hired hands will take two hours to do an errand that should take twenty minutes. I'm better off leaving them working at my place while I handle things myself. That's how I stay a successful rancher."

The old-timer snorted out a short laugh. "Ain't

that the truth. With the kids I got working here, it's easier to take care of things my own damn self."

"I hear ya." Rohn couldn't agree more. Besides, he'd left the three clowns digging fence post holes. Given a choice between driving to town in his air-conditioned king cab pickup, and digging holes in this heat, there was no question which task Rohn was going to delegate and which he'd be more than willing to take on himself.

"So how many posts and two-bys do ya need, boss man?" Rod took the pen from behind his ear and stood waiting to write up the order on the pad in front of him.

This was the kind of place Rohn liked. A nice family-owned business that knew the customers' names and used a good old pen and paper to take orders instead of some fancy computerized shit. Small-town living at its finest. It was a comfort knowing that even if he didn't have a woman in his life, he still had plenty of good friends.

He also had a ranch to run. Time to get back to work. Rohn glanced at his handwritten list. He rattled off the lumber he needed while Rod wrote it all down in his usual chicken scratch. After the order was totaled, Rod turned the invoice around to face Rohn. "Put this on your account?"

"Yes, sir. That'd be great." Rohn scribbled his signature at the bottom.

"All right. You're all set. Just drive around back to the yard." Rod tore off one of the two copies from the pad. "Give this to Jed and he'll load it up for you."

"Thank you much." Rohn nodded. "Don't work too hard."

Rod let out another snort. "No chance of that. You, either."

"I'll try my best. Thanks." Rohn nodded and turned toward the door and the yard where he'd parked the truck.

Errand complete, and in under a quarter of an hour, too. If he'd sent Tyler, who Rohn was pretty sure had been in school at the same time as Jed, this one stop at the lumberyard could have taken an hour if the two got to shooting the shit. Today's youth— no work ethic. Not how it used to be in his day.

The thought gave Rohn pause. When had he become such an old stick in the mud? He was beginning to sound more and more like one of the old farmers he'd worked for when he'd been a much younger man and used to take whatever job he could find.

Rohn had spent four summers wrangling cattle for Mr. McMann before the old man had died. A stint in Vietnam hadn't gotten the old rancher. Getting knocked down and trampled by a bull hadn't killed him. Needing to walk with a cane in his last years didn't defeat him. A microscopic blood clot in his brain had.

But even when the old man was nearing the end of his life, he wouldn't have put up with half the shit Rohn's ranch hands got away with. Rohn was no-where near the end of his days—God willing—but his guys got away with more shit than he cared to think about.

Then again, this was a different time. Hired hands could be few and far between. Ranches were lucky to be in business at all nowadays, let alone turn a profit. Maybe Rohn should relax before he gave himself a stroke. He could cut the kids some slack and still get the job done.

Cut himself some slack, too, because playing the big boss all the time was exhausting. Especially when there was no feminine comfort for him at the end of the day. Hell, aside from his trips into town or the stock sales, the only other people he saw regularly were his hired hands.

With that thought in mind, he decided to go ahead and treat the boys to something they'd enjoy. Him, too. He'd pick them all up a good lunch. Not a bag full of greasy fast food, either. He knew exactly where to go to get what he needed.

After the lumber was loaded, he headed in the direction of Tyler's favorite barbecue spot. When the shack and trailer came into view, Rohn swung the truck into the lot and parked.

The place looked like nothing. It basically amounted to a wooden lean-to that housed the smoker, a building the size of his office with a few picnic tables inside, a few more tables outside, and the trailer where the employees served up customer orders. It might not look like a five-star restaurant, but damned if it wasn't the best food he'd had in a good long time.

The smell of that day's batch of meat in the smoker was enough to have Rohn's mouth watering before he'd even cut the engine and climbed out of the truck's cab.

Tyler could be an ass some days, but he hadn't steered Rohn wrong when he'd brought him to this place and claimed Rohn would never eat barbecue anywhere else after tasting the food here. He didn't like to give Tyler credit for being right too often—

it might give the young cowboy a swelled head—but as he anticipated his first bite, he had to admit the kid knew his barbecue.

Rohn had just stepped out of the truck when a woman who looked too familiar to be a stranger caught his attention. He squinted through the midday glare, frowning, until recognition hit him like a sledgehammer to the chest.

A smile bowed Rohn's lips. It had been a long time, but it was her. Yeah, she had changed a bit. She was older, a bit curvier, but he'd recognize her anywhere. From the blond curls that had tickled his cheek, to the curve of the hips he'd held on to tight in the bed of his truck where they'd first made love, he knew her. Even twenty-five years later.

In deference to the heat, she wore a tank top that showed enough of her creamy white skin he could see she was still as fair as ever. Her shoulders were pink on top, proving that she'd still freckle and burn rather than tan.

Back in the day she would have been wearing cutoff shorts. Daisy Dukes that showed off her legs to such advantage that Rohn had been able to think of nothing else but having her thighs wrapped around him. Today, she wore knee-length khaki shorts, but that didn't stop him from picturing what lush curves were hidden underneath.

Gone were the cowboy boots she used to love to wear on the farm, even in the summer. In their place were sandals that let her toes peek out.

She stood with her back facing him as she held the door open for an older couple walking out. When they stopped to say thank you, she turned her head so he could see her face.

If he hadn't been one hundred percent certain before, he was now. He took a few long strides in her direction. "Bonnie?"

She turned at the sound of his voice. When her eyes widened, he knew she recognized him, too. "Rohn. Uh, yeah. It's me. So you are still in town."

"Yup. Never left. I own a place not far from here. Cattle ranch."

"Oh. Nice. Good for you."

It was a shock, and a coincidence since he'd just been thinking about her recently. "Bonnie Blue Martin. Back again."

She let out a short laugh but it somehow lacked humor. "I haven't heard anyone call me that since high school."

"That's good to hear." Rohn cocked one brow. "I don't know how I'd feel about some other guy using the name I'd given you."

"No worries about that." A look close to guilt crossed her face as she shook her head. "So how have you been?"

"Good. And yourself?" he asked.

"I'm doing all right."

As they made meaningless small talk, Rohn absorbed everything that had changed about Bonnie, and all the things that had remained the same. She still seemed shy, though that naïve innocence that had cocooned her back then seemed to have been stripped away by time. She seemed harder somehow. Less delicate. More guarded.

The ready smile she'd always had for him was a whole lot more reserved now. It eluded him, just as her gaze did. She barely glanced up, not holding eye contact for more than a few seconds, but rather looking around at anything but him.

"What are you doing in town? Are you back home for good after all these years?" As time had passed, and the decades slipped by, he'd given up hope of ever seeing her again.

That he could feel this good about seeing Bonnie again surprised Rohn. It wouldn't always have been the case. Her leaving without saying good-bye had cut his young heart deep. It had been hard to remember the good moments for a long time.

But that time was past. Seeing Bonnie was a welcome sight today. Running into her unexpectedly had brought back good memories of that summer and his youth. Memories he needed right about now to remind him he'd had another life, another love, besides Lila. And with any luck, he'd find one again now that Lila was gone.

That hope soothed him like a gentle rain after a long drought. Perhaps time really did heal all wounds.

"I'm only back temporarily to handle some things." She raised those blue eyes to meet his before she yanked her gaze away again. "My father died."

His mouth dropped open in surprise. Here he was joking, borderline flirting with her—or at least thinking about doing it—and she was grieving. "Jesus, Bonnie. I'm so sorry. I hadn't heard."

"It's okay, Rohn. There's no reason why you should have heard. I know he kept to himself mostly."

Rohn dipped his head. "That he did. Private man, your dad. I used to see him at the auction occasionally. Not for the past couple years though."

"Yeah, I understand that he sold off the lower field. He couldn't plant any crops the last couple seasons. He couldn't handle the work. Not with his diagnosis."

"Diagnosis?" Rohn raised a brow at the word.

"Throat cancer," Bonnie elaborated.

Rohn sucked in a breath between his teeth. "Sorry to hear that. I lost my wife to cancer five years ago."

"Oh, I'm so sorry. I didn't know."

"Thanks." There was no reason why she should have known. He brought the subject back to her grief. "When did your father pass?"

"Last week." Bonnie's answer surprised him.

"Wow." He supposed Bonnie's losing her father in his later years was completely different from his losing Lila before she'd even reached the middle of what should have been a very long life. "Again, my condolences."

She lifted one shoulder in a shrug. "It's not like it was a surprise, chewing tobacco the way he did for most of his life."

Rohn tipped his head. "That I do remember."

Bonnie's father always had a wad of chaw in his mouth. It was still difficult to reconcile that the intimidating man had been taken so quickly. Then again, Rohn knew firsthand the quick devastation cancer could wreak.

"So anyway, I'm here to take care of things." She drew in a big breath and blew it out, sounding weary. Looking that way, too, now that he took a second glance and noticed the dark shadows beneath her eyes.

"What are you planning on doing with the old place?"

She let out a snort. "Good question."

"You don't know?" he asked.

From what Rohn remembered, it was a decent piece of land, even if the lower field had been sold. If memory served, her father had put in a good-sized crop of wheat in the field behind the house.

"No. Not really."

They'd been holding this conversation while standing in the doorway. As a man pulled into the lot, parked, and came toward the door, Rohn moved to the side, out from the shade of the awning and into the heat of the sun. Bonnie followed him.

"Are you in a position to keep the property?" The thought of Bonnie moving back to town woke an interest inside Rohn he'd long since buried. Maybe the first love a man had never completely left him.

"And run it by myself?" Her brows rose high before she shook her head. "No. But I'm not sure now is the right time to sell. The economy sucks and the real estate market's so depressed. I can't imagine farmland is all that valuable at the moment."

"You could maybe try finding a renter. Someone who's interested in farming but doesn't want to take on a mortgage right now. Or rent the house separately and then find a local farmer looking to expand his crop beyond his own acreage."

"I guess. You interested?" She asked it with a smile and he could tell she was only half-joking.

"I wish I could say I was, but wheat isn't my choice of crop. I got cattle at my place and I've got my own hayfields. The extra bales I need to get through the winter I buy from my neighbor."

"Know anybody who might be interested? I've been gone so long, I feel like I'm a stranger around here."

It had been a long time. "Plenty has changed. Then again, there's plenty that's stayed the same. But if you're thinking about looking for a renter, I guess the best thing to do is put an ad in the paper."

"That's a good idea. Thank you." She eyed him, those blue pools finally focusing on him from beneath her blond lashes. "Everything else seems to have changed, but not you. You still look just like you did back in high school."

"Do I?" He laughed. "Then that brings to light one more change right there—that you need glasses." Rohn grinned as she rolled her eyes at his teasing.

For the first time during the encounter, the smile she flashed him seemed genuine and not forced. "I don't need glasses. It's true."

"Well, you don't look the same."

She lifted her brow high. "Well, it has been twenty-five years."

She'd taken the comment as an insult, but she was wrong. He hadn't meant it as such. Rohn was at the age he knew experience created beauty, not youth.

"I meant, you look even better than you did back then."

"I'm not sure I believe you, but thanks." She smiled again, softening a bit, warming up to him.

He wanted to see her relax, even for a little bit. Throughout the whole conversation she'd seemed a little stiff. A bit like she'd rather be anywhere but there talking to him. Her words were polite enough, but there was something about her. A stiffness in her spine. A shift in her gaze as it darted away from his whenever their eyes met. A nervousness he sensed in her when there was no need for it.

They were old friends. Hell, so much more than friends. For one summer, as seen through the eyes of teenagers, they'd been each other's worlds—until she'd gone off and never came back.

If she hadn't left, what would have happened? There was a good chance he never would have met Lila. He probably would have married Bonnie. If he had, would they still be together today instead of him being alone and lonely?

Rohn pushed the traitorous thought aside. Guilt hit him hard for even thinking it. He wouldn't trade the years of happiness he'd had with Lila for anything in the world. Even as lonely as he was now without her.

He drew in a breath, centering himself, and forced his mind back to the here and now and the woman in front of him. "So, anything I can help you with at your father's place? Moving boxes? Fixing things? I'm strong and I'm pretty handy when I put my mind to it."

"No, thank you. I couldn't accept your help."

He drew his brows down. "Why not?"

"I wouldn't feel right."

"Nonsense. That's what old friends are for."

She waved off his offer. "I'm just going to rent a truck for a day or two to haul some stuff from the house. I'm going to have to make a few trips to the dump. And I figured I'd donate the clothes and some of the furniture to the church."

"I've got a truck you can borrow."

"No, Rohn. I couldn't—"

"I insist."

Bonnie hesitated. "Okay. But I'm paying you for using it."

"Nope. No payment necessary." He shook his head.

"No, I insist."

"Bonnie, I won't take your money."

"Then I won't borrow your truck." She folded her arms, standing firm and stubbornly.

"A'ight. We'll discuss that later." No way was he letting her give him money to use his truck, but that could be battled out at a future date.

"Yes, we will."

"I got three young guys working for me with good strong backs, too, if you need 'em." When she opened her mouth, he held up one hand. "We'll discuss your trying to pay them later, too."

She couldn't move heavy furniture by herself. If she insisted on refusing free help, the least he could do was offer her his hired help . . . and if he happened to stop by and check on the guys while they were there and got to spend some more time with Bonnie, that wouldn't be so bad, either.

Finally, Bonnie dipped her head. "All right. Thank you. I might take you up on that since I don't know anybody in town to hire."

"Good. Glad to hear it. And if you need anything else, a friendly ear to bend about, I don't know, the market for sales of farmland, or the current state of interest rates, give me a call. My phone number's listed. Lerner comma Rohn, spelled with an *h*. Remember?"

She rolled her eyes toward the sky. "I remember."

Rohn realized he'd held her outside in the heat for a long time. "You here to eat?"

"Yeah."

"Want some company?" Damn, that was presumptuous of him but he wasn't letting this chance pass him by.

"Um, I was going to grab something to take out. You know, get right back to work at the house. So, is this place new?" She'd effectively declined his offer and changed the subject.

The question was, why? What was making her so uncomfortable? The situation she had to deal with or him?

While he figured out the answer to that question, he'd have to keep things casual. Play it cool. God, he hated being in this position. It was like they were back in high school again. Playing games.

"Eh, I guess it opened about six months ago. Best barbecue around as far as I can tell. My ranch hands love it, and considering the amount of barbecue they can put away, that's saying something."

"Sounds good." There was that look again, like she wanted to escape.

This time, Rohn decided to let her. "Actually, I'm bringing lunch back to the crew so I should probably go in, get what I came for, and head back to the ranch."

The breath she drew in seemed filled with relief.

"Me too. Best I get moving myself." She motioned toward the door.

He nodded. "One bit of advice, the brisket and the jalapeño mac and cheese combo is the way I'd go, if I were you."

"Thank you. I'll keep that in mind." She turned for the door and he followed her inside.

Bonnie Blue. The first girl to steal his heart and

the first girl to break it. He watched her move toward
the counter. Her back to him as if they hadn't been
as close as any two people could be once upon a
time. He should let her go about her business while
he went about his. Just be happy they'd had a chance
to say hey and catch up, and leave it at that.

That would be the smart thing to do.

Sometimes, Rohn wasn't so smart. It seemed that
was especially true when it came to Bonnie.

Summer, 1990

The tractor cut wide swaths across the dirt, sending whirls of dust into the dry Oklahoma air. Rohn
felt a bead of sweat roll down his cheek. He wiped
the back of one hand across his face.

Today's job entailed plowing the field to prepare
the soil for a crop of hard red winter wheat that would
be planted this fall for harvesting next spring.

It was a hot one today. He hit the brake with his
booted foot and pulled back on the throttle, letting
the engine idle as he swiped off his hat. He took out
his handkerchief and wiped the perspiration from
his forehead.

He glanced across the field, squinting through the
glare of the sun as a figure came out of the house
and began the walk toward the freshly plowed field.

Talk about hot . . . the sight of Bonnie Martin in
her cutoff jean shorts made the temperature ratchet
up another twenty degrees or so. He watched her
pick her way across the field in her boots.

When she got closer, she waved to him. Rohn lifted
a hand and waved back. He could hop down and go

meet her halfway, but truth be told he was enjoying watching her walk.

The sway of her hips as she traversed the field was a sight to behold. So was the way she kept glancing at him and then away when she realized he was watching her. She was shy. He didn't know many girls at school who were. Most were the type to expect a guy to look their way, and get pissed off when he didn't.

Finally, she reached him and glanced up. "Hey."

"Hey. What's up?" He leaned forward, bracing against the steering wheel.

"I thought you might be thirsty." She held up the glass of sweet tea she'd carried out with her. Funny, he'd been so busy watching the girl that he hadn't even noticed what she held in her hand.

Her mamma's tea was good. He'd had it the other day when he'd come to meet with her dad to get this job. But the tea could never be as sweet as Miss Bonnie Blue herself. He'd like to sample her lips and see if she tasted as good as she looked.

He reached down and took the tea, pressing the cold glass to his parched lips. Swallowing, he felt the cool liquid wet his throat. It washed away the dust and dryness.

One thirst was quenched, but not his other one. He had a hankering for some more of Bonnie. Time alone with her was something he could definitely do with, and now was the perfect time to lay the groundwork for that.

"So, I was thinking about going to see that new movie playing in town. You think you'd like to go and see it with me tonight?"

Her eyes widened at the invitation. "Um. Okay."

It wasn't an overwhelming response. He would

have liked better if she'd said, *hell, yes.* But it was still a yes, and that was just as good. He'd take an okay any day over a flat-out no.

Biding his time to stretch out this little visit, he took another swallow of tea before he said, "I think the show starts at seven. So I'll pick you up here between six fifteen and six thirty?"

"No." She surprised him with the intensity of her *no.* "I mean, I'll meet you at the theater. If that's okay."

"A'ight." He didn't know why she wanted to meet there rather than have him come and get her, but he was willing to work with her to make her happy. "Out front?"

"Yeah, that's good."

"Okay. I'll see you then." He chugged the remainder of the tea and handed the glass back to her. "Thanks for that. I appreciate it."

"No problem. Anytime." She focused her blue eyes on him and then yanked her gaze away. He hoped by the end of tonight, she'd stop being shy around him, but for now, it was kind of cute.

"I better get back to work. Don't want your father getting mad at me."

"No, you don't. So I guess I'll see you later then."

"That you will." He waited for her to move so he could start plowing again, but she stayed standing right there.

"Rohn, maybe don't mention the movie to my mother or father."

"Okay. I won't." He wanted to ask why, but he didn't. He really did have to get back to work. He'd ask her outright later if she didn't volunteer the information.

She looked relieved. "Thanks."

"Sure." He nodded. "No problem."

"All right. So I'll see you later. At the theater."

"Yup."

Finally, she turned and after one backward glance, made her way back.

He could have shifted into gear and gotten right back to work the moment she was clear, but instead he watched her walk away all the way to the house. Only when she'd gone inside did he glance around him.

Good thing Mr. Martin was nowhere to be seen or Rohn might have been in trouble for slacking off.

Rohn eased his foot off the brake and hit the throttle. He heard the sound of the engine react to the change. The machine jerked into motion and Rohn made his way down the row.

The job was monotonous, but now he had something to occupy his mind. He'd have plenty to think about for the rest of the day thanks to his date with Bonnie on the horizon.

And hell yeah he'd have even more to think about tomorrow, because that would be the day after his first date with Bonnie Blue. The first date of many, he hoped. If things went well, he'd have lots of good memories to relive as he bounced in the tractor seat tomorrow.

With the taste of the sweet tea still on his tongue, Rohn hoped to have the taste of Bonnie there shortly.

Chapter Six

Bonnie drove up to her former home for the second time in less than a couple of hours, but this time, the paralyzing dread wasn't riding her.

Maybe that was because of the incredible smell of the barbecue takeout that filled the car's interior. It was like an invisible yet physical hug surrounding her.

It was called comfort food for a reason, she supposed. Even just the scent soothed her nerves. Of course, she could also be feeling different after coming face-to-face with Rohn. It hadn't been as horrible as she feared. He'd been pleasant. Friendly. Maybe he didn't hate her for leaving the way she had.

The overwhelming guilt from the past was still there, but surprisingly she'd also felt pleasure at seeing the familiar face of her old boyfriend who seemed to only get better with age.

The goofy smile of his youth had turned sexy and

alluring. His hard football-player's body had filled out a bit, making him look even more solid and strong. And those eyes—his steely gaze still had the power to captivate her.

She sighed. Her moment of diversion was over. She opened the car door and grabbed the bag of food and her purse. Time to get back to reality.

Inside the house seemed stifling. Mentally. Physically. The clutter made the walls feel too close even as the hot air pressed against her. She probably shouldn't have turned off the A/C to open all the windows on a day this sweltering, but she couldn't bear feeling so contained. So trapped.

Maybe once some of this stuff was out of the house it would seem better. Once the heavy curtains were taken down and the rooms bare, she'd feel better.

There was a lot of work ahead of her, but first, food.

Rather than let the smothering atmosphere of the house ruin her meal, she carried the bag of takeout outside. There was still an old picnic table in the yard. She walked to it now and noticed the grass had been recently cut.

Given the state of her father's health, she had a feeling she had one more thing to thank Andrew for next time she saw him.

That brought up another concern—future maintenance of the property until she sold, or rented, or did whatever she decided to do with the place.

This gift from her father, this bequest, was not a welcome one.

It was almost as if he knew it would be a burden on her. Then again, maybe she was being paranoid. Lack of food could do that to a person.

Her blood sugar was probably too low at this point, after the long drive and nothing but an energy drink in her system for the last few hours on the road.

It didn't help her hunger that the food smelled good enough to make her mouth water, but she had chosen to drive all the way home before taking even one bite.

That could be corrected pretty fast. She broke into the bag and saw they'd put both paper napkins and a plastic fork and knife in the bag. Good, because she'd been in such a hurry to get out the back door, she hadn't thought to stop and grab those items from the kitchen.

Opening the lid of the container, she got the first look at what she'd been smelling for long enough to have her stomach grumbling in protest.

She'd ordered what Rohn had recommended— the combo plate. Scooping up a forkful of mac and cheese, she took her first taste.

The flavor filling her mouth was like sunshine. Bonnie couldn't help but smile. She had doubted it could be as good as Rohn had promised, but it was. She'd remember not to doubt him again.

There was no need for the knife, since the smoked brisket was so tender it broke apart with the fork. She took a taste and one more time she was struck with an explosion of sensation. It was as if her senses had been dormant and just now had awoken.

How could a takeout combo plate of barbecue accomplish all that? Though maybe it was more than the food. Maybe she had put herself into a state of hibernation—a method of self-preservation when she'd fled this place all those years ago. It took coming home to bring her back to life.

She must have been hungrier than she'd thought because though the portion was generous and she had been sure she'd have to put the leftovers in the fridge, she finished every last bite. All that remained was a partial container of barbecue sauce.

The problem was now that Bonnie was done with her food she had no more excuse to sit idle, aside from not wanting to go back inside the house.

Rallying the motivation to force herself into motion, she hoisted her stiff body off the old wooden bench. She put the garbage into the takeout bag and carried it to the trash can.

Walking through the kitchen door, she realized it wasn't as overwhelming being in the house as it had been before. Each time she walked in, it affected her a little less.

By the time she finished and was ready to sell, she should be immune to the place and its memories.

Bonnie moved down the hallway past what had been her parents' room years ago. How many nights had she heard the battle raging inside that room during their years of marriage? All while she hid her head beneath the covers with nothing but her teddy bear for comfort, even when she was well into her teens.

Her own room was just beyond. She couldn't bring herself to start with it, either. Too many memories. She turned back around and headed back to the kitchen.

The kitchen was the heart of the home, and she'd need it to be clean and serviceable while she stayed there. Most importantly, nothing bad had happened in the kitchen, probably because her mother served her father's meals in the dining room. The kitchen was her and her mom's domain and she was going to bring it back to the way it used to be.

Summer, 1990

"Mom." Bonnie came through the back door, but her mother wasn't in the kitchen.

She made her way through the house and back toward the bedrooms. She heard raised voices. Her parents' bedroom door was open, but she hesitated to go inside. It sounded as if her mother and father were fighting, but she couldn't tell about what. The more she considered, the more she realized she didn't want to know. She just wanted the argument to stop.

"Mom." She said it again to let them know she was there, hoping it would put an end to whatever their heated discussion had been about.

Her mother came out into the hallway. "Yes, baby."

"I was wondering if I could go to the movies tonight. There's a new show playing in town. I could take my bike. You wouldn't have to drive me. It starts at seven so I wouldn't be out too late."

"Sure you can go. With who?"

"Um." Bonnie knew it was a risk telling her mother about going with Rohn. What if her father objected? What if he fired Rohn for asking her out? He wouldn't want to see her ever again after that.

Her mind scrambled, but there was really only one

thing to do. Lie. Only one person would be believable in this scenario. "I'm meeting Melody there."

"Oh, that's nice. She's a nice girl."

"Yeah, she is." Poor Melody was nice, and now also Bonnie's cover for her secret date with Rohn.

Her father came out into the hallway. "What's going on?"

"Bonnie's going to the movies in town tonight." Her mother answered for her and Bonnie was happy to let her. When her father wore this expression, there was no way to make him happy.

"Who with?"

"Melody." Bonnie took over answering the questions. She felt guilty enough about the lie. She didn't want her mother to have to repeat it.

Her father seemed to dismiss her evening plans after that, as he moved to the kitchen to glance out the back window. "That kid about done with that field yet?"

"Um, almost. He's got like two more passes." Bonnie realized she probably shouldn't know in such great detail what Rohn was doing. Even if the truth was she watched him every second she could. "At least that's what it looked like the last time I walked past the window."

Jeez, she had to be more careful. The most amazing thing of her life had just happened. Rohn had actually asked her out. She'd dreamed of this day and it had really happened. She wasn't going to jeopardize it by having her father decide she shouldn't be dating the hired help.

Though she had a feeling her father wouldn't like her dating anyone, no matter who it was. Yes, she'd turned eighteen last month, but he was the kind to remind her often enough that while she lived under his roof, she also lived under his rules. If he said she couldn't see Rohn, then that would be it. She wouldn't be able to go.

Lying was the only option. She'd have to hide their relationship.

Relationship.

Even thinking that word seemed premature. She could only hope and dream that meeting him at the theater tonight would turn into a relationship.

It could be nothing more than Rohn not wanting to be alone in the movies. Or maybe it was a group thing. He could be meeting his friends there and thought she might like to come along. She tried to remember the exact words he'd used to invite her and couldn't. She'd been too shocked and excited to think at the time.

She couldn't think more about that right now. Her father was frowning, his focus on the view outside the window of the field Rohn was plowing. "I probably could have finished it myself in half the time."

"You have years more experience than he does, honey." Her mother stepped in to smooth things over. "He tries his best. He's a real hard worker and he's eager to learn. By the end of the summer he'll be better at it, I'm sure."

"Yeah. I guess he's working out all right. And for what little I'm paying him, I reckon I can't complain. The other guy who came about the job wanted double what I'm paying this kid. I was surprised he settled for what I offered him."

That was interesting news to Bonnie. She dared to comment on it. "I guess he really wanted the job."

"Or he needed it bad enough. Who knows?" Her father sighed. "I'm gonna go work on that machine that needs fixing. Call me when dinner's ready."

"I will." Her mother stood on her tiptoes and pressed a kiss to her father's cheek. He didn't even acknowledge the endearment before he turned to walk out the back door.

Bonnie watched it all, happy the fight between them seemed to be over, but vowing she'd never marry a man who didn't love her as strongly, as passionately, as she loved him.

Her mind went back to what had been revealed in the kitchen just now. Rohn had taken the job for shitty pay. Why?

Her heart sped at a crazy notion. Maybe because he'd wanted to be near her? Could it be?

There had to be plenty of jobs available for a young, strong guy willing to work hard. In fact, a couple of Rohn's friends were working for a landscaping company, getting paid to cut lawns. Rohn had said so himself. They worked early in the morning and then quit for the rest of the day, going fishing, or hanging out around town. All while he continued to labor until dinnertime on her father's dusty land.

Farming was a tough job. Harvesting the wheat. Plowing and planting the fields for next season. Not to mention Rohn had to put up with her father's demands.

But if he was here, doing this all to be near her . . . Bonnie nearly passed out at the thought. Deep down, she loved the idea, even if it might be just in her crazy imagination.

And—oh my God—tonight they had a date. She needed to find something to wear. She headed for her bedroom.

Six thirty couldn't come fast enough.

Chapter Seven

Summer, 2015 (Present Day)

The drive from town to the ranch was fairly short, but it was long enough for Rohn to replay his conversation with Bonnie at the barbecue place over in his head more than once.

With the distraction occupying him so completely, he drove the familiar route on autopilot. He didn't realize he'd made it all the way home until he was almost passing the mailbox at the end of his drive. He slowed in time to make the turn into his place.

The tires crunched the gravel beneath them as he crept past the house, past the barn and onto the dirt path leading out to the field where he could see the guys working.

After coming to a stop, he threw the transmission into reverse and backed the truck up to where the fresh holes were dug for the new fence line they were putting in. He'd gotten the lumber they needed, but the kids could unload it.

Since he'd made the decision to purchase Janie's

hay harvest to help her out, he could take one of the fields he'd formerly reserved for that crop and turn it into grazing land. With more space available, he'd decided to expand his stock.

His guys might be a pain in his ass some days, but he happened to have three hands working for him who knew their way around horses. Justin especially could saddle break a horse like nobody's business. And Tyler was crazy enough he'd jump on the back of anything, including the wildest bronc.

They'd discovered Rohn owned some good bucking stock, thanks to Tyler's inability to say no to a challenge and willingness to ride anything, be it horse or bull.

Tyler was working the closest to where Rohn had parked. He came ambling toward the truck, wiping the sweat out of his eyes with the hem of his T-shirt as he walked.

It was a hot one today. The guys should be good and ready for a break and something cold to drink. The barbecue lunch he'd bought would be a welcome surprise. Rohn reached over and grabbed the takeout from the passenger seat.

"Whatcha got there?" Tyler's eyes widened when he saw the telltale paper bag Rohn held as he stepped away from the truck.

"Just picked up a little lunch for myself from that barbecue place you like so much." The bag was so full and heavy, Rohn had to use two hands to support the bottom of it. When Tyler's brows drew low, forming a line above his eyes, Rohn could see the confusion and disappointment written in his expression. Smiling, he added, "I bought enough for you guys, too."

Like a kid on Christmas morning when he found out there was one more present under the tree, Tyler grinned wide. "I'll get Justin and Colt."

"You do that." These kids were too easy to tease. Rohn chuckled to himself as Tyler spun on his boot heel.

Tyler whistled to the others and yelled, "Hey! Take a break. Rohn got us barbecue."

At that information, the two cowboys dropped their tools to the ground, leaving them where they landed. They jogged toward Rohn as he shook his head. Just like a pack of puppies, these kids were. Whistle, shake the bag of food, and they'd come running.

If he'd had kids back when he and Lila had first gotten married, they wouldn't be all that much younger than these guys were now . . . *if* she'd been able to have kids.

She'd miscarried three times, the last one well into her second trimester. That's when Rohn put a stop to the emotional roller coaster they'd ridden for years and insisted they stop trying. He couldn't stand seeing the overwhelming sadness every lost baby brought to their lives. Hated seeing the guarded hope colored by anxiety in Lila each time that pregnancy test came back positive and she lived with the fear she'd lose it.

In spite of the doctor's assurances, she always blamed herself, questioning if the laundry basket she'd lifted or the cold she'd come down with had done something to cause the miscarriage. Beating herself up that she should have taken better care of herself. Gotten more rest. Taken more vitamins. Stayed off her feet and in bed for nine months.

The reality was, it simply wasn't meant to be. Rohn accepted that, though it didn't keep him from wondering what if?

What if he'd had sons? Would they be like Tyler—hardworking and kindhearted but easily tempted to be wild and out of control? Or like Colton, more of a follower than a leader? Then there was Justin—all jokes and smiles on the outside, when on the inside Rohn could see the darkness he tried to hide ever since his brother had been killed in action.

Then again he could have had a daughter. Good Lord, that was a frightening thought. Given what he knew about guys in this day and age, he wasn't sure he'd have been able to handle the stress of having a daughter to shield from the world and all its horrors.

Thinking it over as they all walked into the house together, Rohn realized maybe he wasn't missing out by not having kids of his own. He had his hands full already just with his three young hired hands.

In the kitchen Rohn put the bag on the table. "Dig in. I'll get the water."

By the time Rohn had reached into the freezer for ice to put in the water pitcher, the mad grab had begun. In the battle for food, Tyler was the quickest. He got to the bag first, grabbing the top takeout container for himself along with a plastic fork and napkin the girl had thrown into the bag.

Rohn shook his head at the lack of manners in a boy he knew had been raised better by his mamma. "Tyler, you know you could have taken all the containers out instead of just claiming your own. There's plenty for everyone."

Tyler sat in one of the kitchen chairs. "They can get it out themselves."

It was apparently every man for himself. The brisket didn't stand a chance against three hungry hired hands.

Justin grabbed his portion and sat. "No worries, Rohn. Ty's looking a little scrawny lately. He needs the food."

Colton snorted out a laugh and sat on the opposite side of the table. "He's got you there, Ty."

The joking around was all in good fun. Boys would be boys. They could all see Tyler was as solid as a brick wall, kind of how Rohn had been back in the day.

"Well, we all can't be Mr. Universe like Justin here. Pumping iron in the garage at night to get the blood moving because he's got no girl to do that for him. And I'll have you know, I don't hear Janie complaining about my size . . . anywhere."

Still standing at the sink, Rohn let his lids drift closed and tried to block out the picture Tyler had put in his head. That was something Rohn didn't need to imagine—Tyler naked or him getting busy with Rohn's longtime friend and neighbor, Janie.

He flipped off the faucet and turned to carry the pitcher of ice water he'd filled to the table. The boys were well into their lunch. He figured he'd better grab the glasses out of the cabinet quick before they tried to steal his food.

Finally settled, everyone with barbecue and water, Rohn opened the lid of his lunch and inhaled the aroma that had been teasing him for the better part of the past half hour. He sniffed and appreciated it for a few seconds more before stabbing the first piece with the plastic fork. He should have gotten up and grabbed real cutlery from the drawer rather than try to eat with this inferior plastic stuff, but the meat had been smoked for so long it fell apart as he lifted it to his mouth.

Good barbecue didn't require a knife or a metal fork, but it did demand a man take his time enjoying the nuances of it. The taste on the tongue. The smoky flavor that seemed to hang on in the back of his throat even after he swallowed.

These boys wolfing down their food like they hadn't eaten in days couldn't be appreciating it as it deserved. Then again, these boys were getting plenty of pleasures in their off hours that Rohn wasn't, so they didn't need to absorb every ounce of satisfaction they could from a plate of meat.

Rohn had just moved on to the jalapeño macaroni and cheese, marveling at the smooth, creaminess of the cheese in contrast to the bite of the pepper flavor, when Tyler glanced his way and asked, "So, what are you doing tonight?"

With the empty fork poised above the mound of orange macaroni, Rohn said, "The same as usual—nothing. Why?"

"Janie called to tell me she's making fajitas for dinner. She asked if I'd invite you over to eat with us."

Watching Tyler and Janie play the happy couple was probably the last thing Rohn could think of wanting to do at the end of a long day. But unless he cooked it himself, he wasn't getting homemade fajitas.

Home-cooked meals were hard to come by nowadays. He mostly got takeout and lived off the leftovers for a few days.

Tyler waved a hand in front of Rohn's face. "Um, hello? It's not a hard question."

"Oh, sorry." Glancing up, he saw all eyes on him. Caught without an excuse not to go, other than that he was a poor sport who wasn't sure he wanted to see them happy when he wasn't, Rohn said, "Yeah, sure. Sounds good. Thanks."

"We're not invited?" Colton frowned.

"No." Tyler's answer was short, but definitive.

Colton drew his brows down lower. "Why not?"

"Hell, I don't know." Tyler scowled at Colton's questioning. "She didn't tell me to invite anyone but Rohn."

"So you could invite us on your own. You're living with her, right?" Colton apparently wasn't letting it go.

"No." Tyler scowled. "I'm not living with her."

"Nope. He just sleeps—or *doesn't sleep*—there every night." Justin grinned. "You see, Colt. If Ty here wants to keep getting what he's getting over there, he's gotta do exactly as the little woman says. Otherwise"—Justin made a slicing motion across his neck—"He gets cut off. *Comprende?*"

"Yup. Got his balls in a jar on the windowsill for safekeeping, she does." Colton smirked.

"Yeah, yeah." Tyler rolled his eyes. "Joke all you want. I'll be the one laughing all the way upstairs to the bedroom tonight."

Rohn had had just about enough of this kind of talk. It was interfering with his being able to concentrate on the enjoyment of his food.

"Good God Almighty. Do y'all talk about anything other than sex?" Rohn's age might be showing but, jeez, enough was enough.

He knew the woman they were joking so disrespectfully about. He'd been her husband's friend before he'd died. He didn't need to hear all this about her ever, but especially not over lunch.

Tyler raised a brow. "Sure, we do. We also like to talk about food. Good barbecue. Thanks for getting it." He lifted his fork to Rohn in a salute.

Food and women . . . that just about covered the scope of concerns for these boys working for him.

Missing those carefree days of his youth a little himself, Rohn let out a sigh. "You're welcome."

Summer, 1990

Rohn was nervous as he stood waiting outside the movie theater for Bonnie. He'd parked his pickup truck and was standing on the curb so she'd see him. He would have liked to have picked her up and driven her here himself, but she'd said to meet her instead.

He couldn't count how many times he had imagined her riding shotgun in the passenger seat of his truck since the night he'd first talked to her at their prom. He dreamed of glancing over and seeing her there.

More than that, he imagined pulling up to the river where all the guys parked with their girls. Cutting the engine, turning to her, and kissing those sweet lips of hers.

Sometimes, often actually, he thought about doing more than kissing her. At night, alone in his bed, he imagined doing so much more with sweet Bonnie Blue.

Working at her dad's farm, seeing her all the time, only ramped up his need for her. Of course, he was an eighteen-year-old boy. It was no surprise that he obsessively thought about girls. But it wasn't girls—plural—that he fantasized about. It was only one. Bonnie.

For some reason, his thoughts turned to her cute little sunburned nose, covered in freckles. He remembered her today as she squinted against the glare of the sun and looked up at him in the tractor seat.

That memory was cut short when he turned and saw Bonnie had arrived, but it was a welcome interruption.

She was wearing a sundress that showed off her shoulders and arms. It ended just above her knees so her lean legs were displayed to perfection. She had on sandals with a little heel that lifted her higher and gave her hips a little bit of a sway as she walked toward him.

He did love how she ran around the farm in cutoff shorts and cowboy boots, but the dress was a real nice change. One he could get used to. Especially if he could run his hands over that soft cotton, down her body, and all the way until he hit the heat of the bare skin of her legs.

Rohn swallowed away the lump in his throat that image had caused and fought the urge to adjust the stiffening length in his jeans.

Instead, he took a step forward and hoped she wouldn't notice the bulge. "Hey. I'm glad you could make it."

"I said I would."

Yes, she had, but sometimes things came up, and he wasn't sure she was as into this date as he was, given her hesitation when he'd asked her.

"Ready to go inside?" he asked, anxious to get this night with her started.

"Sure." She nodded and gripped the strap of the small, backpack-shaped purse looped over her shoulder.

"Okay. Let's go." He moved across the sidewalk to the window and asked for two tickets. As he pulled his wallet out of his jeans Bonnie stepped up next to him and dug inside her bag.

She pulled out a ten-dollar bill and held it toward him. "Here. For my ticket."

He wrinkled his brow and pushed her hand and the money back toward her. "No, I've got this. I asked you out. I'm paying."

She reacted to that with a mix of what seemed to be awkwardness and embarrassment. He didn't want her to feel anything but happy to be there with him, so he added, "I do appreciate your offer, though. I know some girls like to pay for themselves, but I guess I'm an old-fashioned kind of guy, so I'd like to get it. Okay?"

"Okay. I just wasn't sure . . ."

"You weren't sure about what?" He glanced at her as he grabbed the tickets and his change, shoving the bills into his jeans pocket rather than taking the time to put them away in his wallet properly. He'd probably be buying popcorn inside, anyway.

"If this was a date." She said it so softly he'd had to listen extra hard to hear.

That she hadn't been sure this was a date was interesting information. She wasn't anything like the other girls he knew, which was one of the things he liked about her.

Bonnie wasn't the type to assume anything. He

liked that, but he should probably make himself more clear in future. That was easily solved. He'd just let her know things straight out, plain and simple. He could do that, starting right now.

Rohn reached out and took her hand, lacing his fingers through hers. "This is a date as far as I'm concerned. Is that okay with you?"

Her cheeks grew pink as she nodded. "Yes."

"Good. Come on. Let's go inside and find a good seat."

He handed the two small stubs to the ticket taker and led her by the hand into the dimly lit theater. He almost asked her where she liked to sit, but thought better of it. He needed to take charge of this date.

From what he knew so far about Bonnie, he figured she wouldn't like the pressure of making the decision. More importantly, she might very well choose the wrong seat. At least, the wrong place to sit in his opinion and for his goals for tonight.

The movie that was playing looked all right, and he wouldn't mind seeing it, but that was not the goal of this evening. Getting to know Bonnie better was. In all ways.

He wanted to know what made her laugh. What she thought about. What her favorite food was. And yeah, he also wanted to discover what her mouth tasted like, what her skin felt like, what she'd do if he leaned over in the dark and kissed her.

If he found out even one of those many things he'd wondered about over the week since he'd begun working for her father, he'd consider the night a success.

If he was lucky enough to have all of that revealed

to him, then hell, he'd be the luckiest guy on earth. He might never come down from the high of it.

He chose the row against the back wall and when he led her to the seats all the way in the back corner and sat, she glanced at him but didn't say anything.

It was a good start. So far, so good.

"You like action movies?" he asked.

"Yeah."

"For real or are you just saying that to make me happy?" He had a feeling that was totally something she would do.

Rohn wanted something real with Bonnie, and even though he didn't have all that many long-term relationships under his belt, he knew open honesty was a good start.

She laughed. "Both. I do like action movies, but I figure you'll be happy about it since that's what you asked me to see."

"Bonnie, I want you to always tell me the truth. Okay? Even if you think it won't make me happy."

"Okay." She agreed too quickly for Rohn's liking.

"No, I'm serous. Promise me."

"Okay. I promise." This time she sounded sincere and he hoped she meant what she said.

He wanted this to work with her and the way to do that was to start off on the right foot. Honestly, about everything. That's how his parents had been happily married for over twenty years and that's how he intended his life and his future to be as well.

Maybe Bonnie was the girl he'd end up with, and maybe she wasn't. No matter how much he liked her, he was grounded enough to realize that.

The lights dimmed and the screen lit up. Rohn had been hoping they'd have a few more minutes to talk, but apparently the theater started showing the previews before the movie start time.

Being in the dark pressed close to Bonnie in the narrow theater seats was no hardship. He could talk to her later, after he convinced her to go out with him for ice cream.

He liked that idea. Movie, ice cream, maybe a ride to the river to talk—or to kiss—either one. He would be good with either.

The previews didn't hold his attention. No surprise when he had her to look at. She'd left her hair down tonight. He tried to think whether he'd ever seen her blond waves not confined in a braid and he couldn't come up with any time. He liked her hair loose and free.

He knew well how the sun bounced off her halo of gold. He'd seen it often enough when he'd been watching her from the seat of the tractor. But he didn't know how it felt. Seeing it down now made him want to reach out and see if it felt as silky between his fingers as he imagined.

She was pretty all the time, but with her hair falling in soft waves around her face, she was more beautiful than her usual girl-next-door pretty.

In the darkened theater, lit only by pale security lights and the big screen way down in front of them, he wished he could see her freckles and the sun-kissed glow of her cheeks more clearly.

He couldn't see her well in this light, but he could let her invade the rest of his senses.

Slumping down in his seat, he leaned a bit closer and angled his face toward her head. She smelled incredible, an odd mix of light floral scent and fresh air, like girly-girl and outdoors all wrapped in one.

They both moved to use the armrest at the same time and their elbows collided. The heat from the bare skin of her arm seared into his memory and elicited imaginings of what it would be like to be pressed against her, skin to skin.

No clothes between them. No people around them. Just him and her.

Damn. He had to stop thinking like that. Good thing it was so dark. His body was embarrassing him. He needed a distraction. Maybe a tub of popcorn would take his mind off her. It would at least cover his crotch, if nothing else.

He leaned close to her ear and whispered, "You want something? Popcorn? Soda?"

She jumped, as if surprised he'd spoken so close to her. She turned her head so her mouth was closer to his ear. He angled his head and leaned in so she could whisper to him.

"Don't get up. You'll miss the start of the movie." The heat of her breath against his ear had him getting harder. So much for hoping for a distraction to get his mind off the growing situation inside his jeans.

"I don't care about that. If you want something, I'll get it."

"No, thank you. I'm good."

He was starting to see how she was. Bonnie would go out of her way not to put anyone else out. From now on, he'd just get her what he thought she'd like and not ask, because he sensed that inevitably her answer would always be the same. *No thank you. I'm fine.*

His prom date had had no problem ordering him around that night. *Get me soda. My feet hurt. Bring the truck to the door.* He'd been pretty sick of that when he'd dropped Lena off at her house that night. He hadn't even tried to take her to the river to try and score some action.

Bonnie was the exact opposite, but her inability, or maybe just reluctance, to express what she wanted was going to be a challenge. He was up for a good challenge, especially when it came wrapped in such a sweet, enticing package as Bonnie Blue.

The long string of previews finally ended and the main event began. He'd never been less interested in what was happening on the screen in his life. His full attention was on the girl next to him, fidgeting in the seat, so close he could sense every breath she took and every move she made.

Her foot tapped against the floor. She moved from clasping her hands in her lap, to putting them on the armrests, only to move them off again.

She was nervous. He was, too. Or at least he had been until he saw how uncomfortable she was. That was the last thing he wanted. He wanted her to have a good time with him. To be completely comfortable with him.

It was ridiculous for them to be uncomfortable. Thanks to the job he'd landed, the one he'd stolen from Brian by showing up first and accepting such low pay, Rohn had seen Bonnie six days in a row. They should be better alone together than this, yet she was clearly nervous.

Resolved to change that, Rohn reached out and took her hand in his, holding it firmly, letting her know that she could fidget and tap her foot all she wanted, but that hand was his for as long as he chose to hold it.

He glanced over and saw her gaze cut to him before she brought it back to the screen in front of them. She didn't protest. She didn't pull away. That was good enough for him.

Smiling, he leaned back in the seat and slumped a little lower, wishing the theater gave him a few more inches as his knees hit the seat in front of him. But as long as Bonnie was next to him and he had her hand in his, he'd deal with the cramped conditions. He'd put up with a lot for her.

He tried his best to keep up with the story playing out on the screen. He really did. But he was far more interested in the real live girl next to him than the one larger than life on the big screen.

Rohn leaned low again. "You enjoying the movie?"

She angled her face to his. This time he didn't turn his ear toward her. He stayed right there, facing her.

They were so close he could feel the warmth of her breath when she said, "Yes."

She watched him from the small distance, moving her gaze from his eyes, to his lips, then back up again. He moved in a tiny bit farther. She didn't pull back but he heard her draw in a sharp breath.

He was breathing a little faster himself, his heart pounding as he leaned in a tiny bit more. He hovered just shy of her lips before braving the final space between them and pressing his mouth to hers. He knew immediately from the first taste of her that one tiny kiss wasn't going to be enough.

Chapter Eight

Summer, 2015 (Present Day)

"Hey." Tyler leaned into the doorway of Rohn's office.

Rohn glanced up and frowned. "I thought you left for the day."

"I did. I ran home . . . uh, I mean to Janie's. I showered and changed there."

"A'ight." Rohn still didn't know what Tyler was doing back here.

"I came to get you."

Rohn frowned. "Why?" He knew he was expected for dinner. And Janie's place was right next door. It wasn't like he'd get lost.

"Because I know how you are. You don't come up for air once you get to working on that thing." Tyler tipped his chin in the direction of the computer on Rohn's desk.

"You're right about that." Even with as much as Rohn hated paperwork, he did tend to lose himself in it for hours.

Little did Tyler know that Rohn hadn't been working just now. He'd been checking out the half a dozen private messages sent to his profile on the dating site that he still couldn't believe he'd joined.

Rohn sighed and closed the browser window fast before Tyler decided to get nosy and look to see what he'd been working on.

"So, you about ready to head over to Janie's?" Tyler asked.

"Is it that late already?" He glanced at the time in the corner of his computer.

It was going on dinnertime.

Damn. Time had slipped away while he'd been staring at all the women who wanted to meet him, and realizing that not a one piqued his interest. Not like Bonnie had during their five-minute conversation outside the barbecue joint.

Tyler dipped his head. "Dinner's in an hour. I thought you'd like to come and hang out for a bit first. You know. Have a beer. Shoot the shit."

Whether Rohn was up for socializing with the newly happy couple or not, it would be rude to just show up and eat. Besides, a cold beer sounded damn good right about now.

He shut down the computer and stood. "A'ight. Let's go."

Tyler frowned as his gaze took Rohn in from head to toe. "You wearing that?"

Rohn glanced down at his T-shirt and jeans. These were the clothes he'd worn all day, but they weren't dirty. He hadn't done any real work today. Hell, he hadn't even broken a sweat.

"I was planning on it. Why? Is this a formal occasion?" He cocked a brow.

"No. I mean I just thought since you don't get out much that you'd dress up a bit. Maybe put on that nice pearl-snap shirt I've seen you wear."

"Thanks for reminding me I don't get out much." Beneath the insult, there was something else in Tyler's tone that made Rohn suspicious. "What's going on?"

"Nothing is going on. Never mind about changing. Just come on. Janie's waiting on us." Tyler tipped his head toward the hall.

"Fine. I was ready to go until you started talking about fashion." Rohn scowled as he led the way down the hall and out the back door.

Both his property and Janie's were large, which meant neighbors or not, it was a hike to get from one house to the other on foot. It was doable, but Rohn had never made the trip without a horse or truck.

Rohn paused with his hand on the door handle of his vehicle as Tyler strode to his own. "I'll meet you over there."

Tyler lifted his hand in a wave and climbed into the driver's seat.

Rohn watched Tyler pull the old pickup out of the driveway ahead of him.

The kid drove a truck as old as he was—on purpose. Meanwhile Rohn, almost twenty years older than Tyler, traded in his own vehicles every two years. Rohn made a decent living. He could afford a new truck.

Besides, keeping a business running smooth so he could make a good living meant he was too busy to be tinkering under the hood the way Tyler always seemed to be.

The kid lived to be covered in engine grease—or

at least he used to before he had Janie to occupy his time. It would be interesting to see which won out if it ever came to a choice for Tyler—time with Janie or his old piece of crap.

Rohn pulled into Janie's driveway and parked behind Tyler's truck.

Getting out, he eyed the shiny coupe parked by the front door of his neighbor's house. Friends and neighbors always parked by Janie's back door, knowing she'd be more likely to be in that end of the house, in the kitchen. The front door led to the formal living room that she and her late husband rarely used.

Maybe since Janie knew he'd be coming over she didn't want her car to block the parking spot by the kitchen so she'd pulled it out of the way to allow him to park there. That still didn't explain the new car. Last he'd seen, Janie had been driving her late husband's truck.

Rohn caught up to Tyler. "Did Janie buy a new car?"

"Um, no." Tyler's hesitation had Rohn drawing in a steadying breath as what was really going on here became apparent.

"Christ. This is a fix-up, isn't it?" He ran a hand over his face.

"Uh, maybe?" Tyler cringed. "Don't be mad. It was Janie's idea as much as mine."

Nice of Tyler to throw his girlfriend under the bus.

"I don't care whose idea it was. I told you, I don't want to be set up on some pity date with God only knows who. I'll find my own damn woman if and when I want one." Rohn kept his voice down so anyone inside wouldn't hear but he was sure as hell going to make sure that Tyler understood how pissed he was.

"I know. Please, Rohn, she's here now and expecting you. Just come inside for a little while. Please don't embarrass Janie in front of her friend."

That might be the one thing Tyler could have said to get Rohn in that door. The kid wasn't as dumb as he acted sometimes. "Fine. I won't embarrass Janie. And make no mistake that I'm doing this for her, not for you. But the minute this dinner is over, I'm out of here."

"A'ight. That's fair. Thank you." Tyler seemed genuinely grateful and more than a bit relieved.

As he followed the young cowboy to the back door, Rohn had to wonder if Tyler would still feel as grateful after all the shit jobs he was going to have to perform over the next week or so.

Anything and everything that the boys bitched about doing at the ranch was going to be assigned to Tyler. Colt and Justin were going to have a very good week, coasting along with the easy jobs at the expense of their friend.

Call him spiteful, but that thought lightened Rohn's mood considerably. He was almost giddy over his plan for revenge against Tyler by the time they reached the kitchen door and the boy turned to shoot him a glance.

"You sure you're gonna be okay with this?" Tyler asked.

"Are you asking if I'm going to humiliate a friend and neighbor I've known for years?" Rohn pressed his lips together unhappily. "Of course, I wouldn't do that to Janie. I'm capable of being cordial even while I'm pissed off at you."

"A'ight." Still looking a little concerned, Tyler opened the door and headed inside.

Rohn drew in a bracing breath and followed. The problem with this scenario was that even if the woman was perfectly nice, he was already primed not to want to like her, thanks to Tyler's underhanded deception.

Oh, well. He'd do his best to act as he'd promised— be pleasant to the woman, even if he wasn't on board with this whole setup. Maybe, hopefully, she'd surprise him. Who knew? She could be the perfect one for him.

Pfft. Doubtful.

He'd just have to consider this practice for the time, if ever, that he went on a date with one of those women who'd messaged him online. He could certainly use some experience in the dating arena.

After all these years, he was more than rusty. Getting back on the horse would take guts.

"We're here." Unnecessarily, Tyler announced their arrival as the screen door slammed behind Rohn.

Janie was seated at the kitchen table with another female. It didn't take a great leap for Rohn to draw the conclusion that Janie's guest was his date for the evening.

Janie was already beaming just at the sight of Tyler but she turned her smile toward Rohn. "Hi, Rohn. I'm glad you could make it."

"Sure. Thanks for the invite."

It took Tyler's puppy, Daisy, all of two seconds to come skidding across the kitchen floor, tail wagging, to get to Rohn. He bent to pet the spotted cattle dog. She spun beneath his hand, not much more than a ball of fur and energy.

"Hey there, girl. I miss seeing you at my place."

The dog was a good excuse to ignore the stranger in the room. But he knew he couldn't ignore her for long, especially when Tyler stood between them and began making the introductions. "Rohn Lerner, this is Tilly Crowe."

Rohn drew in a breath and straightened up. He noticed all eyes were turned to him, including Tilly's. Ignoring the puppy still scampering around his boots, even though he'd far rather play with her than meet his blind date, he pasted on a smile. "Nice to meet you."

She smiled, her bright red lipstick drawing his attention to her mouth, but not because he longed to kiss her. More because he was wondering what he'd look like if he did and all that red crap ended up smeared all over him.

Probably like a clown.

"And it's very nice to meet you." Tilly stood and took a step toward Rohn, arm extended.

As he shook her offered hand, he noted that she wore her clothes just a bit too tight. Whether that was because she thought it looked good, or because she'd gained a few pounds since buying the skirt and blouse, he didn't know.

She was small compared to his six-feet. Even in shoes with heels so high he wasn't sure how she was standing in them, she was still a good half head shorter than he was.

He didn't mind a petite woman. Hell, Lila had been tiny next to him. But he'd always loved how Lila didn't give a crap even if she could walk beneath his outstretched arm without ducking. She'd run around the house in flip-flops or mucking boots and not worry about trying to appear taller. . . .

And here he was comparing Tilly to his dead wife, just as he'd feared would happen if and when he ever tried dating again.

His making the comparison wasn't fair to Tilly. It still didn't change the fact that he wasn't feeling it with this woman. His pulse didn't pick up speed. Parts lower hadn't stood up and taken notice either, in spite of the cleavage she was showing.

Funny, but he'd been plenty interested in Bonnie this afternoon outside the barbecue place while she was standing in the hot sun in shorts and a cotton shirt. She'd been wearing nothing all that notable. Nothing tight. Nothing showy, yet he'd imagined—and remembered intimately from their past together—what her body felt like beneath his.

Apparently it was the woman wearing the clothes, not the clothing, that was important. All the money and shopping sprees in the world couldn't change that.

"Let's all go sit down in the living room." Janie smiled.

Great. They were moving on to the socializing portion of the evening, which would last who knew how long.

Tyler caught Rohn's unhappy gaze and said, "Supper'll be done shortly. I'm sure Janie will want us all out of her kitchen so she can work her magic."

Rohn had heard Tyler use the term *shortly* plenty of times a day at work and he knew it could mean anything from five minutes to five hours. But he didn't argue as he followed Tilly's wobbly gait through the winding path in Janie's home that led to the living room.

He'd sat in this room in this house exactly once,

just over a year ago on the day of his friend's—Janie's husband's—funeral. Hell of a depressing memory that was.

On the bright side, just a few months ago Janie had been in the same boat Rohn was in. Unwillingly single because they'd both lost their spouses too soon and to the same disease.

But Janie was younger than Rohn, still in her midthirties. It probably didn't feel as daunting for her to start fresh in a new relationship. Not the way it felt for him at forty-three.

Enough feeling sorry for himself. The immediate need was to get through tonight. He was going to have to rally a good mood to do it.

Rohn sat on the sofa, which looked fairly new from the front, but showed its age on the back and arms where the sun had faded the deep rose-colored fabric to a paler hue. He supposed after all these years he wasn't looking all that great from all angles anymore, either.

In fact, he should probably get out and help the boys in the field more. He needed to keep in shape now that he was considering putting himself back out on the market. God help him . . .

"So what do you do for a living, Rohn?" Tilly smiled sweetly, but the streak of lipstick on her front tooth was so distracting, he had to think twice to comprehend she'd asked him a question.

"I own the stock ranch next door." He tipped his head in the general direction of his place.

"That's nice. So what do you do there?"

This was not a country girl, by any means. He regrouped and put himself in the mind-set he used when talking to city folk.

Dumbing it down to the bare minimum so she'd understand, he said, "I buy and sell livestock."

"Oh. Good for you." Tilly looked less than impressed.

Rohn shot Tyler a glance that told him he'd swung and missed with this one. There was no way this woman would be comfortable being a rancher's wife.

That thought gave Rohn pause. Was he in the market for another wife?

He hadn't thought about it. He knew one thing. Wife, girlfriend, friend, whatever she turned out to be, he wanted a companion so he didn't have to eat dinner by himself. He needed someone to settle in front of the television with at night. Someone in his life so he didn't have to go to bed alone. Sleep alone. Wake up alone.

Another glance at Tilly told Rohn that Tyler probably hadn't been thinking of fixing him up with Mrs. Right. More like Ms. Right-for-One-Night.

Where did he and Janie even find this woman? Tilly and Janie seemed like complete opposites.

Rohn knew how to find out. "So, Tilly, how do you know Janie and Tyler?"

"I cut Janie's hair. At the salon in town."

That explained a lot. The perfectly coiffed head of hair, dyed dark blond with lighter blond streaks sporadically run through it. The long, polished nails. The perfectly applied makeup—except for that one wayward smear of lipstick still on her teeth.

Tyler and Janie would have done better trying to find Rohn a date at church, or even better, at the stock auction, not at a beauty salon. He was lucky he remembered to clean the dirt from under his fingernails at night before bed. Never mind handling a high-maintenance female. He didn't live the kind of life a woman like that would take to easily.

He glanced up and found Janie and Tyler silently watching the interaction. Seeing Rohn looking at him, probably with a plea for help clear on his face, knocked Tyler into action.

Tyler jumped up from where he'd been sitting on the love seat next to Janie. "Can I get anyone anything to drink? Beer. Wine. Sweet tea?"

"Beer, please." Rohn realized his response sounded a bit too enthusiastic, but damn, he needed something. It was going to be a long evening. "In fact, let me help you with the drinks."

"No, stay. I can—"

Rohn interrupted Tyler's protest. "Don't be silly. You can't carry all four yourself. Let me help." He turned to the woman sitting right next to him on the sofa. "Tilly, what can we get for you?"

"I'd love some red wine, if you have it. With a couple of ice cubes, please."

"A'ight. Red wine on the rocks, coming right up." Rohn stood.

He didn't usually drink wine. Not if there was beer around instead. Even so, he was still pretty sure that wasn't how most people drank red wine, but who was he to question Tilly's preferences?

The escape from his unwanted date in the living room accomplished, Rohn reached the kitchen and let out a breath.

"It's not that hard, you know."

Rohn looked up at Tyler's comment. "What's not?"

"Talking to a woman."

Rohn drew his brows low at the insult. "I can talk to women just fine, thank you."

"Then why are you acting like I took a branding iron to you rather than just invited a good-looking woman over for dinner?" Tyler shook his head, his mouth set in an unhappy line. "You know, you might have a good time if you'd just let yourself."

"Ty, I'm just not—"

"Ready?" Tyler suggested. "Rohn, it's been a long time since Lila passed."

"I know and I wasn't going to say that. I am ready, I'm just not interested in *her*." Rohn had lowered his voice to a whisper but still glanced at the doorway to make sure no one had heard. Tilly wasn't the one for him, but he didn't want to hurt her feelings.

Tyler considered that in silence for a moment, his eyes never wavering from Rohn. Finally, he dipped his head. "A'ight. I understand."

Rohn lifted his brows high. "Do you?"

"Hell, yeah. If there's no chemistry, then it would never work out between you two in the long run. But you know, not every woman is looking for forever. Some of them, like the ones who just got divorced and dress up real fancy for a casual dinner, might be looking for just a little loving. Nothing more."

Tyler was suggesting a one-night stand. Rohn's face heated. "I don't want to talk about this with you."

The young cowboy shrugged. "Suit yourself. All I can do is bring the horse to the chute. It's your choice whether you wanna climb on and ride."

The rodeo analogy made Rohn cringe. Things were only getting worse. "Let's get those drinks and get back in there, please."

"I'm on it." While Tyler turned toward the fridge, Rohn decided he'd stay for dinner and then make his excuses and get out, fast and clean.

As Rohn waited for Tyler to find the corkscrew to open the wine, his mind drifted to Bonnie. She'd be spending her first night in the house tonight. All alone.

Maybe he should stop by quick and just check on her. That's what a friend would do.

Yup. A friend, because that's what they were now. Old friends.

Even Rohn didn't buy his own lie . . . but maybe that was okay.

Chapter Nine

Bonnie looked around her. After hours of work, the kitchen actually looked habitable.

The trash bins outside were full to overflowing, but at least she'd be able to cook and eat in the kitchen now.

It looked and smelled deep-down clean. She'd have to go to the store and pick up more cleaning products to get through the rest of the house. The heavy-duty, industrial kind since there was years of dirt and grime to get through.

She needed a shopping list so she didn't forget anything once she got inside the store, which was what always seemed to happen to her when she went shopping without a list.

Bonnie pulled open the drawer that had always held pens and paper when she was a kid and sighed. It was packed full of crap, just like the rest of the house. She wasn't going to be able to find what she needed easily, and she was too tired to look. She was about to slide it closed and save that chore for another day when something caught her eye.

It was an old photo. Just the corner of it peeked out from beneath a Chinese food takeout menu but she knew immediately what it was of. The bottom of the yellow dress was too familiar for her not to recognize it.

Shuffling things out of the way, she pulled out the picture and saw herself, twenty-five years ago, smiling so her mother could finish the roll of film before the prom.

Her father had kept this picture of her all these years?

Though, she shouldn't be surprised. It seemed he kept everything.

Her curiosity piqued, she dug further and found the program from her graduation ceremony. And in its folds, the tassel from her cap.

The drawer was like a time capsule and she wasn't sure she was ready for that trip back into the past quite yet. She shoved the items back in and closed the drawer.

Out of sight, out of mind. She could live with that.

Moving toward the spot where she'd left her purse on the countertop, she rummaged through. She found a pen and a scrap of paper to write on and scribbled down a couple of things she needed.

As she wrote, she realized how sweaty and disgusting she felt. Thank God she'd had the foresight to tackle the bathroom before she'd started on the kitchen. There was no way she'd have the energy to clean the shower stall now.

The cool water on her skin did much to wash away the heat of the day along with the dirt. She'd thrown in a load of laundry earlier, too, so she had clean

towels for her shower, and fresh bedding for later—
wherever she decided to sleep.

She wasn't sure she could stand being in her old
bedroom. Certainly not in her father's bedroom.

The sofa in the living room might have to do, but
she hadn't started cleaning out that room yet. Just
knowing the clutter was there might keep her awake
in spite of the over-the-counter sleeping pills she'd
bought.

Then again, maybe she was too damn tired to care
about anything. She felt the bone-deep weariness
settle over her now that she was clean and dressed in
a T-shirt and soft cotton shorts. She could probably
sleep on top of the piles of old newspapers in the
living room and not even notice.

Being busy was a good thing. Being busy had kept
her mind off the strangeness of her homecoming.
Kept her mind off the bad things and the good
things—like coincidentally running into Rohn.

What the heck was she going to do about him?

Nothing. That's what. She'd rent his truck, clean
this place out, and then head back to the life she'd
built for herself in Arizona. There was nothing else
for her to do.

She was on her way into the kitchen to get some
cold water to take the sleeping pills with when she
heard a knock on the front screen door. She jumped
at the sound and then heard the deep, masculine,
"Hello?"

The sun had set a while ago, and in hindsight, she
probably should have closed and locked the front
door long before now, but that was less of a concern
to her than who stood silhouetted in the doorway.

If she hadn't recognized the voice, she would have

recognized his height, and the cowboy hat she'd seen earlier that day.

"Rohn. Come on in." When had her voice gotten so breathless?

It became apparent that keeping things just friends between her and Rohn was going to be an issue, judging by how her heart pounded at the sight of him at her door. Especially if he made a habit of dropping in unannounced while she was dressed for bed.

"You sure?" He pulled the screen door open and popped just his head in. "I don't want to disturb you."

She let out a short laugh. There were many other things to disturb her in this house. Rohn would just be one more. "It's fine. Come on in . . . as long as you don't mind the mess."

Bonnie had momentarily forgotten about the state of the house. She couldn't forget now as she watched Rohn's gaze sweep the clutter in the room. He came all the way in and let the door slam closed behind him. "Looks like you got your work cut out for you here."

"Yes, it does." She glanced at the brown paper bag in his hand. "What have you got there?"

He flashed her that grin that had won her heart so many years ago. "Ice cream."

She couldn't help the wide smile as good memories for a change bombarded her. "What flavor?"

"Strawberry cheesecake." He watched her closely, waiting for her reaction to that information.

How could she not react? After all these years he'd remembered she loved that flavor. The place in town had served it that summer as their seasonal special.

The mist of nostalgia clouded her vision in the form of unshed tears. "Thank you."

Rohn's brows drew down. "What's wrong?"

He put the bag down on top of a stack of newspapers and came to her. He ran one hand up and down her arm. His kindness in light of how she'd left, what she'd done, broke her.

"Nothing's wrong. I'm just tired."

"I should go." His voice was soft, gentle. That, in combination with the mingled concern and heat in his eyes when he looked at her, had her insides twisting.

"No. Stay. I'm fine. Just silly and nostalgic."

"You were never silly. And sometimes nostalgia is a good thing." He raised his hand to brush it across her cheek, lingering just long enough for her to feel the warmth of his touch against her skin.

God, she was going to crack. His kindness would break her. In the face of all she'd done, his being sweet would surely do her in.

He dropped his hand away from her face. "You wanna eat that ice cream before it melts?"

Bonnie breathed in relief. She'd needed his hand off her so she could get herself together.

"Okay."

Feeling his touch was too bittersweet for her to deal with. Going to the kitchen to grab spoons would provide a much-needed distraction. She led the way and he followed her.

"Wow. This room is a hell of a lot different from that one." He hooked a thumb in the direction of the living room.

While pulling open the utensil drawer, filled with cutlery she'd run through the dishwasher just today, she glanced back at him. "I spent a good couple of hours in here."

"It shows."

"Thanks." She carried two spoons over to him. "Let me get two bowls."

He grinned wide. "Nope. I want to eat it right out of the container the way we did that night we picked up a pint and ate it in my truck by the river. Okay with you?"

"Yeah. It's fine. Do you want to sit in here and eat? Or outside?" she asked.

A sly smile tipped up the corner of his mouth. "We'd better stay inside. I remember the last time we shared a pint of ice cream outdoors."

Bonnie drew in a breath, pulled out a kitchen chair, and sat, but had no comment. She remembered, too. They'd ended up making love in the back of his pickup overlooking the river. After the first time, that was what they did every chance they could get alone.

Rohn reached into the bag and emerged with a familiar white pint container with the flavor scribbled on the lid in red marker.

She smiled. "I see things haven't changed much."

He pulled the other chair closer to hers and then sat. "Nope. Same except for the price. And that, like most everything over the years, has doubled." Rohn pried the lid off and let out a low, grumbling, "Mmm. It'll be well worth it, though."

Getting over her discomfort at being around him again, Bonnie reached out and took a scoop off the top with her spoon.

Creamy and cold, the flavor she remembered from her youth filled her mouth. Taste buds definitely had a memory. Hers remembered enjoying this treat like it was yesterday. "Mmm. You're right. It's exactly like it was back then."

He scooped himself a mouthful. "And soft and half melted."

"Just the way I like it." She smiled and grabbed another big spoonful.

"I know." Rohn laughed and scooped more for himself.

That had been a debate between them that night they'd shared the pint in his truck. How she could prefer to eat the ice cream when it was so melted it was almost liquid, while he liked it firm and solid right out of the freezer.

Maybe this was good, easing back into getting used to each other again so they could be friends. She glanced up and caught him watching her, his eyes focused on her tongue as she licked off her spoon.

Her heart twisted with an unrealistic hope that they could be more than friends. Parts lower twisted as well, with a need, a desire, long banked.

If only . . .

"So, how are the bedrooms?"

Bonnie whipped her attention to Rohn at that question just when she'd been thinking about sex. "The bedrooms?"

"Yeah. I'm assuming you're planning on sleeping here tonight, but if the bedrooms are in the same condition as the living room . . ." His lifted his dark brows, which were beginning to show a bit of gray, and let the sentence trail off.

On Rohn the touches of silver looked sexy. She wrestled her mind back to the question. "The bedrooms are pretty bad. I figured I'd sleep on the couch in the living room."

"Uh, the living room's pretty bad, too."

Dipping her head in a nod, she couldn't deny the truth of that. Rohn had seen the shambles with his own eyes. "It is. I'll be okay."

A frown creased Rohn's forehead. "Come stay with me."

She paused with ice cream in her mouth and her empty spoon in midair. She swallowed. "What?"

"Just for tonight. Tomorrow, I'll loan you my guys. You can get this place cleaned up and sleep in your old bed tomorrow night."

The last thing she wanted to do was sleep in her old bed, only second to sleeping in Rohn's house and all the feelings that would raise, but she couldn't tell him any of that. "No."

No, to everything. To spending the night under Rohn's roof with all the emotions pinging around inside her. To him loaning her his employees to help her. Definitely no to sleeping in her old bedroom.

"Why not? It makes sense. Besides, it's hot as blazes in here. Is the A/C broken? Do you want me to take a look at it—" He was in the process of standing when Bonnie stopped him.

"It's not broken. I turned it off. I wanted the windows open . . . to air the place out."

He nodded. "Understood."

It was a good excuse. A place that looked this cluttered would need airing. Rohn didn't need to know it was the demons haunting her that had Bonnie throwing open the windows and doors the moment she'd gotten inside.

"I still don't think there's any reason for you to sleep here tonight. I have two empty guest bedrooms at the ranch."

"No, Rohn." She shook her head to emphasize how adamant she was about her decision. "But thank you. I appreciate the offer."

He paused, watching her before he nodded. "A'ight. I won't push. But if you change your mind, or need anything at all, day or night, here's my number."

Her shopping list was on the table. He picked up the pen she'd left there, tore off a piece of the paper bag, and scribbled his number. Handing it to her, he said, "Promise you'll call if you need me."

"I promise." Her heart swelled with what could have been. What never could be.

How could any man be so damned sweet? Just as her taste buds had remembered the flavor of the ice cream, her heart remembered what it had felt like to love Rohn. Or at least what her eighteen-year-old self had thought was love.

"You want any more of this?" He tipped his head toward the ice cream they'd both stopped eating.

"No, thanks. I'm good."

He nodded and reached for the cover. "It'll make a nice cool snack for you tomorrow while you're working." He moved to the fridge and pulled open the freezer door, before glancing back at her. "I see there's plenty of room."

She cringed as he put the pint container into the completely bare freezer. "I tossed everything. I didn't know how old it was. I'm planning on going shopping tomorrow."

Rohn slammed the door closed and came back to her. "Then that ice cream might end up being breakfast."

"I wouldn't mind that one bit." Bonnie smiled.

"No. I know you wouldn't." He laughed. "I'm going to go so you can get to bed—or to the sofa . . . If you can find it."

"I'll be fine." She followed him through the living room and to the front door.

Rohn turned as he reached for the knob. "Last chance for a comfortable bed and nice cool A/C."

"Thank you, but I'm good here."

"Yeah, I had a feeling you'd say that. A'ight. I'll see you soon. Borrow that truck anytime you need."

Glancing around, she let out a short laugh. "I think I'm going to need to take you up on that offer."

"I hope you do." Cupping her face with his palm, he leaned down and pressed a soft, quick kiss to her cheek. "Good night, Bonnie Blue."

Barely able to breathe after even that brief, chaste kiss, she managed to say, "G'night, Rohn."

Summer, 1990

It was like a dream but it was very real. In the darkened movie theater, Rohn was actually kissing her.

Her first real kiss.

She'd never admit it to him, but except for a quick game of spin the bottle in eighth grade during a birthday party, she'd never been kissed.

How pitiful was that?

This kiss made up for the delay. For all the years she'd waited for it. It was perfect.

Bonnie couldn't wrap her head around any of it, but maybe that was better. She didn't want to think. Only to feel.

She wanted to memorize every single nuance of

this moment so she could relive it over and over, because who knew if it would ever happen again?

There was stubble on his upper lip that scratched her skin. She loved the feel of it. It was a very real reminder that she was really kissing him and not just imagining it.

He tasted like gum. She realized he must have been chewing it, until he pulled away from the kiss, spit the gum on the floor, and then came back to her. This time he turned in his seat so he was angled toward her, like he was settling in for a long kiss. She hoped he was.

The theater was dark, but they were by no means invisible, even in their back corner. Anyone who was looking closely enough would see them, but she didn't care. She would kiss him in broad daylight, if he wanted. She'd do pretty much anything this boy wanted her to do. Anything at all.

He brought his hand up and cupped her face, before he slid his fingers beneath her hair to cradle the back of her head. He held her close, pressing her mouth tightly against his.

Rohn leaned back just a bit. "Your hair is so soft."

Nervous, she forced a smile. "Thank you."

She didn't have to say more. His mouth was back covering hers. His hand remained tangled in her hair, his fingers moving in a slow massage against her head that had her scalp tingling from his touch.

He ran the tip of his tongue along the seam of her lips, gently at first, before thrusting it into her mouth. Just because she'd never done this before didn't mean she didn't know about French kissing. She knew enough to open her mouth and let him take over.

The kiss got more intense. He leaned his whole

body in closer as if he would love to crawl into the seat with her if they'd been anywhere else.

He plunged his tongue into her mouth, stroking it against hers. She'd liked the soft, closed-mouth kisses before but this was a whole new level of kissing.

Judging by Rohn's reaction, including the increase in his breathing, he liked it, too. She liked knowing that.

Finally, he pulled away. He watched her for a couple of seconds before he leaned close to her ear. "We better cool it for a little while."

Cooling it was the last thing she wanted to do but she agreed. "Okay."

The guy who came into the theater to check on things with his flashlight would be coming through eventually, anyway. She didn't need him to see them making out. Then there was the fact this was a two-hour movie. Rohn had gone from calm to panting for breath in a matter of moments. A hundred and twenty more minutes could do untold things to him.

He turned in his seat to face the screen, but reached into her lap to pick up her hand. She liked the feel of his big, rough hand holding hers. She felt warm and held, and as if he would be there for her no matter what, protecting her.

They could face anything together, as long as he held on to her. She loved that idea. She could love Rohn.

Heck, she was afraid she already did.

Rohn didn't kiss her again for the rest of the movie. He did move his arm around her shoulders and pull her closer to him before he rested his head against hers.

The move felt as intimate as a kiss. Like he was

claiming her. As if he wanted everyone to know she was his.

Was she? He'd told her this was a date and kissing him had made it feel like one, but was it more? Was she his girlfriend now? She didn't have the nerve to ask, but she could hope.

The closing credits rolled up the screen, but Rohn didn't get up. Neither did she. He waited until the lights had been turned on and the theater was emptying before he turned to her. "You wanna go out for ice cream?"

"Um . . ." Yes, she wanted to go out for ice cream, but she was also worried about getting home late, especially since she'd lied to her parents about who she'd be with tonight.

He waited for her answer and she decided to at least explain her hesitation. She didn't want him assuming it was him she objected to.

"Do you know what time it is? I just don't want to get home too late."

He glanced at the watch on his wrist. "It's eight forty. The movie wasn't even two hours long." He looked up at her. "What time did you promise your parents you'd be home?"

"I didn't say."

"Do you want to call home from the pay phone in the lobby? I have some change in my pocket you can use."

"No, it's okay." She didn't need her mother asking any questions she wasn't prepared to answer. "It'll be fine. We can go get ice cream."

Rohn's lips tipped up in a smile. "Good. I won't keep you out too late. I promise."

She kind of wished he would keep her out late, but

that would have to be for another time when she'd come up with a better lie. She'd need to pretend she and Melody were doing something else together. She would think on it.

Right now, all she wanted to think about was how good Rohn's hand felt on hers.

"Come on." He stood, tugging her out of her seat after him.

The ice-cream shop was just down the road so they walked. She was grateful for that. He wouldn't see how she'd chained up her bike to the rack on the sidewalk like a little kid.

All the cool girls had cars, but she still had the first big girl bike she'd gotten for Christmas more than eight years ago.

The ice-cream place was packed, not surprising since it was a beautiful summer night. There were families with kids out for a treat, and also couples on dates, like her and Rohn. That thought made her smile.

What was a surprise, and kind of a relief, was that they didn't see anyone from school. It was a small town, but not so small that she knew every single person who lived in it.

Tonight she didn't know anyone in the ice-cream shop, and that was just fine.

The part of Bonnie who waited for the other shoe to drop, the half of her that kept whispering doubt and telling her not to be too happy because it couldn't possibly last, had her fearing that if Rohn ran into one of his guy buddies he might dismiss her. He could pretend they were just friends. He might stop holding her hand and looking at her like he couldn't wait to kiss her again. She didn't want that to ever stop.

They seated themselves at a booth. She slid in first and instead of sitting opposite her, Rohn instead slid in next to her.

She felt the heat of his thigh through the denim as he pressed close to her. "What are you having?"

Bonnie hadn't even looked at the menu. She grabbed it now.

"I think a small cone." She was too nervous to be able to fit much of anything in her fluttering stomach, but ice cream in small amounts should go down smoothly enough.

"What flavor?" he asked.

That might be harder to narrow down. She was such a fool for him she'd forgotten this place had dozens of choices.

"Um . . ." She glanced down at the menu.

One flavor jumped out at her. It had a red banner next to it that read *Seasonal Special—Strawberry Cheesecake—cheesecake-flavored ice cream with strawberries and bits of graham cracker crust.*

Hungry or not, she found her mouth watering just from the description alone. "This one."

He leaned over to read the line on the menu she was pointing to and lifted his brow. "Wow. That sounds really good."

Satisfied with her choice, she asked, "What are you getting?"

He glanced down at his own menu, but only for a second before he pushed it to the other side of the table. "I usually get mint chocolate chip. I'll probably just stick with that."

That statement, and the fact that he barely had to

look at the menu, had Bonnie wondering how often Rohn came here and how many girls he'd brought. She couldn't think like that.

Against all odds, like a scene from her wildest dreams, he was with her now, and that was all that mattered. That and making sure her parents didn't find out she'd lied about whom she was meeting.

Maybe she should have just told her mother the truth. That Rohn had asked her out, but her father was so weird sometimes. The littlest things could set him off, depending on what mood he was in.

The year of the big drought when they'd lost so much money and her mother had to get a job at the grocery store, Bonnie had walked around on egg-shells. They both did, trying to not do anything to anger her father and send him into a rage.

Nope. It was safer this way. Who knew how he'd react to Rohn and the date. In fact, it had probably been risky to agree to come to the ice-cream shop. Though if she knew one thing, it was that her father had never set foot in here as long as she could re-member.

Glancing around, she didn't see anyone he was friendly with or talked to, either. They were most likely safe.

She looked over at Rohn and found him watching her. He smiled when he caught her gaze. "Awful lot of thinking going on in that pretty little head of yours."

He'd called her pretty. She swallowed away the mixed nervousness and excitement that caused. "I was just thinking . . ."

He waited expectantly as she searched for the right words. Finally, he prompted, "About?"

"How we shouldn't mention anything about tonight to my parents."

His brows rose. "Okay. Why not?"

Because she'd already lied about whom she was with. Bonnie kept that to herself and shrugged, trying to look casual as she made up an excuse. "I'm not sure if my father would like me going out with you, because, you know, you work for him."

Rohn frowned. "You don't think so? I thought he liked me."

"He does. At least, he seems to . . . I don't know. He's just strange about things like that."

"A'ight. If he's one of those fathers who doesn't think anybody is good enough to date his daughter, then I understand."

"Yeah." She agreed, even though she didn't think that was it at all.

It was more like her father just liked to control things—her life included. And he really didn't like any change. He hadn't even wanted her going to Arizona for college. He and her mother had argued long and hard about that subject. If Bonnie's grandmother didn't live in Phoenix, and Bonnie wouldn't be living with her instead of in the dorms, she had no doubt she'd never have been allowed to enroll there.

She caught Rohn's gaze. "So, you think we can just keep tonight a secret?"

"Sure." He tipped his head and then smiled. "It's kind of fun, actually. You and me, secretly dating."

His comment made her think there was going to be more than just this one date between them. Feeling giddy, Bonnie said, "Like Romeo and Juliet."

He laughed. "Yes, but let's hope we have better

luck than they did. You know, since they both ended up dead."

She smiled. "Yeah, let's hope."

The waitress came to the table and interrupted their conversation, but Bonnie continued to beam with happiness on the inside, and probably on the outside, too. She was dating Rohn. She was Rohn Lerner's girlfriend.

Who knew? One day she could even become Bonnie Lerner. Yes, it was premature since this was their first date and all, but it could happen.

She tamped down her crazy dream for the future and watched him order for both her and him—just like men did for their dates in the movies. Feeling more adult than she ever had, Bonnie tried to assume the air that this happened all the time.

Meanwhile, she was bubbling over inside.

With all this excess energy, she'd practically fly home on her bike. But before that happened, she'd have to say good night to Rohn. With any luck, there'd be a good-night kiss.

Her heart fluttered with anticipation.

The waitress left, and Rohn reached out to grab her hand in his again. She'd never forget this night as long as she lived.

Chapter Ten

Summer, 2015 (Present Day)

Sitting in his office, Rohn glanced at the pile of mail on his desk. He hated going through the mail. It was always the same thing. A lot of crap he'd have to toss, mixed in with bills he'd have to pay. There was nothing fun about that.

Deciding it could wait, he stood. There was something else he needed to do, anyway. Something more important.

Tyler was in the kitchen pouring himself a cup of coffee. Rohn lifted a brow. "I thought my coffee sucked compared to Janie's."

"It does."

"So why you drinking it?"

"Let's just say we were running a little late this morning and we didn't get around to having coffee over at her place."

He held up one hand to stop any further explanation. "I don't need the whole song and dance."

Rohn could very well guess what had Tyler and

Janie running late this morning, and he sure as hell didn't need to picture it.

Tyler's lips twitched with a smile. "You asked."

"I know, and let's forget that I did. Anyway, I need y'all to finish up with the stock and then come see me right after. I got something for you to do."

"Sure. What's up?"

Rohn really didn't want to answer that question. Tyler was too intuitive sometimes for a young guy who seemed to live only for trucks and sex. Rohn knew he was going to suspect something was going on the moment the subject of Bonnie came up.

The clues would all be there. For one, Rohn was going to pull his entire crew and one of his trucks from a day of work at the ranch and send them to Bonnie's house.

For another, Rohn hadn't shown any interest in Tilly, even though she was clearly interested in something with him. As the night had gone on, and the wine started to hit her, she got pretty flirtatious, not to mention handsy.

Good thing Rohn had played football in high school. He knew how to evade offensive maneuvers when necessary. He'd evaded Tilly's advances, in spite of Tyler's suggestion to grab himself a little loving with no strings attached.

Even if Tyler didn't know he'd gone over to Bonnie's directly after dinner, by way of the ice-cream shop, he'd still know that Rohn had left Janie's house alone.

There was nothing to be done about it. Bonnie needed the help, so Rohn plowed ahead. "I need you, Justin, and Colton to head on over to a friend's house and help her out."

"Her? As in a woman?" Tyler widened his eyes.

Rohn drew in a calming breath. "Yes, her, and get any crazy notions out of your head right now."

"Why? If there's a woman in your life—"

"There's not. I went to high school with her. She just lost her father and she's trying to clean out the house all by herself. I thought it might be nice to lend her a little help."

Tyler sobered at the news of Bonnie's loss. "Understood. Of course, we'll help her out. No problem at all."

Finally, Tyler was doing what he'd asked, and without complaint.

"Thank you." Rohn nodded. "Take the truck. There's a ton of shit in the house that needs to get hauled to the dump."

A ton might not be too much of an exaggeration, based on what Rohn had seen the night before. Bonnie's father sure had collected a lot of stuff over the years. *Collected* being a nice term for what he'd seen. He didn't know how Bonnie had slept in that mess. He couldn't call to ask her, either, since she'd never given him her cell phone number, nor had she called him or texted him on his.

Of course, there was a good chance her dad had kept their old house phone and number. He liked that idea enough to give it a try.

"Let me know before you leave," he told Tyler.

"Will do." As Tyler took off toward the barn carrying his cup of coffee, Rohn headed toward the office.

Rohn closed his office door behind him. The boys would come busting in even with the door closed, but at least he'd have a little bit of privacy. He sat at the desk and grabbed the big yellow phone book the phone company still delivered annually, even though half of the folks around there no longer had house phones and used only a cell.

He flipped to the *M* section of the residential listings and from there to Martin. There it was, in black and white. Bonnie Martin's father's name and address.

Thinking how nice it was that even with all the change, some things stayed the same, Rohn pulled out his cell and punched in the digits.

It rang a few times, and then he heard her voice. "Hello?"

"Good morning, Bonnie Blue. It's Rohn. How'd you sleep?" He heard the telltale sound of her stretching. Realizing how early it was, he cussed. "I woke you up, didn't I?"

Here he was, worrying about her sleeping, and he was the one to wake her.

"No, I was mostly awake. I just didn't get a whole lot of sleep last night so I couldn't motivate myself to get off the couch."

Beneath his breath he cussed again at the news she'd slept on the sofa when he had a perfectly good guest room for her to sleep in.

"Bonnie." Frustrated, he shook his head even though she couldn't see it. He was more upset with himself for allowing her to be uncomfortable all night than at her for making the choice to be that way. "I should have insisted that you sleep here."

"You could have insisted all you wanted, but I wouldn't have done it. I was perfectly fine here. Honestly. I sleep best in my own bed, and that happens to be in Arizona. It wouldn't have mattered whether I was in your guest room or here."

He didn't completely believe that. Sleeping in a nice comfortable air-conditioned bedroom had to be better than the sofa in that sweltering pigsty he'd seen. Hopefully, she'd at least turned on the A/C before she turned in for the night.

It seemed the years had made his Bonnie Blue stubborn. Gone was the compliant girl he'd known. He liked a woman with spunk and a mind of her own—he liked it on Bonnie, even though she was no longer his—but not when it caused her to make needlessly foolish choices.

"Well, it's not going to happen again tonight."

"Rohn, I'm fine—"

"We're getting that place cleaned out today, Bonnie." Rude or not, he cut off her protest. "Then tonight you can sleep in your own bed—or at least your *old* bed."

"We? And who is this *we?*" There was a smile in her tone as she picked up on the way he'd phrased his declaration.

"I got three guys and a truck coming to your place. They'll be there in probably an hour or so. You might want to put some clothes on. I don't want them staring at that cute little T-shirt and those shorts you were in last night. They won't get any work done." Rohn smiled, knowing the compliment would put her off guard.

He was right, because it took her a few seconds to reply, "Okay."

"You want breakfast?"

"Rohn, please don't bother—"

"I'll take that as a yes. See you soon." He hung up before she could protest further.

Rohn had been waffling about whether he should

go over to her place right away or give the guys a bit of time and check on her later.

He didn't want to look too pushy, but hell, he supposed that horse was already out of the barn since he was sending over help whether she wanted it or not. He might as well be there, too, and make sure she ate something other than ice cream for breakfast.

Happy with that plan, he smiled and reached for the pile of mail. He'd have to give her a bit of time to get herself together before going over. He could get the nasty task of going through the mail completed, and then head to the diner and grab a couple of egg sandwiches.

He'd better get enough for the boys, too. At their age, they could eat all day and still not be full. Plus, he owed them. They were doing him a favor even if he was going to pay them for the day. Pawing through and hauling away what could very well be twenty-five years' worth of garbage was definitely not what they'd hired on for.

They were good kids. They'd do whatever Rohn asked of them. They might grumble the whole time, but they'd do it. And unlike having his own children, he could send them home at the end of the day.

Chuckling at that thought, he tossed the first piece of junk mail into the trash can below his desk and picked up the square white envelope below it. Frowning, he tore open the flap and then pulled out a thick invitation.

A few days ago he would have groaned at what he read. Today, it brought a smile to his face. His twenty-fifth high school reunion . . . and Rohn knew exactly who he was going to ask to be his date.

They'd missed going to the prom together because they'd met too late, but they could certainly go to this.

Summer, 1990

Rohn sped across the field, bouncing in the seat of the tractor, pushing the machine to the maximum speed he dared.

Only when he reached the barn did he lower the throttle he'd kept on high. He turned the key in the ignition to off and hopped to the ground. He spun toward the house and was surprised to see his boss standing right in front of him.

"You're finished early today."

"Yes, sir." Rohn dipped his head in response to Mr. Martin's observation. What he didn't mention was that he'd worked his butt off to finish early so he could go home and change for his secret date with Bonnie.

"You got a hot date tonight or something?" The older man grinned and then spat a stream of brown tobacco-tinged spittle to the ground. Meanwhile, the accuracy of the man's guess nearly had Rohn choking.

"Yeah, something like that." Rohn hoped he didn't sound as guilty as he felt.

"Well, go on then. Don't let me hold you up. You're done with your work, so you can go." Mr. Martin turned toward the house, where Rohn's truck was parked.

"Thank you for letting me go a little early." Rohn cut his gaze sideways at Mr. Martin as they walked side by side toward the house.

He and Bonnie were still keeping their relationship secret from her parents and it was starting to wear on him. Especially at times like this when he had to speak directly with her father and fudge the truth.

"You earned it. You're working real hard here. Besides, a good-looking young guy like yourself should have a little fun once in a while. You're doing a good job, son." Mr. Martin slapped Rohn on the back.

All the compliments did was raise Rohn's level of guilt over deceiving the man.

"Thank you, sir." They'd reached the house and the last thing Rohn wanted to do was run into Bonnie and have to hold a conversation with her in front of her parents, all while pretending he wasn't secretly meeting her in town in a couple of hours. He stopped before they reached the back door and hooked a thumb toward the driveway where his truck was parked. "I'm gonna head out."

"All right. Have a good night."

"I will. Thank you." He turned on a boot heel and was about to sprint for his truck when Mr. Martin called his name. Heart pounding, Rohn stopped and turned back. "Yeah?"

"If you need to come in an hour late tomorrow, that'd be fine."

"Um, probably won't need to but thank you. I'll keep that in mind." Jeez, he hated this deception.

Rohn wasn't sure why Bonnie felt they needed to keep their dates secret. She was eighteen. So was he. Surely her father would allow her to date at this age.

All they'd done was go to the movies and the

ice-cream parlor together a handful of times. Yeah, they'd kissed, and a tiny bit more, but that was it.

Maybe he'd talk to Bonnie tonight about finally telling her parents about them. But even as he thought that, he realized they were in too deep already. What would they do? Lie and tell her parents they were just starting to date now? They certainly couldn't admit they'd been lying for weeks, sneaking around to see each other behind her parents' backs.

They'd created an impossible situation. It was probably best to just continue as they were and hope her father didn't figure it out before she left for college. He wouldn't be able to monitor what she did then.

The thought of Bonnie leaving for Arizona twisted Rohn's gut. He hated the idea of her going away. Not just because he was going to miss her, but because he didn't want her so far from him or surrounded by all those college guys. Guys who would surely appreciate a pretty little thing like her. But there was nothing he could do about that.

He couldn't help but glance at the front windows of the house as he started his truck, hoping to catch a glimpse of Bonnie Blue's sweet face.

Disappointed when he didn't spot her, he turned in the seat and backed the truck out of the drive. He'd be meeting her in town tonight and he could barely stand to wait the few hours.

He made himself drive the speed limit through town, so he got home safely and without getting pulled over. Once home, he showered and then ate dinner with his parents. All the while, he watched the clock, waiting for the moment when he could leave to go meet Bonnie in town.

Finally, the agonizingly long minutes clicked by and it was time he could leave without arriving ridiculously early. "Bye, Mom. Bye, Dad."

"You're leaving?" his mom called from the kitchen.

"Yeah." Ready to bolt, Rohn forced himself to stay put and wait to see what his mother had to say.

"Meeting the guys?" his mother asked.

He moved to the doorway so he could see her. "Yeah. Probably. I'm not sure who will be there."

Lying to Bonnie's parents meant he also had to lie to his, just in case they ever met in town. Luckily, his parents weren't all that concerned. They trusted him and as long as he didn't abuse their trust, they couldn't care less if he met Brian and Pete in town, or Bonnie.

"Okay. Have fun. Be careful."

"Yes, ma'am."

She didn't question where he was going or when he'd be back. She treated him like an adult, which he was. Why couldn't Bonnie's parents be as understanding?

Actually, her mom probably would be. He knew it was her father Bonnie worried about. Rohn drew in a breath as he climbed into the truck, hoping one day, he could come right out and tell the man he was dating his daughter.

Hell, Rohn was more than dating her. He was falling for Bonnie pretty hard.

Enough that his heart beat faster just thinking about her. Of course, he'd never tell another living soul that little detail. Not his guy friends, anyway. They'd laugh at him for sure. But Rohn was hoping to finally get to show Bonnie off to his friends tonight at the party. If she still wanted to go to it. He supposed he'd find out soon enough.

Bonnie was chaining up her bike to the usual rack near the theater. Shaking his head at her insistence on riding that thing instead of letting him pick her up at her house, he pulled the nose of the truck up to the curb right behind her. He saw the moment she realized it was him in the truck idling just feet from her.

She turned and smiled, then bounced down off the curb and over to the passenger side of the truck.

He'd learned she'd have the door open and would be inside long before he had time to get out of the truck, run around the hood, and open the door for her. Not that he hadn't tried it. He had. She'd just giggle at him from her seat and tell him she could open the door herself. At which point he'd box her in with his arms on either side of her and treat her to a big kiss in exchange for her sass.

Come to think of it, just for that kiss it was well worth the effort of running to open the door for her, even if he did fail every time.

"Hey." He smiled and turned to her as she hopped into the truck.

"Hey." She buckled her safety belt and then angled herself to return his smile.

A mouth that pretty deserved a kiss. Cupping her face, he leaned in and took one. He pulled back just enough to say, "Anytime you want me to start picking you up at the house so you don't have to ride—"

"I know, but I don't mind riding." She gave him her usual answer, just as he'd expected.

"A'ight." He pulled back and gripped the steering wheel. "Ready for the party?"

"Yup." She didn't look all that excited.

That wasn't so surprising. She wasn't the party type. She liked quiet dates for the two of them. Watching a movie. Sharing the strawberry cheesecake ice cream she'd become obsessed with. So much so he'd begun to order that flavor for himself, because invariably she'd finish the small cone she insisted on, and he'd let her finish his.

"Do you not want to go?" he asked her.

"It's fine. We can go."

He turned off the engine and spun in the seat to face her. "That's not what I asked. I want to know what you want to do."

"You want to go so—"

"Bonnie . . ." He imbued the one word with enough warning that she clamped her mouth shut midprotest. "Tell me what you want to do."

She hesitated a second before lifting one shoulder in a shrug. "I kind of would rather just be alone with you. But I know you want to go, so we can go."

He did want to go. Not because he wanted to drink the beer Brian's older brother had bought for the party since their parents were out of town, or to hang out with his friends, but because he wanted to show off Bonnie as his girlfriend. He couldn't wait to walk in there with her on his arm and let everyone know she was his girl. But more than that, he wanted her to be happy, and if she didn't want to go, then he didn't need to be there, either.

Rohn debated making a deal with her. They could stop by the party for half an hour, say hello to everyone, and then leave. But he knew how things would go. Once his friends and the rest of the guys on the football team grabbed him, he would be hard-pressed to get out of there before midnight, or before the cops showed up, whichever came first.

That was another consideration—there was a very real chance this party could get busted by the police. That was the last thing Bonnie needed, considering they were already lying to her parents.

The final point, which clinched the decision for Rohn, was that Lena and her friends would be there. His prom date likely wouldn't take kindly to his dodging her all summer. Nor would she welcome Bonnie into her fold of girlfriends. There would definitely be hard feelings because Bonnie was dating him.

Girls could be vicious, and Lena and her clique were among the worst.

Nope. His Bonnie Blue didn't need any of this shit just because he was proud to have her on his arm.

"Okay." He spun back to face the steering wheel and reached for the key in the ignition.

"Wait, okay what?"

"Okay, we don't have to go to the party." He started the engine and put the truck in reverse.

"But then where are we going?"

"You said you'd rather be alone, and I agree. I just happen to know someplace where we can be alone." He glanced and saw the expression of surprise on her face, but he didn't explain further. She'd see where he was taking her soon enough, and if he knew her at all, she'd love it.

Chapter Eleven

The surprise early-morning phone call from Rohn was enough to get Bonnie moving for the day, no matter how groggy she felt from the pharmacy sleeping pills that hadn't helped her sleep all that great.

As her mind spun she headed to the bathroom. She needed to dress for the day. Rohn's hired hands would be coming over to help soon and Rohn was apparently delivering breakfast.

Her face burned as she remembered his comment on the phone when he'd told her to *put some clothes on*.

Bonnie hadn't felt attractive, or like a real woman, in a long while. She'd kind of sidelined that portion of her life and concentrated on safer things. Work. Her mom. Their home.

Rohn made it seem as if it would be easy to fall back into things with him. Was he just being friendly, or was he looking to pick up where they'd left off? He wouldn't be if he knew the complete truth.

When—*if*—she ever told him, he'd hate her. No doubt about it.

Keeping that in mind she pulled her hair back and splashed cold water on her face. She needed the icy dose of reality. Because of the past, she could have no future with him. The sooner she accepted that, the better.

Face washed and teeth brushed, Bonnie flipped open the lid of the small carry-on-sized suitcase she had with her in the bathroom—one of the only two clean rooms in the house. Since she'd be cleaning again today, she should put on a T-shirt and shorts. Even so, she had the urge to put on one of her better tank tops.

She wanted to look good and she knew why. Rohn.

Forcing herself to stop trying to be pretty for him, she grabbed the T-shirt instead of the tank. Bonnie had just pulled it over her head when she heard the distant sound of her cell phone ring.

Now what?

Drawing in a breath, she ran for the kitchen, where last night she had plugged the phone into an outlet to charge.

The readout said *Mom*. Bonnie had texted just to say she'd arrived in town safely, but she hadn't had a chance to call her mother yesterday. She'd intended to, but she'd become so involved with cleaning, she'd never gotten around to it.

She grabbed the phone and yanked the cord out, hitting the button to answer the call before it went to voice mail. "Mom. Hi. Sorry, I was at the other end of the house and had to run for the phone."

"Oh, I'm sorry, baby. So how's it going there?"

"It's . . . going." Bonnie glanced around the kitchen. She couldn't bring herself to say it was going well. At least she could say she'd made some progress in the short time she'd been in Oklahoma.

"That doesn't sound good."

Her mother knew her too well. She would know if Bonnie outright lied and said everything was fine. "There's just a lot to be done, that's all. Nothing I can't handle."

"I knew I should have gone with you. I'm going to call my boss and take off work—"

As a teacher, Bonnie had the summer off. Her mother didn't, nor did she have paid vacation time at her job as a receptionist. Their finances were fine, but still things were tight enough that she and her mother needed both of their incomes to live comfortably.

"No, Mom. Really, I'm fine. Actually, cleaning out is kind of cathartic. You won't believe what I found last night in the kitchen drawer."

"What?"

"The tassel from my graduation cap. It was stuck in the program along with my prom picture. I guess you stashed it there twenty-five years ago. Crazy it's still there, huh?"

"Uh, Bonnie. I never put those things in the kitchen drawer."

"What do you mean?"

"I never saw your cap or the tassel for that matter after you graduated. I assumed you had it put away somewhere."

Now that she thought about it, she had. Both the tassel and a copy of the graduation program had been stashed on the top shelf of her closet. She'd been meaning to make a scrapbook and had never gotten around to it before leaving for Arizona. So how did it get in the kitchen and into the program?

"Are you sure you didn't move the tassel into the drawer? Maybe you forgot?"

"Baby girl, I might be old but I'm not forgetful. I never saw that tassel except on your head when you walked up to get your diploma." The conviction was clear in her mother's tone.

"Okay. I believe you."

Could it have been her father who'd gone through her closet and stuck it in the kitchen with the prom picture? That was something she'd need to wrap her head around when it wasn't spinning with shock.

"You sound overwhelmed. Are you sure you don't need my help there? I can look at flights—"

"Really, Mom. Don't waste the time or the money coming here. I, uh, actually have help."

"Colleen and Andrew? They always were so sweet."

It wasn't the neighbors Bonnie had been thinking of, but she didn't correct her mother. "Yeah, they are sweet. They came over to see me right after I arrived yesterday."

"Good. I'm glad you're not alone there."

"Nope. Not alone."

What would her mother say if she knew Bonnie had seen their old farmhand, Rohn? Had shared ice cream with him. Had been invited to stay at his house. That she was about to have breakfast with him.

Knowing her mother, she'd think it was great, because even to this day Bonnie had never revealed that she and Rohn had been secretly dating that summer.

She didn't have time to get into anything with her

mother now. Rohn's guys would be over soon. She should probably wrap this up before they arrived.

"So I was about to get started on all I need to do today. Can I call you later?"

"Of course, baby. Don't work too hard. Okay? And accept help when it's offered. Don't be stubborn."

"I'm not stubborn."

"Yes, you are."

Bonnie drew in a breath. "All right. I'll try."

"That's all any of us can do. Bye, baby."

"Bye, Mom."

She disconnected the call and laid the cell on the counter. That one conversation had raised more questions than it answered. Bonnie yanked open the drawer in the kitchen, curious now as to what else it contained.

Pawing through the menus, pens, rubber bands, and assorted crap, Bonnie finally excavated to a level that revealed more personal things. She pulled out the items she'd found last night and laid them on the counter.

Beneath that she found even older pictures. Photos that could only be from the time period when her father and mother were dating. Before they'd gotten married. Had her father put those there too? Did he miss her mother so much, he kept the pictures in the kitchen so he could look at them?

He had never remarried and Bonnie had always assumed it was because he was such a miserable bastard that no woman would put up with him. But in light of this evidence, she had to wonder, had her father not remarried because he'd never stopped loving her mother?

She pawed deeper. One picture stopped her dead. It was her, as a baby, held in her father's arms, and he was smiling. This baby picture. The one from her prom night. The graduation stuff. Had he actually missed her, too, after she'd left?

A knock on the front door startled Bonnie. She swept all of her finds back into the drawer to deal with later and turned toward the living room.

Unlike last night, she had the front door closed and locked. The only thing she could see was a cowboy hat through the small window, but she knew who was there anyway.

That was Rohn's hat.

Flipping the top lock with one hand, she turned the knob with the other and pulled the door open.

"Good morning." His smile made her heart skip a beat and she knew she was in trouble.

"Good morning." She couldn't help the smile that bowed her lips. "Come on in."

He stepped forward into the room, glancing around as he did so.

"I haven't started working yet today." Bonnie felt the need to explain, to make excuses why the living room was still as cluttered as it had been last night when he'd left.

"We'll get it straightened out today. But breakfast first." He held up the white paper bag in his hand.

She lifted her brows at the size of the bag. "That looks like a lot of food."

He grinned. "I bought enough for the guys. They'll be here right behind me and they can really put away the food. Believe me."

Bonnie followed him into the kitchen. "I'll have to run out and get something for them for later—"

"Stop. I'll grab them lunch later, and if they need anything before then, they can go and get it themselves."

"I don't even have any bottled water for them to drink."

"Bonnie." Rohn grinned wider. "I know you've been away from farm life for a while, and maybe things are a bit more refined where you live now, but I can tell you that these guys are used to drinking straight out of the hose at the ranch. They'll be fine with tap water. Hell, using a glass will be a step up."

She had been away for a long time. It was easy to forget things like swimming in the pond to cool off in summer, and, as Rohn had said, drinking straight out of the hose.

There had been life before bottled water. Sometimes it was hard to remember that. She missed those good old days. Some parts of them, anyway.

"All right. I'm still buying you all lunch though since you're helping me."

"How about we debate that when the time comes?"

"Okay." She had a feeling he'd fight her tooth and nail about buying lunch. She'd have to sneak in a call to the pizza place later and order a delivery before Rohn had a chance to buy something else. But lunch wasn't nearly enough for all he was about to do for her. "I don't know how to pay you back for all your help."

"That's easy. You don't have to."

"No, Rohn, I want to."

"A'ight. If you insist, I have an idea of how you can

return the favor." He pulled out an envelope from the back pocket of his jeans and held it up.

"What's that?" She frowned at it.

"You didn't get one in the mail?" He seemed surprised she didn't recognize the square white envelope that didn't have any identifiable markings on it.

"No." She shook her head. "And my mail goes to Arizona, not here."

"I thought maybe they'd sent it to this address. Anyway, here—" He thrust the envelope toward her.

Still not knowing what it was, she lifted the flap of the already torn envelope and pulled out the thick piece of paper inside. The words *25th High School Reunion* sprang out at her.

"Go with me for old time's sake. Just as friends, and nothing more, if that will make you feel more comfortable."

Comfortable? Being around Rohn made her heart beat faster. Her pulse race. Her mind reel.

Old slippers and worn pajamas were comfortable. Being with him was anything but that.

"When is it?" She eyed the invitation again, supposing if she could get her brain to function, she'd be able to read that answer for herself.

"It's in a couple of weeks."

"I don't know if I'll still be here." She had a life, a job, and her mother in Arizona to get back to. The thought of leaving, of going back to Phoenix and never seeing Rohn again, had her heart hurting.

"If you are still here, will you go with me?" He shrugged. "You know, just to save me the embarrassment of having to go alone."

Why a man like Rohn would ever have to go anywhere alone was beyond her, and suddenly, she felt insanely jealous of any other woman he might choose to go with him if she said no.

It was a bad move. She was crazy, but she said, "Okay."

"Well, a'ight then." His grin made him look twenty years younger. "Let's eat."

"Okay." Her stomach was so twisted from his invitation and her answer she wasn't sure she could eat, but she'd have to try since he'd gone to the trouble to bring breakfast.

At the kitchen table, he reached into the bag and pulled out two wrapped bundles. "I hope you like egg and cheese on a roll."

"Yes, thank you."

"Hello? Anybody home?" A male voice she didn't recognize came from the front door Rohn had left open.

He grinned. "That will be the hungry hordes here to work. I told them I was picking up breakfast to make sure they'd finish up at my place quick and get right over here instead of dilly-dallying."

"Smart man." Bonnie stood and moved toward the doorway. "Come on in."

Three men came through the front door, each one as good-looking as the last. Their presence filled the room, which was already so full it barely accommodated their bulk. All three wore jeans, boots, and cowboy hats, and she had no problem envisioning them working Rohn's cattle ranch.

A cowboy with eyes so pretty she was sure they had won him more than a few girls during his young life was standing closest to her. He smiled and tipped his head in her direction. "Hey, I'm Tyler."

A handsome blond man who was slightly taller

and maybe a little bit older than Tyler moved a step forward. "Ma'am. I'm Justin."

"And I'm Colton." The third cowboy tipped his hat in her direction. He, too, would have any farmer keeping a close eye on his daughter.

She should know. Bonnie had been that farmer's daughter one summer, back when Rohn was the handsome hired hand.

"Nice to meet you. I'm Bonnie."

"Or *Miss Bonnie.*" Rohn had snuck up behind her. "Food's in the kitchen. Eat up. After, we'll figure out a game plan."

He sounded so mature and authoritative that she had to smile. The boys followed his order, albeit with a smirk and a few chuckles.

Rohn watched them file into the kitchen and called after them. "Two of those sandwiches are for me and Bonnie so don't be hogs and eat 'em all."

"A'ight. And it's *Miss* Bonnie," Tyler called back.

Rohn shook his head and mumbled, "Smart-ass."

"Bet he gets away with it, though."

"Yup. And if you tell me how *cute* you think he is, I might have to never talk to you again."

"Oh, he is cute, but I think I prefer men with a few more years of experience under their belt."

He raised a brow. "Oh, do you now? Good to know. And FYI, I got a whole lot of years under my belt." Rohn winked and she had to laugh.

"I'll remember that."

Joking. Laughing. Flirting. What had happened to her?

Bonnie was feeling lighter than she had in years. Maybe the change came from having people in this house. Rohn and his three hired hands chased away the dark, somber aura and brought in the light.

"Come on. Best get in there before they forget their manners and eat everything."

"Okay."

Rohn waited by the doorway so she could enter the room first. Gentleman to the end. Though not always quite such a gentleman. She recalled that well from twenty-five years ago.

Cheeks burning at the memories she went into the kitchen, which was overflowing with men and life and laughter, and realized she was hungry.

Chapter Twelve

"I like your *friend*." Tyler's stressing the last word had Rohn rolling his eyes.

Here it came. The mocking. Rohn did his best not to feed into Tyler's prodding with his response. "That's nice."

"She's real pretty." Tyler, never one to be satisfied with a simple answer, kept pushing.

"Yup." Rohn nodded and continued on the path to the ranch house. After a day of working with the boys at Bonnie's house, he was dirty and needed a shower.

Tyler should have headed to the pasture with the two other boys to throw the afternoon hay to the horses. Instead, he was badgering Rohn.

"You should ask her out."

Annoyance and the desire to put Tyler in his place and shut down this conversation had Rohn saying, "How do you know I haven't?"

"You have?" Tyler's eyes widened. "Did she say yes?"

Crap. Rohn hadn't expected a follow-up question. "Yes . . . if she's still in town."

Tyler shot Rohn a look. "What do you mean *if* she's still in town? When the hell did you ask her out for? Next New Year's Eve?"

Perhaps opening up that can of worms had been a bad idea. "No. For our high school reunion in a couple of weeks."

"Why don't you ask her to dinner tonight? She's got no food in that place of hers and she's gotta eat. That's a guaranteed yes in my opinion."

"I don't know about that." A yes wasn't guaranteed in Rohn's opinion. "And how do you know she's got no food?"

"Because I opened the fridge today looking for a bottle of water."

There went Rohn's whole lecture to Bonnie about how the boys were happy drinking out of a hose. Kids nowadays. Soft and spoiled, every last one of them. And without the manners their mammas taught them, apparently—rummaging through someone's fridge without asking first. "Well, if you won't stay out of her fridge, then you definitely should stay out of her business and mine."

"Seriously, though, Rohn. Just ask her out. I bet she's lonely over there in that mess of a house all by herself." Tyler, obviously ignoring Rohn's remonstration, plowed right ahead and gave his opinion where it wasn't wanted or needed.

Rohn sighed. "It's not as simple as all that."

They had a complicated past, he and Bonnie. A history Tyler knew nothing about, and one Rohn had no intention of sharing.

"Why isn't it? It's just a date, Rohn. Ain't nothing complicated 'bout that. I'm not telling you to marry her. I'm saying ask her over for a damn dinner so the woman doesn't faint from hunger. I don't wanna find her unconscious and buried under a pile of stuff next time we go over there. Do you?"

In the face of Tyler's direct questioning, it was hard for Rohn to come up with a good reason not to ask Bonnie out for dinner. Or even over to his house. He'd noticed the dark shadows beneath her eyes. She wasn't sleeping well at her place.

That could be because she'd slept on the sofa, or it could be because that empty house was just that—as empty of people as it was crammed full of shit.

Maybe if he could get her over to his place, she'd agree that his guest room was a perfectly good option for her to stay in for a few nights, or the whole time she was in town.

Tyler was right. There was no good reason not to call her right this minute and ask her to come over for a home-cooked meal—except that she could say no.

Of course, she could also say yes, and then break his heart again when he got attached to her and she eventually went back to Arizona.

Who was he kidding? He was already getting attached to her.

Just like it had been in high school, a few minutes in Bonnie's presence was all it had taken.

From the day he'd hired on to help her daddy at the farm, and he'd gotten to know her better, she'd eclipsed all else in his universe.

Rohn wrestled his mind off those memories and to his wayward hired help. "Get out of here and go help Justin and Colt."

"You gonna call her and suggest dinner?" Tyler asked, his brows high with expectation.

"Yes. Now get." Rohn widened his eyes in warning.

Grinning, Tyler did as told for once, while Rohn shook his head. He thought he'd learned his lesson not to take love advice from kids. On the other hand, that kid was very happy. He had himself a smart, beautiful woman who also happened to own a damn nice house and piece of land to go with it, so who was Rohn to question Tyler's advice?

He watched and waited to make sure Tyler had gotten all the way to where Justin and Colton were loading hay into the back of the truck to drive out to the horses before he went into the house.

In his office, he sat down and took out his phone to call Bonnie for the second time that day. She was already becoming a big part of his daily life and damn, he was going to miss that when she left. Maybe if they could get her house and the field looking good enough, he could convince her to stay in Oklahoma.

With that pipe dream in place, he dialed her house number, pressed the cell to his ear, and listened to the ring.

"Hello?"

"Hey, Bonnie Blue."

"Hi, Rohn."

He heard the smile in her voice and smiled himself. "So my nosy farmhand tells me you have no food in the fridge and he's concerned we'll find you passed out from malnutrition, so I figured I'd relieve his worry and, you know, feed you."

"You already fed me breakfast, and ice cream last night."

"And you fed me and the guys pizza for lunch, so I figure it's my turn again. Come over to my place for dinner tonight." He didn't give her a chance to say yes or no and plowed ahead. "Six o'clock okay?"

She hesitated for a second before finally drawing in a breath. "Yeah, that's fine."

"My spread is just outside of town. Remember the old Jackson place?" He was sure she would know where he was talking about. When they'd been dating, they'd go parking along the river not far from where he lived now.

"Yeah, I know it."

"That's it. That's where I live."

"You bought the Jackson ranch?" Her tone rose.

He laughed at her surprise. "I did."

"Wow."

Rohn shook his head, glad he'd impressed her with something because his cooking sure wouldn't do it. "So I was thinking to make hamburgers on the grill. Maybe some corn on the cob. Three bean salad. That good with you?"

"Sounds wonderful. Thank you."

"Don't thank me until you've had my cooking."

She laughed. "All right. See you later."

"See you later." Rohn couldn't erase the smile from his face all the way outside. He had nearly reached the truck when the three stooges who were his ranch hands intercepted him.

"Rohn, you wanted them left out for the night, right?" Justin hooked a thumb toward the horse paddock. "It's not supposed to rain tonight and it's too hot to put 'em back in the stalls."

"Then you answered your own question. Leave the horses out, but make sure they have fresh water. You were gone all day so those tubs never got scrubbed and refilled."

"A'ight. We're on it. I'll get the hose." Colton turned to go take care of the task.

Justin followed, saying, "I'll grab the brush from the barn."

Tyler wasn't lazy, but he also was never one to jump to work too quickly. He waited for the other two to be out of earshot before he turned to Rohn.

"So, where are you off to?" Tyler's amused smirk had Rohn not wanting to answer the question.

He did anyway. "The grocery store."

"To buy something to cook for dinner tonight?" Tyler asked.

"Yup. A man's gotta eat." Rohn wasn't about to give Tyler the satisfaction of providing any more information than the basics, though he was sure the kid was doing plenty of guessing on his own.

"You might want to pick up a pint of vanilla ice cream while you're there."

"Vanilla ice cream? And why is that?" Rohn asked.

"I just talked to Janie. She's baking today and she made an extra cobbler for you two for dessert tonight." While Rohn was busy being appalled that his private plans had already gotten passed on to his neighbor, Tyler continued, "Though actually, whipped cream goes with cobbler, too. And you know, whipped cream could come in mighty handy for other things later on. . . ."

Good Lord, this kid thought of nothing but sex. And now, thanks to that comment, Rohn couldn't get it off his mind, either. "Tyler—"

"I'll bring the cobbler over right after work and

be gone long before she gets here, so don't look so worried."

"I'm not worried. And I'm not buying whipped cream." Rohn added that last part as an afterthought.

Tyler shrugged. "Suit yourself. You're too old for that kinda stuff anyway, I guess."

Rohn saw Tyler smirking and decided there was no winning this conversation.

"Go check on the new bull, Tyler." When all else failed, Rohn could always assign this pain in the ass something to do.

"A'ight." Still looking much too pleased with himself, Tyler headed for the far field, and Rohn turned toward his truck.

He had a lot to do and not a whole lot of time to do it in. Shopping. Cooking. Cleaning. All because of Tyler and his crazy idea.

Summer, 1990

The spot they were headed was private and beautiful. A secluded place along the river, accessible only by a dirt road, but that was no concern. They would have no problem getting there in Rohn's truck.

Any other time there might be a chance one of his friends could be parked there with a girl, but not now. Tonight, he knew exactly where they'd all be. At Brian's party. He and Bonnie would have the spot all to themselves.

He knew it was plenty private there. It had to be, considering some of the shit his buddies claimed they did with their girls by the river. That consideration—

being all alone with Bonnie where no one could see them—had Rohn's gut twisting.

That wasn't why he was taking her there. He just didn't know where else they could be alone. But damn, the possibilities—if she was ready for them to take things a little bit further—were enough to have him rushing to park.

Even if all she wanted to do was look at the stars, he could get into that. No problem. Their time together was so limited, just being together was good enough for him. Though being together with a nice make-out session thrown in would be pretty damn good, too.

Rohn reached over and covered her hand. She turned her palm up and laced her fingers through his and he squeezed a bit harder. He knew if he put his arm around her shoulders, she'd snuggle right up to him, but that would have to wait until later because it was almost time to make the turn and he might need both hands on the steering wheel, depending on how rough the dirt road was.

This was his first time actually driving all the way down to the river in the dark, so he flipped on the truck's high beams and slowed to a crawl. She didn't question the fact that they were obviously driving way off the beaten path. Bonnie wasn't the type. She trusted him and knew he'd never take advantage of her.

At least, he hoped she knew that. He'd make damn sure she did. Yes, he'd made the first move kissing her in the back of the movie theater, but he'd already decided that tonight Bonnie would be calling the shots.

Her breath caught as the river came into view with the moon rising over it. "It's beautiful."

He had to agree with her. Soon, when he turned off the headlights, the moon and stars would be the only light. He wouldn't mind the darkness one bit, but he was glad she got to see the view in the last moments of daylight.

After releasing his hold on her hand, he spun the truck in a tight circle and then threw it in reverse. He backed as close to the edge of the bank as he could safely before putting it in park and cutting the engine.

"I figured we could lower the tailgate and sit back there. There'll be more of a breeze than cooped up in here with just the windows open."

"Okay." Now Bonnie looked genuinely enthusiastic, unlike before when she'd tried to pretend she was all right with going to the party.

She reached for the door handle and was out of the truck before he could get the keys out of the ignition. He thought about it and turned the key to accessory. He rolled the windows down and then turned the volume on the radio a bit louder.

No reason why they shouldn't enjoy a little music while they took in the view. They were so far from any houses, the sound wouldn't attract any attention.

Bonnie was already standing behind the truck gazing at the river, so engrossed she didn't even seem to hear him walk up to her. Rohn smiled. This was how he liked to see her. Relaxed. Totally at ease.

He stood close behind her and wrapped his arms around her waist as he kissed the back of her head.

"You're right. This is nicer than a loud, crowded party."

She turned in his arms to face him. "Mmm, it is. I love you." Her eyes widened immediately after she said the word *you*. Her mouth opened and then closed, making it obvious that the confession had slipped out. "I meant *it*. I love it."

Her confession knocked the air right out of Rohn's lungs so that he sounded a bit breathless as he said, "I love you, too."

"You do?" Bonnie bit her lip and looked close to tears.

"Yeah. I do."

It was crazy. He'd barely been aware of her existence a month ago. He'd never noticed her until the prom, but that one meeting had been enough to hook his interest.

Throw in a handful of dates and countless hours thinking about her while they were apart and looking for her while he was at the farm, and that was it. His heart didn't stand a chance. He didn't want it to. He was ready and willing to fall for Bonnie. Thank God, she was too.

The relief that she felt the same had a smile bowing his lips. That smile didn't go away even as he pressed his mouth to hers.

Her arms around him, Bonnie squeezed him tighter, pressing as close as two fully clothed people could get while standing.

He could kiss Bonnie forever, but it would be easier on both of them if she was sitting on the tailgate and closer to his height. As it was, with her a head shorter than him, he had to bend way down to reach her.

Rohn pulled back from her lips. He smiled again when he saw her beautiful face lit by moonlight. It was all he could do to take his arms from around her so he could turn and open the tailgate. Quick enough, he spun back to her and lifted her easily so she was sitting on the tailgate and eye level with him.

Stepping between her legs, he rested his hands on her waist, more than ready to get back to kissing her. She must have had the same idea. She fisted the fabric of his T-shirt and pulled him closer as her mouth crashed against his. She thrust her tongue between his lips and kissed him deeper.

The initial surprise that his little Bonnie Blue had let her inner hellcat loose soon gave way to sheer enjoyment as her tongue wrestled with his.

He was already breathless and getting hard from the intensity of the kiss even before she reached between them and he felt her hands on his buckle. She leaned back and their gazes met before she looked down to focus on her hands on his belt. His stomach rose and fell with his breath as he watched her open his buckle, then the button on his jeans, and then his zipper.

He was shaking by the time she reached her hand inside his underwear and he felt her gentle touch on him.

Her hand never leaving him, she brought her eyes up to meet his. "Rohn."

"Yeah?" His voice shook as hard as his body.

"Can you climb up here with me?"

Hell, yeah. As long as she kept touching him, he'd

do naked summersaults, if it would make her happy. "Okay."

With his jeans hanging open and his underwear exposed, he hopped onto the tailgate. Sitting next to Bonnie, he wrapped his arms around her, kissing her while taking them both down until they were horizontal in the bed of the pickup.

She moved over him. He watched as she straddled his legs.

Bonnie above him was an amazing sight. Bonnie unbuttoning her jean shorts while over him was enough to make him fear he might pass out.

"You know, we, uh, can take our time if you want." He made the offer even as he got so hard he could feel his pulse throbbing all the way through his erection.

"I know." She wiggled out of her shorts, pulling them off each foot over her flip-flops, before she tossed them to the side.

He drew in a shaky breath as Bonnie, in nothing but a tank top and underwear, decided to pull that underwear off. He somehow forced his eyes to stay focused on her face, which was a pretty amazing feat since she was naked from the waist down.

She reached for him and pulled his length out of his underwear. The warmth of her hand in contrast to the cool breeze blowing had him shivering.

So did the knowledge of what they were about to do as Bonnie lowered her body over him.

He reached up and held her back with a hand on each of her shoulders. "You sure?"

"Yes. I've never been more sure about anything in my life. I love you and I want this."

He wanted this—with her—more than she could possibly know. "I love you, too."

His words brought a tiny smile to her lips before she leaned low and pressed a kiss to his. He didn't question her again. There was nothing more to say, and when he felt the warmth of her body surround his, he wouldn't have been able to form a coherent thought to speak, anyway.

Chapter Thirteen

Summer, 2015 (Present Day)

Bonnie knew she shouldn't be there, but there she was, standing outside Rohn's house about to go in for dinner. With him. Alone.

Why? For the same reason she'd said yes to his invitation to go with him to the reunion. Because it seemed the teenage girl who'd had a crush on him twenty-five years ago was alive and well inside her. All these years later she still couldn't resist Rohn Lerner.

Reason and good sense abandoned her when Rohn was near—or even on the phone. That voice, deeper now than it had been when she'd known him, funneled directly into her ear, caused a shiver to travel through her, no matter how hot the thermometer said it was.

There was no use fighting it, so she might as well go inside and enjoy herself. Later, she'd worry about the future. Pushing that away, she strode to the front door.

Not wanting to arrive empty-handed, and knowing

if she asked what she could bring he'd say *nothing*, she carried a six-pack of beer in her hand. She had no idea what he drank. That summer they'd dated neither of them had been legally old enough to buy a drink. The law had raised the legal drinking age to twenty-one just a few years prior to their turning eighteen.

Standing in front of the door without knocking or ringing the bell wasn't going to get her inside anytime soon. And procrastinating was only making her more nervous. She raised her fist and knocked.

The sound of Rohn's quick, heavy footsteps reached her before the door opened and she saw him, smiling but looking a little frazzled and very domestic.

She let her gaze drop to the dish towel, creatively tucked into the pockets of his jeans to form a makeshift apron. "Nice apron."

He rolled his eyes and pulled the towel from its perch. "I'm sorry. Things took longer than I thought they would."

"I can help you."

"Nuh-uh. You're not helping. I won't allow it. You're a guest. Besides, I'm pretty much done anyway. Come on in." He tipped his head and took a step away from the door.

She held out the beer after she stepped inside. "Here. For you."

"You didn't have to bring anything, but thank you." Rohn took the six-pack from Bonnie's hands.

"You're welcome. And are you kidding? My mother would have a fit if she knew I came to dinner and didn't bring something."

"You're right. How is your mamma doing anyway?"

"She's good. Enjoying the Arizona climate. It's good for her asthma." Bonnie responded to Rohn's inquiry with her stock answer as he led her through his home.

The house was interesting. As Bonnie looked around her, she had trouble seeing Rohn in it. She'd entered through a door that led to a hallway.

There was a living area off to the right. Silver picture frames decorated the polished wood side tables. More frames were interspersed among the books on the shelves. A dining room was to the left, filled with a heavily carved wooden dining table and eight matching chairs, a sideboard, and a buffet.

Both rooms seemed so unlike the Rohn she knew. Then again, he'd been eighteen when she'd known him. It wasn't as if they had experience decorating a house together. What teenage boy would know or care about home decor?

It wasn't until they got farther into the house, to the kitchen, that she started to be able to see Rohn living here. Bonnie could picture him making coffee at the counter. She imagined him leaning against the sink and watching the sunrise out the window over the sink.

More, she could imagine herself standing there next to him.

Bonnie yanked her mind off that fantasy, putting a screeching halt to what was a dangerous and pointless dream. She was cleaning out her dad's house, selling or renting it, and leaving . . . but not tonight.

Tonight she was going to enjoy this dinner with Rohn. One look at that smile of his when he'd opened the door had her heart beating faster and she knew there was no way not to enjoy spending time with him.

Rohn put the six-pack on the counter and then tossed the towel onto the edge of the sink. "Something to drink?"

"Sure. What are you having?"

"I think I'm going to indulge in one of those nice cold beers you were kind enough to bring."

"That sounds good to me. I think I'll join you." Alcohol could only help the ridiculous nervousness she felt around him.

Rohn reached out and pulled a bottle from the six-pack while glancing at Bonnie. "You want a glass?"

"The bottle is fine."

He twisted the cap off and handed the longneck to her. The condensation on the cold bottle made her hand wet as she took a closer look at the kitchen.

A vase full of fresh wildflowers on the table caught her attention. Rohn must have picked flowers. The image of that—Rohn bent over in the field grabbing handfuls of Queen Anne's lace, cornflowers, and daisies—made her smile.

He carried the remainder of the six-pack to the fridge, opened the door, and slid the carrier onto the top shelf. "I did pick up a couple bottles of wine, too, in case you wanted some. One red, one white, in case you get tired of the beer. The guy at the store said these two were good, so . . ."

"Rohn, believe me, I'm no wine expert. The few times a year when I buy a bottle for Mom and me to drink, I usually choose by which has the nicest label."

He lifted one brow. "And how's that work out for you?"

She laughed. "Surprisingly well."

"Good to know." He lifted his bottle to his lips and swallowed, his eyes on her the entire time. "It's good to have you back in town, Bonnie Blue."

"For now." She had to remind herself as much as him that she was leaving. Eventually.

"For now." He acknowledged that with a nod and then pushed off from where he'd been leaning back against the cabinets. "Come on out to the patio with me. I gotta throw on the burgers."

Rohn looked so domestic flipping hamburgers on the grill that it had Bonnie feeling sad for the loss of what could have been. If she hadn't left. If she hadn't withheld probably the most important information of their lives from Rohn. If she hadn't made that decision and done what she'd done . . .

Summer, 1990

The sun was setting earlier and the nights growing cooler. All that did was indicate that Bonnie needed to enjoy each and every second she had left with Rohn before she left for college.

She slipped her hands beneath the hem of his T-shirt and ran her palms over the bare skin of his lower back as he loved her. He thrust into her one last time, groaning, before he rolled to the side to lie next to her on a blanket spread in the back of the truck.

There was a sheen of sweat on his face in spite of the chill as he gazed down at her, a smile tipping up the corner of his mouth. She hoped he didn't see the tears that just thinking of leaving him, even for the semester, had caused.

"Did you see the moon?" he asked.

"Yes."

"It's almost full. Just like it was the first night we were here together." He rolled onto his back to stare up at the sky, but his hand remained on her stomach and he left one leg tossed over hers.

He was right. The moon had been almost full that first time they'd had sex, which meant that was a month ago. Bonnie didn't need a calendar to see that her period was late.

Her heart knocked against her rib cage as realization crept in. They hadn't been careful that first time. Or the second time, for that matter. It wasn't until Rohn had snuck away to another town where no one knew them and bought a box of condoms that they started to use protection.

"Um, it's getting late. Can you take me back to town?" She had to get to the drugstore before it closed and buy a test.

Rohn groaned. "I hate dropping you off in town and letting you ride that bike home. It's not safe in the dark."

"I'll be fine." Roadway safety was the last concern on her mind.

Finally, he sat up. He handed her the shorts and underwear he'd stripped off her an hour ago, before reaching for his own.

She was silent as they drove back to town as the fear gripped her. She somehow managed to hide her fear from Rohn as he kissed her good night and left her alone with her bike.

That's when the adrenaline kicked in. Shaking, she rode directly to the drugstore and prayed she didn't know the clerk or see anyone else she knew inside. Hiding the pregnancy test beneath a magazine, she carried both to the counter. She was happy to see it was some young guy she didn't know manning the register.

Even so her heart pounded as she said, "Hi. Just these please."

He didn't look twice at her as he tossed both items in the bag and took her money.

Bonnie stashed the test into the waistband of her shorts, beneath her shirt, just in case and then rode home as fast as she could. Her parents were in the living room watching TV as she came through the door.

"I'm home." She turned toward her room.

"Did you have fun? What did you do?" her mother asked.

"Melody and I went to the diner and shared a plate of fries and then we went to the drugstore and bought a new magazine. It's the fall fashion issue." She held up the plastic bag with the magazine inside as proof. Bonnie had become quite good at lying. "I'm going to brush my teeth and then head to bed early I think. I'm kinda tired."

"Okay, baby."

Luckily, her father hadn't even bothered to glance in her direction. Instead he'd focused on whatever was on television and let her mother ask all the questions.

She headed first to her room, where she closed the door and pulled the box from its hiding place beneath her shirt.

Holding it beneath the edge of her desk in case anyone walked in, she pulled the desk lamp closer and read the instructions. She'd have to take the test to the bathroom with her and then wait for the results.

In two minutes she'd know if what she suspected was true or not. And God help her if it was.

Chapter Fourteen

Summer, 2015 (Present Day)

Rohn wished he had some whiskey. Or tequila. Or vodka. Hell, a single shot of anything that he could down to take the edge off.

Around Bonnie, he was as nervous as a schoolboy on his first date, but worse because now he was an adult and knew all that could go wrong in life and love.

Nope. The beer wasn't cutting it. He took another swig from the bottle, anyway.

"So the boys who work for you are nice." Bonnie glanced up from her plate.

They'd chosen to eat out on the patio. He appreciated that decision even more now as the warm breeze ruffled the hair around her face and the sun low in the sky cast a warm glow across her cheeks.

"They can be, when they aren't busting my chops."

She laughed. "Yeah, I could see how they might like to stir up trouble. That Tyler especially."

Rohn let out a snort. "You ain't kidding about

that. He liked you, too, by the way. He said you were very pretty."

"Really?" She looked surprised and embarrassed at the same time. "That's sweet, especially since I think I might be double his age."

"Not quite, but yeah, I know what you mean. Makes a man feel old around all these young bucks."

"I think you hold your own, all right."

"Thanks."

"I like your house," she said, leaning back in her chair and looking relaxed compared to how he felt.

Good thing Bonnie was so good with the small talk. If it were up to Rohn, they'd be in trouble. He feared that he'd been out of the dating game for so long that if he couldn't talk to her about cattle or this year's hay crop, he'd be hard-pressed for a topic of conversation. They could talk about the past, he supposed, but given their history together, that was a bit of a minefield.

He dipped his head to acknowledge her compliment. "Thank you. I did a lot to it right after Lila and I bought it. Structurally it was sound, but it felt . . ."

"Like old man Jackson had been living here for the past sixty years?" she suggested.

"Yeah." He laughed. "Lila was really great with fixing the place up."

"I can see that. The living room and dining room are lovely."

"And you can tell I had nothing to do with decorating them." He grinned.

"Pretty much." Bonnie looked so beautiful when she smiled like that. Just like she had when she was eighteen. If only he could get her to do it more often.

Rohn drew in a breath and, with enough beer in

him to make him brave, launched into what he wanted to know. "You ever take the plunge, Bonnie Blue? Ever get married?"

"No."

Her answer was as interesting as it was encouraging. "Why not?"

"I guess I just never made it a priority." She shrugged.

"What did you make a priority?"

"My career."

"What did you end up doing, anyway?" Rohn couldn't believe he hadn't already asked what she did in Arizona.

It was as if he knew her, but at the same time, he didn't know her at all. They'd been as close as two people could be all those years ago. Aside from those shared memories, they were strangers. He really did suck at communicating.

"I'm a teacher."

He smiled at her answer. "That's what you always said you wanted to go to school for."

School. That had been what had taken her away from him. Or at least he liked to think it was. It had been easy to blame the university in Arizona and the academic scholarship she'd gotten rather than turning his attention to something closer to home. Like the possibility she'd just outgrown him and that was why she'd never come home for summer or winter breaks.

Of course, her parents had divorced about that time. With her mother moving out to Arizona with her, it probably felt silly for her to come back to Oklahoma for school breaks.

Still, there was the phone. He'd called a couple

of times but when he'd seen it was one-sided—that he'd do all the calling and she'd do all the avoiding—he'd eventually stopped.

A man could only take so much rejection. Especially at that young age.

"I bet you had all those college boys wrapped around your little finger." Maybe she'd disappeared so completely from his life because she'd met someone.

Bonnie shook her head. "No. Not really."

That made no sense. She'd had a pretty good hold on him, all those years ago. And judging by how he couldn't stay away from her the past few days, it appeared that now was no different. He'd do anything she asked him to, including clean out that mess of a house of hers. He'd spend day and night there just to make her happy, and with the hope of seeing more of her.

"How long were you and your wife married?" Bonnie's question interrupted his thoughts.

"We were going on sixteen years when she died. Hard to believe it would have been our twenty-first anniversary later this year."

"So you met and married her a few years after high school then?"

"Yup."

If Bonnie was asking him how long it took him to get over her, that answer was a good long while.

Lila was by no means a rebound girl. He'd started dating her after the hurt had faded, but he also hadn't had another serious relationship in the middle. He'd been too skittish for too long after what had felt like such a world-altering love and loss with Bonnie.

He had bought Bonnie a promise ring that summer. He'd been waiting for the perfect time to give it to her, but she'd left before he got a chance. He'd wondered for years if his giving it to her would have made a difference.

Would that microscopic chip of a diamond set in a gold circle have kept her here and saved him a world of hurt?

"So, what grade do you teach?" Time for small talk again. His beer-soaked heart wasn't enjoying these particularly painful memories.

"Fifth grade."

"Nice." Not that he knew all that much about kids. He wished he did.

"Dinner was really good."

"Was it?" He laughed.

"It was. I don't think you do yourself justice. The burgers were perfect. And everything else was really good too."

"Everything else I bought premade at the store, but thank you. I do have some skills in the grill department. And there's even dessert."

"Dessert?" She lifted a brow. "I'm impressed."

"Don't be. Tyler's girlfriend made it."

"Girls his age bake?" She looked surprised.

"No. His girlfriend is closer to our age."

"Tyler's dating an older woman? Why am I not surprised?" She laughed.

"Yup. I guess I shouldn't call her a girlfriend then, should I? Lady friend? Woman friend?" He wrinkled his nose. "I'm not loving any of those."

"Society hasn't really come up with a good alternative for people our age, has it?"

"Not really. No. Wonder what that says?" Rohn thought the message was pretty clear. That single women in their thirties and forties should just give up and be old and lonely.

"I think it's just that the world is changing but not everything has kept up. It's sad, really. There are a ton of people dating later in life. With divorces, and widowers, people are dating at all ages."

He nodded. "Yet we only have the terms *girlfriend* and *boyfriend* to work with."

"Or *significant other.*" An adorable wrinkle creased the bridge of her nose.

"You have a significant other, Bonnie Blue?"

She raised her gaze to his before answering. "No. You?"

That she was interested enough to ask lightened his heart considerably. He answered happily, "Nope."

She nodded, and a silence fell over them. All this serious personal talk had put a damper on the lighter conversation.

Uncomfortable with the silence, he said, "Anyway. Ready for dessert?"

"Can I have a tour first?"

"A tour? Sure. What would you like to see?"

"Your animals. I don't know. The whole place." She lifted a shoulder.

"Okay." He glanced at her feet and the open sandals she wore. "You good to walk in those? Wouldn't want you stepping in something unpleasant and ruining your shoes."

She laughed. "I'll take my chances."

He stood. She did the same. As he turned toward the field the bulls were in, he glanced sideways at Bonnie. "I remember a day when you wore exactly two kinds of footwear. Cowboy boots or flip-flops."

"Not true. I had real shoes for the prom, dyed to match my dress."

"Yes, you did. And you were the most beautiful girl there."

She rolled her eyes. "Thank you, but I think that official honor belonged to the prom queen. Marie whatever her name was."

"Jorgensen."

She cocked one brow and glanced at him. "So, you remember her name, do you? Did you have a little crush on her maybe?"

"No. The moment you and I talked that night, I only had eyes for you, Bonnie Blue." He watched the blush creep across her cheek. "I remember her name because her son works loading the trucks at the feed store in town. She's not exactly prom queen material anymore, but bless her, she's got four good, strong, healthy kids in exchange."

Bonnie's eyes widened. "Four. Wow."

"Yeah. All boys. She wanted to try for more—looking to get a girl. Her husband told me he put a stop to it. Told her he wasn't going to have a basketball team trying to get a cheerleader." At that, Bonnie laughed. The sound made him smile. "I always thought you'd have a bunch of kids, Bonnie."

"Me? Nope. Nice-looking bulls." She walked a little faster as they approached the fence. If he wasn't mistaken, she was avoiding the subject of children. If she wanted the subject dropped, he'd let it go.

"You know bulls, do you?" he asked.

"No. But they're still nice-looking." She cut him a sideways glance.

"Let me give you the rundown on who's who. This guy right here, giving us the stink eye, has made me a ton of money. He's a real good bucker. Tosses the riders in the dirt nine times out of ten. I just started selling his sperm. I get a good amount of money for each straw."

Her brows rose. "I had no idea. So you're like a pimp. And he's the gigolo."

"Kind of. Except he doesn't get to have any of the fun with the lady bulls. Never even gets to see them. I ship the stuff to whoever orders it."

"So how do you get, the um, you know . . . stuff?"

Rohn laughed. "Let's just say, I'm thankful to have Tyler, Justin, and Colton around to do the dirty work when the time comes. You probably don't want to know the details."

She considered that a moment and then shook her head. "Yeah, you're right. I think I'd rather not know."

This conversation had taken them into whole new territory. But it wasn't the talk of bull semen getting to him. It was the fact the attraction between him and her was still as strong today as it had been twenty-five years ago. Back when he'd been a hired hand and she'd been the farmer's daughter.

That summer had been a hot one, and their love ran even hotter. Those were some powerful memories.

"Bonnie."

"Yeah?"

"Tonight was just two friends having dinner, but I'd like it if we could go out on a real date."

"Rohn, I'm only here for a little while and then I'm leaving again."

He took a step forward. "Bonnie, you can make excuses all day long, but it's not going to change the fact that there's something here between us. Whether we choose to ignore it or enjoy it is up to you. I know what I wanna do. Even if it's just for the time you're here."

"I don't know."

"Let me help you decide." He reached out and rested his hands on her waist. It felt as familiar as it did strange to be touching her again.

When she didn't retreat, he leaned lower. She raised her gaze to his and he saw a need to match his own in her eyes. There was no stopping him then. He closed the final distance between them and kissed her.

Fireworks on the Fourth of July had never seemed as bright as the sparks rocketing through Rohn at the feel of Bonnie's lips beneath his. It felt like he was eighteen again and damn, he never wanted the feeling to end.

She kissed him like she was as desperate for him as he was for her, then she pulled back. Fast, and far enough his hands fell to his side.

"I can't." She shook her head.

He nodded. "I understand. We can take things slow."

"No. That's not it. I mean I can't ever. I'm sorry. Thank you for dinner. I gotta go." She turned and ran.

"Bonnie." He took a single step after her before he stopped himself. She was literally fleeing from his kiss. It wasn't in him to stop her.

Rohn watched Bonnie drive away until the taillights of her car disappeared. Only then did he turn back to the house and head for the kitchen. There he saw the remnants of the dinner preparations.

The dinner that had ended pretty disastrously, in his opinion.

Forget about the mess in the kitchen. It would still be there later. Instead, he turned toward the office.

Sitting in the desk chair, he booted up the old desktop computer. He drew in a breath of frustration as it took too long to come to life, and then a couple minutes more before something happened on screen and his browser window finally came up.

Tomorrow, he was looking at new computers. If he was destined to be on the damn thing more often, like it or not, he might as well make it less painful. And it was becoming quite obvious he *would* be online a lot more. After Bonnie's rejection tonight, he was hurt enough to go back to his damn online matchmaking account.

If her telling him she couldn't be with him, ever, and then running away wasn't rejection, he didn't know what was. He was mad and he was hurt, but he'd get over it. He had before after the last time she'd run out on him. He would again.

That didn't mean he had to sit idly by waiting for time to heal all wounds. If Bonnie didn't want him, he knew where there were women who did. Rohn might loathe this online stuff, but tonight he was motivated.

Hating with every fiber of his being that this was what his life had become, he clicked to the in-box area of his profile and saw new messages had arrived. Proof there were women in the world who found him attractive.

That was nice to have reaffirmed after tonight.

Systematically, Rohn went through the half a dozen

or so messages. He even found one from a woman he wouldn't mind meeting. He hesitated for a solid minute, staring at the screen, deciding if he really wanted to go down this path.

He was still deciding when headlights from a vehicle pulling into his driveway had Rohn's mind racing as fast as his pulse.

Had Bonnie changed her mind and come back? He strode out of the office, and all the way to the back door.

One glance told him it wasn't Bonnie's car. It wasn't a car at all. It was a pickup truck pulling up to the barn.

What the hell was one of the boys doing here this late at night? Frowning, Rohn strode over to find out.

By the time he arrived, the driver's-side door was opening and Justin was stepping out. "Hey, boss."

"Hey. What're you doing here?" Rohn couldn't help but think that had Justin arrived an hour earlier, he would have walked in on the tail end of the dinner with Bonnie.

He might have been witness to that hot and heavy kiss out by the bull pasture. Or perhaps to Bonnie's tearful, speedy departure. He wouldn't have been happy about Justin seeing any of it. Rohn couldn't guarantee he would have noticed a steam train barreling down upon him in the heat of the moment, much less Justin's pickup truck in the drive.

Justin tipped his head toward one of the vehicles parked off to the side. "I forgot my wallet. Left it stuck in the dashboard of the truck today while we were working. I need my ID and cash."

ID and cash—every young cowboy's requirement for a wild night out. "Going out, are you?"

"Yup. Colton talked me into it. He made me feel guilty because I haven't gone out with him in so long, and Tyler won't come out anymore, for obvious reasons." Justin grinned.

Rohn imagined that smile of Justin's won the single guy lots of ladies, at least for one night. "Well, y'all have fun."

Justin nodded. "We will sure try. No doubt. Have a good night, boss."

"Thanks." Doing dishes and then trying to find something on the television until he could fall asleep? Yeah, real fun.

As Justin strode toward the ranch truck to retrieve his wallet, Rohn turned back toward the house. But he didn't go to the kitchen. Instead he went directly to the computer, intent on getting himself a life.

Doubt or not, he had to make a move. He'd waited too long already to move on with his life. In his profile in-box, he opened the message from a stranger named Margaret. She was nearby. Just in the next town. She was divorced, but that was probably to be expected in a woman who was forty. And she liked horses. Or at least she said she did.

Margaret. It was a nice, wholesome name. He could handle a Margaret. Better than a Tiffany or a Brittany or a . . . whatever the hell name was popular nowadays.

He hit reply to her message and stared at the blinking cursor for a few minutes. Then he just started to type. He couldn't figure out what he wanted to say, so he said that.

I'm not sure what to say. I've never done anything like this before.

That sounded like a line to him. It would be his luck that though he was telling the truth, it sounded like a lie and was probably a line used by hundreds of guys on here disingenuously. He needed to explain.

The reason I've never done this before is because I was married for many, many years. My beloved wife died five years ago and my employees and friends have decided it's time for me to start dating again. Though that's not the only reason I'm on here. I know it's time myself.

Crap. Was this any good? Did he suck at writing? How would he know? He didn't write anything more than invoices or lists for the store nowadays.

Forging ahead, he decided to wrap it up.

If you'd like to meet I'd like that too. Thanks. Rohn.

Well, he was no Hemingway, but at least it was the God's honest truth.

After reading over his message to her, he hit send before he thought better of it. That was it then. For better or worse, the message was on its way.

Rohn stood and headed for the kitchen. He had to clean up. Wash the dishes, put away the leftovers. Maybe dig into that dessert Janie had made that they'd never gotten to tonight.

The memory of why had him feeling less inclined to eat. He flipped on the faucet instead and waited for the water to warm as his mind reeled.

After he was done cleaning, he'd go back to the computer, which he'd left turned on, and see if Margaret had responded yet.

If she didn't reply tonight or by tomorrow? Then what?

Then he'd open every damn one of those messages

he'd received and reply to them. And if those didn't yield him a date, he'd start searching the site on his own.

He'd have to, because it was more than obvious Bonnie was not going to be a part of his future.

Hell, he wasn't even sure they still had a date for the reunion, not that she'd ever given him a solid yes for that, anyway. It had been more like a maybe, *if* she was still in town.

Maybe she'd been giving him hints she wasn't interested all along and he'd just ignored them. Who the hell knew? He'd been out of this game for too long.

He'd never wanted to be alone at this point in his life, but since it had been thrust upon him, he'd have to work with the hand he'd been dealt.

A little while later, when the kitchen was clean and there were no more excuses to procrastinate, Rohn made his way back to the office.

There was a new message in his in-box. It was from Margaret.

Hi, Rohn!! I would LOVE to meet you! When??!!? Where??!! I'm off from work tomorrow so I have all day!! Just let me know. Bye!!

He lifted a brow at the sheer amount of punctuation in Margaret's message. Maybe this was how things were done nowadays. After all, it was hard to convey emotion over e-mail and text messages. The kids must manage to do it with all these exclamation points.

Margaret was no kid, but she'd adapted to this strange new electronic world they were living in. Rohn would have to do the same.

Clearing his throat, he set fingers to keyboard.

Brows drawn low, he contemplated what in the world to say for a moment before he typed:

How about meeting for a cup of coffee and maybe breakfast tomorrow at the diner on the highway at ten?

After a second thought, he added an exclamation point to the end of his single sentence. He stared at the black words on the white screen for a few seconds before he shook his head and deleted the ridiculous-looking and unnecessary exclamation point. He hit send, quickly before he could agonize over this message any further.

Baby steps.

Refusing to sit there and wait for a reply, he stood, but he hadn't even taken one step toward the door when the message alert popped up.

Margaret was one eager lady. He hoped that was because she was so excited to meet him and not a sign of the level of desperation of single, middle-aged women today.

Middle-aged. God help him, he was middle-aged. When the hell had that happened?

Drawing in a breath, he moved back in front of the screen to read her message.

IT'S A DATE!!!

All caps this time, in addition to the multitude of exclamation points. That must mean she was even more excited than before.

Letting out a breath, he hit the buttons to power down the computer and headed for the hallway while the machine was still chugging away as it shut down.

He'd had more than enough of this computer

dating stuff for one night. For a whole lifetime, actually.

With Bonnie's kiss still on his lips and on his mind, along with the memory of her walking away from him yet again, he went back to dip into that apple cobbler of Janie's and contemplate this date.

Chapter Fifteen

"Good morning, Miss Bonnie."

Bonnie smiled at the handsome young cowboy tipping his hat to her. "Good morning, Colton. How are you today?"

"Good, ma'am. Yourself?"

"Fine. Thanks."

She'd slept like crap, but what else was new? This time it wasn't just her house haunting her, or the clutter still surrounding her everywhere. It was her brain refusing to go to sleep.

Her mind wanted to second-guess the decision she knew was the right one. She could not be with Rohn. No matter how much she wanted to be with him. And she did. So much. That deep-seated need hadn't helped her sleep, either.

She glanced past the cowboy in front of her at the truck parked in the driveway. "Who else is with you?"

"I brought my own truck over. We figured we can divide and conquer, and finish twice as fast. We can be loading one truck while the other guy drives to wherever. Ty and Justin are on their way in the ranch truck.

"Good plan. Is Rohn coming too?" Bonnie had meant the question to sound casual, but wasn't so sure it had come out that way.

"Nah. He was still at the house when we left. Told us to put in a day of work here, but to get back to the ranch in time for afternoon chores."

"Oh." The disappointment crashed over her.

He wasn't coming over. She'd hurt him—again—in an attempt to save him. To save herself. She needed to stop doing that, to both of them.

But it was better he wasn't here today. Much better. She couldn't be tempted to do something foolish, like let herself be with him. She couldn't be with him and leave him. And given the secret she'd kept from him for twenty-five years, she certainly couldn't be with him and stay with him, either.

It was foolish to think they could be friends and not have the feelings resurface, so the best thing to do was steer clear of each other until she left. She only wished she'd realized that sooner.

With a sigh, she turned back toward the still-cluttered room. "I can show you what I had planned for today while we're waiting for the other guys, if you'd like."

"That sounds good. They should be here shortly. They were stopping in town to grab breakfast. Rohn said to make sure we fed you or you probably wouldn't eat." Colton's eyes crinkled in the corners with a broad smile.

Even after how she'd acted last night, Rohn was still taking care of her, just from a distance. Her heart warmed at the same time it broke because she'd always have to keep him at a distance.

Drawing in a breath she turned toward the hall. Time to clear out the clutter and with it, the memories. "I think I want to donate all the bedroom furniture to the church. I haven't been around lately. Do they still take donations for the needy?"

"Yes, ma'am. Clothes and house-type stuff."

"Even larger furniture? Like beds."

"Yes, ma'am. They're always wanting beds. Even used ones are appreciated. They've got a furniture warehouse for folks who don't have everything they need. Some company donated the space."

"Really? That's wonderful. I didn't know."

"Yup. It's only about two years old now. Maybe less." Colton followed her down the hallway as he talked. "I helped my mom out after the rummage sale at the church last year. I trucked the stuff that didn't sell over to the warehouse so I know right where to go and who to talk to. They'll definitely appreciate and make good use of whatever you've got."

"Good. I'm glad it will help."

That was one worry gone. Bonnie had decided she couldn't stand being in the house with the furniture from her childhood. The things her father had kept and lived with for all these years, making few changes.

Twenty-five years had passed and it looked like he hadn't replaced a thing. She'd never considered him to be a sentimental man, but the evidence began to indicate he might have been. There was money in his savings account, not much but enough to show he hadn't held on to all this stuff because he couldn't afford to buy new.

There were precious few things that had been

truly Bonnie's from her childhood—her bed and the matching dresser being two of them. But after what had happened on that bed the night she left, she couldn't bear to look at it.

It hadn't been used in decades so the set was still in decent shape. Someone would be able to use it. Someone who had no memories tied to it.

Maybe having that furniture out of sight would also put it out of mind, and that would chase away a few of the many demons keeping her up at night.

The sound of doors slamming out in the driveway caught her attention.

"Sounds like the guys are here. And breakfast." Colton grinned.

"Then let's eat. I ran out to the store yesterday for some supplies, so I've got sweet tea and bottled water."

"Thank you, ma'am."

"No, thank you. I really do appreciate all your help. This isn't part of your job."

Colton shot her a sideways glance as they made their way back toward the front of the house. "It kind of is. We do what Rohn tells us to do. He says come over here and help you. We come here and help."

She cringed. "Sorry."

"No, don't be." He waved away her concern. "I'd far rather load your old furniture into a truck than dig fence posts, which is what he'd have us doing if we were at the ranch. We're getting the better end of the deal. Trust me. The other guys feel the same."

"Are you sure?" The guilt that Rohn's fence had been put on hold still rode her, but she'd like to know that at least his guys weren't unhappy about the arrangement.

"Oh, yeah. Besides, any friend of Rohn's, we consider a friend of ours. We want to help you. I think once this place gets cleaned up, it'll look real nice."

Bonnie glanced around her and hoped, eventually, it would look good enough to sell or rent, at least. Right now, that was not the case. "Maybe."

"No maybe about it. Definitely. It might even be nice enough you'll decide to stick around for a while. You think you might?" Colton's question had her turning to him.

"No, I can't do that. I have a job in Arizona I need to get back to."

"Ah, I didn't know." He tipped his head. "That's a shame. I know Rohn would like it if you stuck around."

She knew she shouldn't ask, but she did anyway. "Did he . . . say that?"

The young man grinned. "Nah. He didn't have to."

A knock on the door had Colton walking forward to open it for his two coworkers, but he'd left Bonnie behind with plenty of questions.

The questions followed her into the kitchen. She and the three men sat at the kitchen table and broke into egg sandwiches like they had the day before, but this time without Rohn. The guys chattered and ate around her.

"I wonder what Rohn's doing today." Tyler's question caught Bonnie's attention.

Colton snorted. "Probably working on the books, like he does all the time."

"Nah, I don't think so." Tyler shook his head. "Didn't you notice? He had on his good shirt."

With half an egg sandwich in one hand, Justin asked, "What good shirt?"

Tyler reached for his bottle of water and cracked it open. "The blue one that matches his eyes with the pearl snaps."

"That matches his eyes? What the fu—" Justin glanced at Bonnie and obviously censored what he'd been about to say. "—heck?"

Colton shook his head, laughing. "Jeez, Ty. What are you, the fashion police now?"

"Yeah, should I text you to see what I should wear from now on? What color matches my eyes?" Justin batted his lashes.

"Ha, ha." Tyler scowled. "If y'all would open your eyes once in a while, you'd notice he only wears that shirt when he's going somewhere special."

"Maybe he's got like a meeting at the bank or something." Colton lifted his shoulder in a half shrug.

Bonnie listened with interest. She was learning more about Rohn without him being here than she would have if he'd come with the guys this morning. She knew they'd never talk this openly if he were here.

"Let's hope that's not it." Justin shook his head. "The only reason to go to a bank all dressed up is to get a loan and if the ranch is doing so bad Rohn needs one of them, we all better start worrying about our jobs."

"He doesn't need money. I've seen the balance in his checkbook. He's doing just fine."

At Tyler's revelation, Colton's eyes widened. "Damn, Ty. You shouldn't be looking at Rohn's stuff."

"What can I say? He left it open on the desk. He should put that shit—" Tyler glanced in Bonnie's direction. "Pardon, ma'am—*stuff* away if he don't want anyone to see it."

She smiled. Their banter provided a much-needed distraction. She was particularly enjoying the way they took care not to cuss in front of her.

"Anyway," Tyler continued. "I think Rohn has a date."

That took her by surprise.

"A date?" She couldn't stop the question that slipped out. She tried to sound casual as she added, "Why do you say that?"

"Because he was wearing his good shirt. I thought he might be coming here to see you all dressed up, even though he keeps saying you're just an old friend. But then he told us to come here and work and that he'd see us back at the ranch later. Now I'm thinking maybe he got dressed up to go see the woman I introduced him to the other night."

"You introduced him to a woman the other night?" Justin frowned. "When? Where?"

Bonnie's throat tightened until she wasn't sure she'd be able to swallow if she dared take another bite. She'd lost her appetite anyway after hearing Rohn was actively out meeting women.

"Remember that dinner at Janie's I invited him to?"

"Yeah, the one he invited Rohn to and not us," Colton added.

"That's the one." Tyler nodded. "And now you

know why I couldn't invite you. It was a fix-up for Rohn and a woman Janie knows from town."

Justin nodded. "Yeah, I had a feeling you were up to something. So how'd it go?"

Bonnie waited and wished Tyler would answer faster.

"I wasn't sure he liked her at the time, but maybe I was wrong if he's going out with someone today. I mean, who else could it be?" Tyler glanced at Bonnie. "Besides you and Janie and Tilly the other night at dinner, I haven't seen Rohn even talk to a woman in . . . forever."

Her stomach twisted at the thought of him with this Tilly woman. It was extremely selfish, her not wanting Rohn to be with anyone else—to be happy— when clearly she couldn't be with him herself. But knowing that didn't change how she felt.

"I don't know. You and your shirt theory sounds like bull to me." Colton tipped his head in her direction. "I think he's interested in Miss Bonnie, here."

That brought her attention around. "Me?"

"Sure. He likes you. I can tell."

"I like him too, but that doesn't mean we can date."

"Why not?" Justin asked.

All eyes were on her when she said, "Because I have a job back in Arizona. And a house."

"You have a house here, too," Justin pointed out.

Colton nodded. "Exactly. You said you're a teacher in Arizona?"

"Yes." Bonnie nodded, not liking being in the spotlight.

"My mamma has a friend who works at the school

here in town. I heard her complaining that three teachers went out on maternity leave at once and they think a couple of them are not coming back, so they're going to have to do some hiring."

Tyler tipped a chin toward Colton after that revelation. "See? You can teach here. You should go and put in an application."

Bonnie struggled to find another excuse. "But my mother lives with me in Arizona."

"Bring her here to live with you. Didn't you grow up here?" Tyler asked.

"Yes."

Colton blew out a breath. "Well, considering how this place never changes, I'm betting your mom's old friends are still around."

"Yeah." Justin nodded. "She might enjoy being back here."

It was hard to protest further, especially with all three men at the table staring at her, waiting for a valid reason why she couldn't stay. "You boys are sure hell-bent on getting me to stay here. I'm not really sure why."

"That's easy." Tyler grinned. "Because Rohn smiles when you're around."

"He hasn't been real nice to work with the last couple of months before you showed up." Colton shot her a glance. "Between you and me, I think he's lonely."

"And he's also private. And he'd flay you if he heard you telling her stuff like that." Justin's tone held a warning.

Colton leveled his gaze on Justin. "I'll take my chances. I think Miss Bonnie needs to know. If it convinces her to stay here forever and makes Rohn happy permanently, then I'll deal with him being mad at me for a bit."

This surreal conversation had gone on long enough. Too long, actually. Words like *forever* weren't in the cards for her and Rohn. She just couldn't tell them why.

"I appreciate all your concern, but I can't stay and that's that."

"Can't and won't are two different things, Miss Bonnie." Tyler focused his gaze on her.

It was easy to think he was just a joker, but as he pinned her with his stare, she had to really listen to what he was saying and absorb the meaning behind his words.

"Just think about it." Colton's stare joined Tyler's.

"And it couldn't hurt to maybe talk to someone at the school about that job," Justin added.

All three were united against her . . . or maybe they were simply pulling for her and Rohn, not knowing it was pointless.

These three, young, good-hearted men didn't know the truth. They didn't know what happened between her and Rohn that summer. What she'd done behind Rohn's back. If they did know, Bonnie had to think they wouldn't be so eager to have her stick around.

Rohn might be happy now, but if she told him the truth that smile his hired hands talked about would disappear and she was afraid she'd never be able to earn it back.

"Okay. I'll think about it." It was easier to appease them and move on from this uncomfortable topic.

But as she said it, she started to actually do it—

think about what it might be like if she stayed. And
think about the fact that if Tyler was right, Rohn
might have a date with another woman. Jealousy—
an emotion she had no right to feel when it came to
Rohn—reared its ugly head. He'd been hers once,
long ago, and she'd left. Just as she'd left him last
night.

In light of that, how in the world could she be
upset now if he chose to date? It was illogical. Unfortunately, love rarely was.

Summer, 1990

The test read positive. She was pregnant. The tiny
pink plus sign in the readout told Bonnie that, without a shadow of a doubt. What it didn't tell her was
what she was going to do about it.

She had to tell Rohn. But then what? What would
they do? She had a scholarship to ASU. And Rohn
had plans to play football at NEO.

He'd give up college to marry her. She knew that.
But then what future would he have? What future
would she have? Would they end up exactly like her
parents? Struggling to survive farming because neither had gotten an education beyond high school.

Pressing one hand to her still-flat belly through
the thin fabric of her nightshirt, Bonnie knew she
was in too much shock to decide anything tonight.
What she did have to do was hide this test and the
box it came in where no one would ever find it, and
protect this secret for as long as she could.

She heard the television. Her parents were still

occupied watching it, so Bonnie took that moment to slip out the back door and into the darkness. With the test and box wrapped up tightly in the plastic bag, she opened the lid of the trash can and shoved it down beneath a bag of trash where no one would ever look.

As she spun back to the house, she found her father standing in the kitchen doorway.

Her heart stopped when he asked, "What are you doing?"

"Throwing something away."

"Outside, in the dark, in your nightgown?" He strode outside and pushed her to the side, flinging the trash can lid open. He pulled out first one bag, then another.

"Daddy, it's nothing." The sound of the blood rushing through her ears was deafening.

He spied the bag from the pharmacy, tied tight. "We'll see if it's nothing." He tore into the bag just as her mother came to the doorway.

"What's going on?" she asked.

"This is what's going on." Her father held up the pregnancy test.

Her mother's eyes widened. "Bonnie. Go to your room."

She ran to the house, happy to get away from the anger she saw in her father's face.

Bonnie had barely gotten to the room when she heard heavy footsteps in the hallway. Her father came through the door, slamming it against the wall. Her mother rushed into the room after him. "Let's talk about this calmly."

"Nothing to talk about." He grabbed Bonnie's shoulder and shoved her facedown onto the bed.

He grabbed her nightshirt hard enough she heard it tear as he pulled it up to her head. While she struggled, facedown on that mattress, he yanked down her underwear.

She felt his knee in her back as he unbuckled his belt, all while her mother begged him to stop.

The first strike of his belt against her skin had her crying out.

His spit flew as he yelled horrible accusations, Saying she was a dumb bitch for letting any boy touch her. For letting herself get pregnant. Saying he'd kill the boy who'd done it.

The leather edge of his belt cut into her raw bare flesh with every insult, stroke after stroke. Worse than the beating was the fear. An emotion no child should have to feel for her father. She was helpless and he was out of control.

Bonnie was gasping for breath and sobbing when he finally stopped. She didn't know if it was because his arm had gotten tired or he'd finally listened to her mother's sobbed pleas for him to stop.

She heard his footsteps down the hall and then the front door slam. The truck engine fired up in the driveway and tires peeled out into the street.

For a second, Bonnie feared he somehow knew it was Rohn she'd been with and she was terrified he was on his way there. If he'd beat his own daughter, what would he do to Rohn?

Her father was a hunter. There were guns all over the house.

Panic and pain warred within her and she flipped over and tried to cover her nakedness. She found her mother, pale and shaking in the doorway.

"Pack a bag, baby."

"What?" Bonnie wiped her tears.

"I'm taking you to the bus station. I'll call Grandma. She'll meet you in Phoenix."

If her mother, always the calming force in the house, felt Bonnie had to get out of the house tonight, then she must be as frightened of her husband as Bonnie was.

"Are you coming with me?" In a daze, Bonnie moved to the closet.

"Not tonight."

She stared at her mother, in shock. "Why not? He's crazy. He could hurt you, too."

"He won't. I'll be fine."

After what she'd seen tonight, Bonnie wasn't so sure.

Chapter Sixteen

Summer, 2015 (Present Day)

Rohn drew in a deep breath, braced himself, and walked up to the only single woman sitting at a booth in the diner. "Margaret?"

"Yes."

"I'm Rohn. It's nice to meet you."

"Oh my God, Rohn, it's so very nice to meet you, too!" Margaret spoke like she wrote. It felt as if every sentence was heavily laden with the emphasis of a half dozen exclamation points.

He wasn't sure he could rally that much enthusiasm about anything at ten a.m. on a hot summer morning when work waited for him back at the ranch.

Dating was too much work. But it wasn't as if he'd be getting a whole lot of paperwork done if he was home. It was too distracting knowing that the boys were over at Bonnie's and he wasn't. That knowledge would be in the back of his mind, no matter what he was doing, just as it was now.

He forced his attention back to Margaret. She was pretty, in an odd kind of way. She looked like she'd spent too much time in the sun and had paid the price. Her skin had that deep, dark, leathery look to it.

Not that he could talk about skin or sun damage. He'd done the same thing to himself by running around outside twelve or more hours a day back before sunscreen was popular.

But he'd had his cowboy hat or a baseball hat on most times so he'd had some protection. And sad but true, he was a man and could get away with a bit more in the aging gracefully department than women could.

Forcing himself to look on the bright side, he figured if she was this tanned, she must spend an awful lot of time outdoors. Something they had in common, and perfect for first-date conversation.

"Please, sit!" She gestured to the side of the booth opposite her with more enthusiasm than the torn, vinyl bench warranted.

"Yeah, thanks." Rohn slid into the seat as the waitress came over. "Can I getcha something?"

It was too early for a drink, even though his nerves sure could use one. "Coffee, please."

"Herbal tea for me, please." Margaret turned to him as the waitress went off to get their order. "I can't have coffee. Too much caffeine."

If the woman had this much energy without caffeine in her system, he could only imagine her after a cup of coffee. He kept that observation to himself and decided to launch into his prepared small talk. "So, your profile said you like horses?"

"Oh my God, I love them. I'm a trainer, actually."

"Really? That's interesting." And explained why she looked like she spent a lot of time outside. It also meant they had something concrete in common.

"I buy horses at auction where they might be sold for meat, then I train them. I get them saddle ready and sell them to folks who want a good horse but can't afford a registered pedigree."

"That's really admirable. We saddle break a few horses a year at my place. A good trainer is hard to find. Using your skills to help save the animals is a wonderful thing to do."

"Thanks. It is satisfying." Margaret smiled. She braced her forearms on the table, leaning slightly forward. "So is that what you do for a living? Train horses?"

Based on her body language, she was into him. Feeling more confident, Rohn answered, "Not for my main business, no. I raise cattle."

"Oh." She hesitated a second. "Dairy cows for milk?"

"Uh, no." He started to have a bad feeling about where this conversation was going.

"Then what do you do with the cattle?"

"I sell them."

She leaned back. "I hope not for beef."

Her body language alone was a warning sign. That, accompanied by the tone of her voice, let him know he was in trouble. "Um, yeah. Some."

"Oh." She pulled her hands, which had been clasped on the table between them, into her lap. "I'm a vegetarian."

"Oh. Well, that's fine. I, uh, like vegetables." He liked them on the side of his plate right next to his beef, but . . . "Only some of my stock gets sold for beef, not all. Some I keep for breeding. And I also raise and train rough stock. Bucking broncs. Bulls."

He'd hoped that information would make her feel a little better. Though when her brows drew low in a frown, he had his doubts.

"You mean like for rodeos?"

Rohn had a feeling things were about to go from bad to worse. "Yes."

"Do you know how cruelly those animals are treated at rodeos? Have you ever been to a rodeo and seen for yourself?"

There was nothing that got Rohn more riled up than this particular debate. "Yes, I have been to many rodeos. Have you?"

"Yes, but I stayed outside the gates in protest."

That wouldn't prove anything to her either way. There wasn't a whole lot she could see from outside the gates, except traffic.

She continued, "It's barbaric how they tie a rope around the animal's private parts to make them buck harder."

He couldn't believe anyone still believed that bullshit. Now that the bigger bull riding events and rodeos were commonly broadcast on television, anyone could clearly see the flank strap was nowhere near being tied to the animal's *privates* as she'd called them.

"Well, I have been to many events *inside* the arena, both as a stock contractor supplying the bucking stock and as a competitor. I've personally flanked my bulls and I can tell you with certainty what you're saying is not true. More than that, I have never seen an animal being mistreated nor have I ever mistreated my own animals."

"Well, maybe you haven't but—"

"No *maybe* about it. First off, if the animal were in pain every time he bucked he wouldn't do it. He'd stand still and not move an inch. He sure as hell wouldn't buck six feet in the air. And besides the fact that's not the kind of man I am, why in God's name would I hurt or allow to be physically damaged an animal that can be worth hundreds of thousands of dollars? Not only while he's on the circuit competing, but afterward as breeding stock?"

"So rodeos exist simply to make men rich? It's all about the money?" Her eyes narrowed with that accusation.

"No, not at all. Most folks in the business barely make a living."

"Then why should the sport, if you can even call it a sport, continue?"

"How about tradition and heritage? How about that it's a wholesome, affordable event that families can attend together? How about it would put a whole lot of folks out of work if the sport, and it is a sport, was to be banned by those ignorant enough to believe it hurts the animals?"

When her brows shot up at his use of the word *ignorant*, Rohn drew in a breath to steady himself. "My apologies, Margaret. I think maybe it's best if we change the subject."

What would be best would be leaving right now and getting out of this date that had gone to hell, but that would be rude. Though he figured he had already crossed that line a few minutes ago.

"I agree." Margaret sniffed in a breath and looked around. She glanced at the specials board behind the counter, at the desserts in the case, at the cars in the parking lot outside the window. She looked anywhere and everywhere except at him.

As the uncomfortable silence stretched between them, Rohn glanced over his shoulder for the waitress, hoping she'd be fast at her job and bring their order, and the check. He was more than ready to get out of there.

An hour later, and not nearly soon enough, Rohn was back home. Thank goodness. The date had been a dismal failure and he'd hated every last second of it.

It served him right. How could anyone know if a person would be compatible with him from a damn profile on a computer? Rohn couldn't, obviously.

A picture and some answers to a few canned questions told nothing. He'd learned that lesson the hard way. Painfully and slowly over stilted conversation on his strained first—and last—Matchmaker date.

With a sigh, he sat at his desk in front of his computer—the cause of all his woes. If he was a man who had less control over his temper, that damn machine would be in a Dumpster by now. As it was, he wasn't feeling too generous toward it.

Gritting his teeth, he opened a browser window and typed in the URL for his Matchmaker account. The old messages loaded along with about a dozen new ones.

Rohn shook his head at the downfall of the human race. How could so many people be willing to put their future happiness in the hands of a bunch of statistics manipulated by some computer geek's program?

Nope. Not him. Not any longer.

"Good-bye, good-bye, good-bye." He said it aloud

with every click of the mouse on the delete button. It was strangely satisfying.

When the messages were all gone, a new one flew into his box from yet another woman. Rohn laughed out loud. The situation was too ridiculous for him to do anything else.

"And, good-bye to you too." With one more click, his box was clear again.

Quickly, before any more messages came in, Rohn searched the information on the screen and found the area for Account Settings. There, he found and hit the button to delete the account.

"Good-bye and good riddance."

They were sorry to see him go, or at least that's what the message read that flashed across the screen. Was he sure? it asked.

Yes, for the first time in a long time Rohn was one hundred percent sure.

He closed the window for the last time, never to return again, and that was that.

Now what?

Glancing at the time, he saw it was midday. That's what he got for setting a date for ten in the morning. Half of the damn day was gone. He'd been too nervous to get anything done that morning, and now, after the morning he'd had, he wasn't exactly motivated to do paperwork.

He wondered how the boys were doing. It was about time they'd be breaking for lunch. He could go over to Bonnie's and check on them.

There was one problem with that plan. Bonnie would be there.

Rohn sighed. He couldn't dodge thinking about last night any longer. He needed to decide what to

do about that particular sticky situation—the fact
that he'd kissed her and she'd kissed him back, and
then told him it could never be. That's what didn't
ring true.

She wanted him as much as he wanted her. He'd
felt it. Only she had pulled away.

Why?

That was the question of the day and he wanted
answers, but there wasn't much chance of him getting one that satisfied him.

Dammit. It didn't make sense. None of her excuses made any damn sense. He wouldn't be satisfied
with anything less than her agreeing to give the two
of them a chance at a relationship.

Okay, maybe he'd be happy with something else,
too. If she'd fall into bed with him, he could work
from there. He could remind her how good they'd
been together, and show her how, all these years
later, they could be even better.

If he could break down her walls, he knew she'd
agree with him that they should try again. Not to
recapture what they'd had then, but to build something new as mature adults who'd lived life and knew
what they wanted.

Sitting there doing squat wouldn't accomplish a
thing, least of all get him Bonnie back.

After pulling out his cell phone, Rohn hit the
button in his contacts for Tyler's phone.

Two rings later, the kid answered. "Hey, boss.
What's going on with you?"

Tyler, as usual, could imbue even a casual question with cocky attitude. Rohn wasn't quite sure how
he did it, nor if he was in the mood for it today.

"Nothing's going on with me. How's it going over at Bonnie's?"

"It went good. We left about half an hour ago."

"What the hell do you mean, you left? Why aren't you still there?"

"Because it's lunchtime. We're at the barbecue place."

"Did she say you could go?"

"Yes, in fact she insisted. She said we'd done all we could do for now and should go."

"That's impossible." There was no way that house was cleaned out already. He'd seen himself the sheer amount of stuff in it.

"Swear to God, Rohn. Call and ask her if you don't believe me."

"But that house was still packed full of shit yesterday—"

"Yeah, and we made another load to the dump and the recycling center, then we made three loads to the church. One whole truckload was just her father's clothes. And just so you don't think we're slacking, Colt even bagged up the old man's clothes for her. She seemed like she wasn't wanting to do it herself."

Rohn felt bad he hadn't been there to support her today. He remembered well how tough it had been on him when he'd finally packed up Lila's clothes. "She's probably still emotional. Her father just died last week."

"Yup, that's what we figured. But after that, she said she had to go through the rest of the stuff and decide what to do with it. She said that could take a few days, so we should go back to working at your place."

"So you went to lunch." Rohn scowled.

"Since it's lunchtime, yeah, we did." Tyler's statement was heavily weighted with attitude. "But I also told her to give us a call and we'll be over as soon as she says the word to get rid of anything else. Gave her my cell number and everything. That good enough for you, boss?"

"Yeah." Rohn felt bad for being so hard on Tyler. "So when you coming back here to work?"

"Jeez, we just got our order. Give us half an hour to eat and drive back."

"A'ight. That's fine." He was in too strange a mood to deal with the yahoos right this minute, anyway.

"Want us to bring you something?"

He thought about it for barely a second. "No. Thanks, anyway." He'd lost his appetite at the diner on the date from hell before the food he'd ordered had even arrived. Even so, he'd forced himself to down it fast so he could get the hell out of there.

"No? What do you mean no?" Tyler sounded shocked. Probably because Rohn had never said no to barbecue before.

"I mean, I already ate."

"Ohhh, okay." Tyler stretched the word out to sound much more suggestive than it should.

Rohn frowned. "What's that supposed to mean?"

"That I forgot you'd probably eat on your date."

How the hell did Tyler know he'd been on a date? "What makes you think I was on a date?"

"Your shirt."

"My shirt?" Confused, Rohn glanced down.

"Yup. That's your good shirt. You must really like

whoever she is if you wore your good shirt, because you refused to wear it the other night to Janie's when I asked you to."

Rohn bit back a cuss, inspired to throw out the damn shirt that Tyler seemed so obsessed over. "First of all, the other night at Janie's wasn't supposed to be a date. It was supposed to be one neighbor having another over for dinner, but you made it a date. Second, stay out of my personal life and my wardrobe."

"I'm just making an observation, is all."

"Well, keep your observations to yourself." Rohn stood, unable to sit while so agitated.

"So, it's a no on the barbecue then?"

"Yes, it's a no."

Though he didn't have anything planned for dinner and he really did love that damn food. Nope, he'd run out and get it himself if he decided he wanted some.

Refusing to give in to Tyler, he said again, "Definitely not."

"A'ight. We'll be back there in a little while."

"Fine. See you then."

He disconnected the call, more miserable than he had been before.

Damn. Tyler knew he'd been on a date. He kept forgetting these guys acted like they couldn't see anything past the end of their own noses, and yet time after time they kept hitting the nail right on the head when it came to Rohn's private life.

Apparently, he was completely transparent. Dammit. He needed to work on that.

Rohn walked through the kitchen and out the back door all the way to the bull pasture. Why? Because that was where he'd kissed Bonnie.

He was like a damned teenage boy. He'd done the
same thing that summer. Sat for hours in his truck
staring at the river where they used to park. It didn't
make him feel any better. In fact, it made the hurt
worse, yet he did it anyway. Often.

Eventually, he'd stopped going, but it took a good
long while. He didn't go there, but he didn't forget
the pain, either. Not until he'd met Lila. She'd healed
him. Loved him. Made him realize there was life after
teenage heartbreak.

And here he was, doing it again, but now he was
old enough that he should know better.

He was more confused than hurt. And he was frustrated. The stubborn woman wouldn't even give them
a chance.

She was holding back for some reason. He could
take a guess why. She probably had some misplaced
noble idea like not wanting to hurt him again when
she left for Arizona.

He was a grown man. He could make his own decisions about what he could handle. She needed to
realize that. He had to prove it to her and soon.

This was his one shot, because if she sold her house
and went back to Arizona, he had no doubt that this
time he'd never see her again.

This second chance with her was a gift and he
wasn't going to squander it.

The sun was high in the sky as he stood beneath its
rays, a reminder that there was a full day's worth of
work to be done, and only half a day to do it. He'd
work with the boys today to get things completed.
That would give Bonnie the space she needed to
get her work accomplished at her own place. But
tonight . . . that was another story.

Tonight, he was heading over to her house and they were going to hash this thing out. He didn't care if it took all night. He wasn't leaving until he made her see the light or she gave him a damn good reason why she was willing to throw away a second chance at happiness.

With renewed energy, he turned toward the house. He needed to go inside and change his damn shirt before Tyler got back.

Chapter Seventeen

The house seemed too empty and quiet after the whirlwind that was Rohn's crew left for the day. It had felt like that yesterday as well when they'd all left.

Too quiet. Too empty. Too lonely.

Bonnie shouldn't complain. The neighbors had stopped by to check on her and see if she needed anything. Colleen had invited her to dinner again, and she'd said no, so if she was lonely, it was her own fault.

She drew in a breath and looked at the stacks surrounding her. All piles of stuff waiting to be taken away.

Her old life, and her father's entire life, fit into three piles. Garbage. Donations. Things to keep. The *keep* pile was the smallest. It amounted to things she thought her mother might want, like their grandmother's Hummel collection, which had been left behind years ago during the divorce. There were also some papers that looked too important to throw away. Bank statements. Income taxes. And of course, the sentimental things she kept finding. Pictures. Her mother's wedding rings. Her own baby spoon.

She would have assumed it was just an oversight on her father's part that all those keepsakes still remained, but she found them in places that made her think he'd kept them nearby so he could look at them. Like in the kitchen drawer. And more in his bedside table. Still more in the top drawer of his dresser right along with his wallet, spare change, and wristwatch.

Every discovery raised more doubt in her mind and made her wonder if she knew the man who was her father at all.

Exhausted, she sat down heavily on the sofa, the only furniture left in the living room. She'd told the guys to take it away with the rest of the stuff but the three had stood their ground and refused, saying she'd have nowhere to sleep if they took it since she'd insisted they haul away both bedroom sets.

She'd finally given in. It hadn't been worth the fight, and the boys were right, anyway. She did need someplace to sit, and lie down.

The only other things she'd kept were the kitchen table and chairs, and the dining room set, and that only because she knew her mother had loved that damn furniture. She had worked a job one summer to save up to buy it.

Bonnie couldn't make the decision to get rid of it without her mother, even if she could still envision her father sitting at the head of that table, his scowl firmly in place if dinner wasn't ready on time. Or if Bonnie had gotten what he considered to be a bad report card. Or if wheat prices were down. Or if the weatherman reported a drought.

There had been no predicting what would put the man into a bad mood that they'd all have to suffer through.

Bonnie's cell phone rang in her pocket and she wrestled it out. It was her mother, whom she'd neglected to call today with all the upheaval happening.

"Hey, Mom."

"Hey, baby. How's it going?"

"Actually, I'm starting to see a light at the end of the tunnel. We have to talk about what you want to do with some of this stuff. Like the dining room set."

"That's a tough call. It costs so much to ship furniture but it is a good set." Her mother sighed. "Let me think about it."

"Okay." Bonnie's gaze hit upon the pile of things to keep. "I'm finding other stuff, too. Um, Dad kept a lot of things. Personal reminders of you and me. Things from when I was a baby."

"You're surprised by that?"

Bonnie let out a snort. "Yes."

"Why? He loved you. I always told you that."

Maybe that was the problem. It had been her mother telling Bonnie he loved her, rather than her father acting as if he did. "A man who loved his daughter wouldn't have done what he did to me."

There was silence for a moment. "Your father was a hard man, Bonnie. I'll admit that. It was how he was raised. But there were other things in play, too."

"What other things?"

"Mood swings. Outbursts. Depression. High highs, and low lows. He should have been on medication, but you know how he was. No doctors. No pills. If he hadn't been nearly crippled by the pain, he never would have gone in for his back."

It was something that a child wouldn't have picked up on, but now that her mother pointed it out to her, Bonnie realized she was probably right.

Stubborn man. A pill a day and her whole life might have been completely different. All of their lives would have been. Rohn's, too.

The sound of someone pulling up to the house had Bonnie glancing toward the front windows. Her heart began to pound when she recognized the truck.

Rohn was there and her body reacted accordingly, just as it always had and probably always would.

"Mom, can I call you back?"

"Sure. Bonnie?"

"Mm?"

"You okay there?"

"Yeah. I am. I'll talk to you later. Bye."

It felt as if a weight had been lifted off her shoulders as the hatred she'd held for her father all these years gave way to understanding. All those years growing up when she'd felt his moods and outbursts were her fault, she hadn't been to blame at all.

Her parents' marriage, which she'd assumed had been loveless, hadn't been at all. It had been troubled, no doubt, but she believed now her father had loved her mother, and probably her, too.

It was all too much to absorb, especially now as Rohn parked his big truck in her driveway.

Glancing down at herself, she sighed when she saw the dirt on her shorts, and the grime on her T-shirt. She could only imagine what her face and hair looked like, but it was too late to do anything about that now.

She went to open the front door and waited for

Rohn to swing the driver's-side door open. He smiled when he saw her standing in the doorway.

Her own smile mirrored his as he walked up the path. "Hey."

"Hey. I heard you sent my boys home early." He strode forward and reached her in a few long steps. "That true?"

"Yes. I needed to take time to go through some things. No use their hanging around here waiting for me when I'm sure there is work to be done at your place." She moved back from the door. "Come on in."

He did and glanced around the living room. "Wow. It's almost empty."

"Getting there. There's still a bit more to do. Then I guess I'll have the real estate agent come in. Once I'm not too embarrassed to have them see the place."

He turned to her, but he didn't seem to be listening to her talk of real estate and houses. Just as she wasn't really thinking about all that, either. She was remembering last night, and the kiss she'd walked away from, and this morning, and the talk of his date with another woman.

Rohn watched her, his eyes narrowed. The intensity of his gaze was unnerving. Even more so when he turned and shut the front door, cutting off a good amount of the last of the day's sunlight and bathing the room in shadows.

"Bonnie."

She swallowed hard. "Yeah?"

"I tried staying away from you. I really did. I couldn't. I'm going to talk and I'd like it if you'd listen."

Heart pounding, she nodded. "Okay."

Rohn grabbed both of her hands in his and took a step closer. He towered over her and she had to look way up to see his face. "I know you're going back to Arizona, and I don't care. I still want to give us another shot."

When Bonnie opened her mouth to protest, he shook his head. "Don't. There is absolutely nothing you can say that will convince me otherwise."

There was. He just didn't know it.

Rohn continued, unaware of the secret standing between them. "One night, Bonnie. Give me one night with no excuses. No pulling away. No walls up between us. If it's not everything we both think it will be, I'll back off."

Her body clenched at just the thought of giving in to temptation and taking that one night.

"Okay."

His eyes widened. "Just so we're clear, what are you saying okay to?"

"One night. Anything you want."

"Anything I want?" His nostrils flared as he drew in a deep breath that swelled his chest beneath his T-shirt. "Be careful what you offer a desperate man, Bonnie Blue. What I want might not be what you want."

"I think it is." Her voice came out sounding so husky, she barely recognized it as hers.

"You sure?" He squeezed both of her hands in his.

The feel of his big, rough hands holding her made her feel safe and warm inside, just like it always had. "Yes."

Rohn drew in a shaky breath. That was the last sound she heard before his lips crashed against hers. He dropped her hands and moved to cradle the back of her head with one large palm while he moved the other hand around her, keeping her pressed close to him.

The man could kiss. She'd thought his kisses were irresistible all those years ago when she'd been young and naïve. Now, as an adult, she knew she'd never be able to resist him or his kiss.

The kiss stole her breath and set her heart fluttering.

It had liquid heat pooling low in her belly as she seemed to throb with need. There was no way she was stopping him this time.

Maybe it was that for the first time in what felt like forever forgiving her father meant there was no more fear or hate filling her. Maybe it was that she knew Tyler was actively setting Rohn up on dates. Maybe it was that he might have actually gone on one this morning.

That brought up something she needed to deal with before the kissing moved to something more. She pulled back. "What about your girlfriend?"

He drew his brows low. "I don't have a girlfriend."

"Tyler said—"

"Fu—" His nostrils widened again but she could tell it wasn't desire. This was anger. His eyes flashed. "I am not with anyone else, Bonnie. I swear to you. Tyler invited me to dinner and sprang a woman on me. I had nothing to do with it. I was polite and got out of there as soon as I could. I told him never to do that to me again."

"What about this morning? He said you had on your date shirt."

He pressed his lips together until they formed a tight line. "I swear I'm gonna throw that damn shirt in the garbage. This morning was a mistake. After you told me we couldn't be anything more to each other than friends last night, I thought I should try to at least give dating a shot. See if I might have some chance in hell of being able to forget you when you're gone."

She swallowed hard, almost afraid to ask. "And? How did it go?"

"It was an unmitigated disaster. I've accepted it's gotta be you for me, or nobody at all. And if I can't have you forever, then I'll take you for as long as I can have you." Rohn ran one fingertip between her brows. "What are you frowning about, Bonnie Blue?"

"Your date."

A smile lit his face, even as the heat she'd thought was lost returned to his gaze. "You jealous?"

"Maybe, just a little."

He ran a hand down her cheek and then cupped her face. "There's no one but you, Bonnie. Not when I was eighteen. Not now."

He kissed her again, his lips possessing hers and leaving no question in her mind that he was a man on a mission, and he was going to take what he wanted. Take what she'd offered him.

No other women mattered. The future didn't matter. He was hers for tonight and for once she was going to let herself enjoy it without worrying about the past or the future.

Tomorrow was a world away. She'd live a lifetime with Rohn tonight. Enough pleasures could be hers to provide memories to last her the rest of her life.

He breached her lips with his tongue, taking her mouth, claiming it as his. As he backed her toward the sofa, there was no doubt in her mind that he'd claim all of her tonight.

Her knees hit the edge of the cushion and buckled.

Then Rohn's weight was on top of her, pressing her into the old lumpy cushions, making her feel what it was like to have a hard, heavy man above her for the first time in more years than she cared to admit.

"Bonnie, I need you." He breathed the words against her ear before he latched his teeth into her neck, nipping at the tender flesh. "I need you so badly." He said it one more time before his mouth covered hers again.

She needed him, too. Needed this. This reckless abandon that made the world go away.

He reached for where her shirt covered the waistband of her shorts and slipped his fingers beneath her clothes. She felt his hands against her bare skin. She wanted to be naked with this man. She should have listened to the boys and kept a mattress.

She pulled back from his kiss. "Can we go somewhere else?"

Rohn's excitement took years off his face. "Where? My house?"

The house filled with his dead wife's pictures and decor? That would be nearly as bad as where they were now.

"No." Bonnie shook her head, until an idea struck her. "Take me to the river."

A smile broke over his face. "A'ight."

Reaching down to grab her, Rohn hoisted her off the sofa.

Bonnie laughed at the speed with which he had her out the door and to his truck. After yanking the passenger door open, he planted two big hands around her waist and lifted her effortlessly into the passenger seat. Rohn literally jogged around the hood of the truck to the driver's-side door, flinging it wide with a force that had the hinges creaking.

"The river it is." He glanced at her with heat in his gaze as he turned the key in the ignition, and she imagined he was thinking the same thing she was. The river had been their place.

It was where they made love for the first time, and for the last time. And there was no doubt in either of their minds it was where they'd make love tonight.

They didn't talk on the short drive. Any conversation would have been ridiculous at a time like this. He did reach over and take her hand in his.

Squeezing her fingers, he held her hand captive in his the whole drive. He didn't let go of her until it was time to flip on the directional signal to turn into the dirt road that led to their place. The river.

Chapter Eighteen

How many times had they parked here together? She couldn't count. Not nearly often enough for her at the time.

There was no more time to think when he made a U-turn and backed up so the bed of the truck faced the water, just like he had all the times they'd been there before.

He cut the engine and glanced at her. "You sure about this?"

"Yes."

"I'm not asking about the sex. More about the place. We took plenty of chances when we were younger, but we're a little old to get caught with our pants down outside in the open like this."

"We never got caught before."

"Nope, we never did." He laughed. "Come on. I got a blanket behind my seat."

Her heart fluttered as if butterflies had taken up residence in her chest as he got down and reached behind his seat to pull out a blanket.

"Don't worry. These days I keep this here in case I break down and need to lie on the ground."

Bonnie laughed. "Don't worry, Rohn. I didn't think you kept it there for . . . you know. This reason."

"If we're gonna make a habit of this, I will make certain to keep a blanket in here from now on for exactly this." He shot that parting statement across the cab of the truck before slamming the door and running around to her side.

With the blanket beneath his arm, he opened her door and helped her climb out of the high truck. When she was standing on two feet, he leaned low and with a groan pressed one short, hard kiss to her lips before he pulled back and reached for her hand.

"Come on, Bonnie Blue." He tossed the rolled blanket into the open back, unlatched the tailgate, and let it down with a creak of hinges and a clang of metal. After a sly glance in her direction, he flipped open the blanket. It drifted with a puff of air and settled slowly into place, covering the bed liner. "Just like the old days."

"Not quite." She ran one hand over the black plastic installed inside the metal bed. "You've upgraded from the old days."

"We can talk about truck accessories and upgrades later. A'ight?" With one brow cocked up, Rohn took a step closer. He moved one thigh forward, wedging it between hers until they stood nestled together like the lovers they had been and would be again.

He leaned low, hovering close to her mouth but not closing the final distance. "I want you, want this, more than anything, Bonnie."

"Me too."

Raising his hand to her face, he held her chin

between his thumb and forefinger and pressed his lips to hers. It was a far more gentle kiss than she'd anticipated now that they were so close to getting what they both had denied themselves.

The kiss didn't remain gentle for long. Every panted breath that passed between them brought more need. He kissed her deeper, angling his head and thrusting his tongue between her lips.

Pressed as closely together as they were, there was no way for her to miss the bulge of Rohn's arousal between them. That physical reminder of how much he wanted her caused a twisting of desire low in her belly. She wanted him just as much, and she had for a long time. Women just hid it better.

The throbbing need inside Bonnie only increased as Rohn thoroughly made love to her with his mouth. The thought of him loving her entire body was more than she could stand. She didn't want to wait for satisfaction any longer.

She reached between them and felt for his belt buckle. It was pressed into her as well, but it was far less comfortable to be against than his erection. His breath hitched in his throat when he felt her working his belt.

The weight of the heavy metal buckle sent the leather belt swinging. After the challenge the buckle had presented, the button and zipper at the fly of his jeans were no problem. She conquered them easily and then was free to slide one hand between his stomach and the waistband of his underwear.

His belly heaved against her hand as he breathed, fast and heavy.

He was still kissing her, and she was blind. Unable

to see, only feel for her end goal. She reached it fast enough.

His stomach jerked when her hand made first contact with his rock-hard cock. She ran one finger along the tip and felt the bead of slick wetness gathered there. He drew in a stuttering breath through his nose, finally pulling back and breaking the kiss.

Rohn rested his forehead against hers and let out the breath. "You're killing me, Bonnie."

"Good." She felt great satisfaction at hearing that.

He let out a short laugh. "You won't think so when I shoot off like I'm a damn virgin again. Though I might as well be. It's been a long time since anyone but myself has touched that down there."

She liked that idea, too.

Kissing the corner of his mouth, she stroked up his length. He let out a long rumbling groan. "Bonnie, I'm serious. I'll come right here in my pants and embarrass myself if you keep that up."

"If I remember correctly, you were always up for a round two."

"Oh, believe me, I still am. Recovery just might take a little longer than it did when I was eighteen." A tremor ran through him when she stroked up his length one more time. "Though, maybe not. The way I feel right now, I might as well be a teenager."

She smiled, feeling as light and free as a teen herself. "Let's see if we can turn back time."

If only that were possible. All her problems would be solved. She pushed the waistband of his underwear down and leaned down low.

Rohn let out a cry when she slid his length between her lips, but he didn't fight her. He widened his stance and braced one hand on the tailgate as the other cupped the back of her head.

He swallowed so loudly she heard it from her position. "Finish this, Bonnie Blue, and I swear I'll more than make it up to you."

She believed him completely, and she couldn't wait to see what he had in mind to pay her back.

It wouldn't take long. He was shaking already, thrusting between her lips, loving her mouth the way she wanted him to make love to her body.

His motion sped up. So did hers as she worked him with hand and mouth. If she was only going to allow herself a little while with Rohn before she left again, she was going to enjoy it to the fullest.

She grasped him tighter and felt the first pulse of his release against the back of her throat as he shook with the climax.

Hearing her name on his lips as he came, tasting him on her tongue, feeling his hands tangled in her hair, she remembered it all—how deeply she had loved Rohn back then.

How easy it would be to fall right back into love. The kind of love that possessed a person completely and ruled all reason, making rational decisions impossible.

It was dangerous, but a love that deep also made the world seem brighter, even as it made the darkness seem even darker in its absence.

She didn't let him go. Even after he was spent she kept him in her mouth, holding him close with a hand around his waist.

Finally, he put his hands on her shoulders and pushed her back. "You okay?"

"Yes."

He reached down and with a hand on each side of her waist, lifted her onto the tailgate so she was sitting with her legs dangling.

It put her closer to his height as he stepped between her legs and reached out to palm her face. "You sure?"

"Yes. It just brought back memories. I wasn't expecting that."

"I know. For me, too." He wrapped his arms around her. "You want to stop?"

"Why? You done?"

He laughed. "No. I'm not done by a long shot."

"Then no, I don't want to stop. Not by a long shot." She was already losing her heart to him all over again. She might as well enjoy it completely.

When he pulled back he was wearing a sly smile. "Then we're going to have to get you out of those shorts."

"Not a problem."

"Lie back, my sweet Bonnie Blue. I want to see if you taste as sweet as I remember."

She did as he asked, watching the darkening evening sky. She felt him unbutton and then unzip her shorts. She tried not to tremble as he slid the shorts down her legs and all the way off before he went back and did the same with her underwear.

He ran his hand over the smooth skin between her thighs. She knew why. She hadn't looked this way twenty-five years ago. "I decided to get laser hair removal."

"I like it." He lowered his head and she felt his

breath, hot against her delicate folds as his thumbs parted her.

For some reason, she felt incredibly nervous. That made her tend to babble. She couldn't believe she was going to tell him this, but she did anyway.

As his tongue made first contact with her, she said, "I did it because I saw a gray hair down there and it made me feel old."

He burst into a laugh against her, vibrating her sensitive spot and making her smile and jump at the same time. Rohn lifted his head just enough to say, "You're not old, Bonnie. Neither am I. And I know what you're doing. You talk when you're nervous. Always have."

"I do not—"

"Hush up, darlin'. You can't concentrate on me making you feel good if you're chattering."

She had no choice in the matter when Rohn went back to his task. It felt as if she couldn't draw enough air into her lungs when he sucked her between his lips and pulled. The glorious feeling had her hips rising like they had a mind of their own. Her mouth opened on a gasp as her eyes closed. She pressed her head back and just felt.

It was amazing. Incredible. Mind-blowing. Freeing. All things she'd barely thought about, forget about actually felt, in far too long.

Rohn had learned a few tricks over the years. Bonnie's eighteen-year-old self had thought he'd been good before, but now every touch had her crying out as her pleasure threshold rose higher.

The man had picked up a few skills, but she tried not to think how he'd learned so much, or with whom he'd practiced. She was the one with him now.

She dragged herself out of her head and back to the present. To the feel of his big, rough hands where they gripped her thighs. To the heat of his tongue as he worked her toward unknown pleasures.

However he had learned his skills, the adult version of Rohn blew away all of Bonnie's teenage memories of their time together. That was saying something since she was pretty sure she'd romanticized the past beyond all reality. She tangled her fingers in his hair because she couldn't stand to not be touching him, even in this position.

Every muscle tightened as her body ramped up for the long-awaited release. She searched for something else to grab as the climax broke over her. She clutched at the blanket but that didn't last and she ended up holding Rohn's head again. She didn't know whether to tug him closer or push him away— the intensity was nearly frightening.

Her hips bucked against him even as she pressed him closer. Like a cowboy on a bronc, he rode out her climax right along with her, managing to stay with her for the entire crazy ride.

She peaked but then went right on soaring higher, directly into another level of pleasure she hadn't known existed until she felt as if she would lose all power over her body.

Rational thought battled for control as her brain told her it was too much, even as her desire told her to let go and see how far he could take her.

Her cries filled the night air. Thank God they were far from any dwellings. No one could hear her. Only Rohn, and she was sure he was working too hard to be worrying about how loud she got.

Finally, the sensations were too much. The need

for control that ruled her life everyday won out over
the reckless abandon her body sought with him. She
shoved him away and lay panting flat on her back.

Senses began to return. She felt the blanket beneath her, scratchy against her skin. Felt the combined
heat of the summer air and Rohn's body pressing
around her.

"Bonnie Blue."

At the sound of his voice, she opened her eyes and
found him watching her. The need was clear in his
eyes. As it was also clear in the hardened length she
felt pressing against her leg.

She reached down and pulled him up. He came
willingly, hovering above her. She pressed a kiss to his
lips before saying, "Love me."

His expression of mingled relief and anticipation
told her that was the answer he was hoping to hear
to his unspoken question. The same one she'd given
him all those years ago when he'd looked at her with
similar desperation. Different truck. Same river. Same
two people, though were they really?

A quarter of a century had passed. They were
different people, yet the same. And she wanted him
as much as she ever had.

He rolled to the side and struggled in his pocket,
his hand emerging with a condom.

Rohn had come to her with at least one condom
in his jeans pocket. That fact intrigued her. Her surprise must have shown on her face.

He smiled. "Yes, I'll admit it. I bought a box yesterday before you came to dinner, just in case. Wishful
thinking on my part, I guess."

"I'm glad you did." They'd been risky in the past.

That she was older now didn't change the fact that they still needed to be cautious.

He sheathed himself and was over her again, staring into her eyes. They were both still half dressed, which was probably a good thing given where they were. The shirts separating them made her hot, and blocked her from easily touching him the way she wanted to.

But he'd lowered his jeans and his briefs to around his ankles and that left her free to grab one part of him she'd always enjoyed. She ran her hands around and clutched at the smooth skin of his butt cheeks. The man was rough all over except for here. Well, here and one other part. The part that was currently enrobed in latex and nudging between her spread thighs.

Lifting her hips put him in exactly the position she wanted him to be. She pulled and he slid inside her.

She gasped at finally getting what she'd longed for as he filled her completely. He didn't seem in any hurry to move, but she didn't mind. It was too amazing being joined with him. She needed to wrap her mind around the fact that he was here, with her, in her, again.

Finally.

Rohn leaned low and pressed his lips to hers. He kissed her with a tender gentleness that had her heart opening further to this man even when she should be locking that rebellious organ down tight.

He intensified the kiss, taking her mouth with his tongue as he began to slowly rock his hips. That region was still so sensitive she felt every one of his strokes tenfold, no matter how slow or small.

"Rohn." She had nothing else to say. She just wanted to say his name to remind herself he was really here with her. That they were really doing this.

He answered her with a groan.

His breaths sped along with the stroke of his body into hers. He groaned on every downstroke. They abandoned trying to kiss. Breathing was hard enough as it was as they both gasped for air.

He opened his eyes and captured her gaze as he stroked into her. She could see his emotions so near the surface. As if there were unspoken words on the tip of his tongue. Then they were gone. He closed his eyes. His body bowed above her as the intensity of his lovemaking deepened.

She closed her eyes, but missed the connection and forced them open again. She wanted to see him as well as feel and hear him.

His strokes sped up. He reached beneath her and lifted her hips. The change of angle had her crying out with her head thrown back.

"You doing a'ight, Bonnie Blue?" His voice was husky and breathless against her ear yet she heard the smile in it. "Don't pass out on me, darlin'. I'm not nearly done yet."

Her eyes popped wide. "You're not?"

"Nuh-uh. Not even close." This time she saw the smile as well as heard it in his proclamation.

"That's because you're holding back." Bonnie had noticed the change in his stroke.

"Yup. I'm not crazy enough to want this to end yet. I might not be young anymore, but I've learned a little bit about control." He grinned. "And that blow job helped me let off a little steam."

"Maybe I should always give you a blow job before we have sex."

He lifted one brow. "If you think I won't agree to that, you're wrong. I'm totally onboard with your plan. Can you handle that?"

"Yes."

A plan for a repeat of this with him—she wanted nothing better. His steady rocking into her, the slide of his body against hers, had clearly made her incapable of thinking rationally.

"Good." Rohn gripped her hips tighter and began to love her in earnest. That ended the conversation.

The noises of the night went on around them. The peepers and crickets filled the air with the symphony of nature only interrupted by another sound—that of two people making love.

Bonnie realized Rohn had been very serious when he said his goal was to make this last. He worked until they were both breathless and sweaty, until her body clamped down around his, primed for another release.

When it broke over her, she cried out and grasped him tight. Needing an anchor, she braced herself with a grip on his forearms.

Her climax broke through his tightly held control. His strokes became short and fast until his groan seemed to bounce back from the dark edges of the night surrounding them.

He collapsed on top of her, a hot, heaving mass of hard-muscled, sweaty man.

The comfortable silence stretched between them as their breath began to even out.

Eventually, he lifted his head from where he'd lain against her chest. He stroked a finger down her cheek. "I missed this with you, my beautiful Bonnie Blue."

Rohn's endearment made her feel as boneless as their lovemaking had.

"Missed what? Sex?" She made the silly joke to take the seriousness down a notch.

"No." He narrowed his eyes at her. "This. Lying in the truck. Your head on my chest while we both stare up at the stars . . . and the sex, too."

She swatted at his chest. "See. I knew it."

"Do you blame me?" He rolled them both over so he was above her. "We're good together. Always were, even that first time when I was a virgin but pretending not to be."

She widened her eyes and lifted her head to try to see his face in the growing darkness. "You were a virgin our first time?"

"Yes." He avoided eye contact, finally bringing his gaze to meet hers.

"I didn't know."

He let out a short laugh. "That's because I didn't want you to know."

"Why not?"

He shrugged. "All the other guys had lost it years before. I guess I was embarrassed to be a late bloomer."

"You were not a late bloomer." She remembered his strong chin and cut, capable muscles. He'd looked more like a man than a boy from freshman year. Of course, that was back when she'd been slyly watching him, while he'd yet to notice her.

"I'm glad I waited for you, Bonnie Blue." Smiling, he drew her closer to him. "Then and now."

Laying her head on his chest, she heard his heart

beat in time with her own. She was falling for him again. Head over heels.

That was probably the worst thing that could happen. What she didn't know was what the hell she was going to do about it.

"So don't get me wrong, I am very happy to be here with you, but damn, it sure is hot." Rohn mopped the sweat from his brow and felt where he and Bonnie were adhered by their wet skin. "I'm sorry. I'm sweating all over you."

"It's okay."

"No, it's not." He cringed as he remembered that sometime during their lovemaking the sweat from his face had actually dripped on Bonnie.

Times like these were why man invented air-conditioning, and he was old enough and successful enough to have a damn good unit at his house. Yet here they were in the bed of his truck, drenched in sweat.

He lifted his head to glance down at her face. "Come back to my place and spend the night. I've got a nice big bed and an air-conditioning unit strong enough to cool off a stadium."

Bonnie wrinkled her nose. "I think I'd better go back to my house."

There was something wrong. Rohn could see it in her expression. Hear it in the hesitation in her words. "Why don't you want to be at my house?"

She shrugged.

"Bonnie . . . tell me."

She hesitated and finally said, "I can feel your late wife everywhere. It was strange being there just for dinner. I know there's no way I could sleep—or do anything else—in the bed you used to share with her."

He contemplated that. Maybe that was one of the reasons why he hadn't moved on even after five years. Not until Bonnie had come back into his life. He could feel Lila everywhere, too. He'd clung to that shadow of her presence after her death.

Now, he realized that comfort he'd depended on just to get through another day might be the very thing holding him back.

"Okay. I understand." He didn't want to let her go. He wanted to hold her all night long, but she had yet to invite him back to her place. Not that it would be comfortable, both of them on that old sofa, since apparently there wasn't even a mattress in the house anymore. Still, he'd do it to be with her.

To be with Bonnie, he'd do just about anything.

She got slowly, gradually heavier against him. Glancing down, he saw her eyes were closed. He could literally feel her fall into sleep. She obviously needed the rest even though she would never admit it and kept refusing his offer of a decent place to lay her head at night.

Where her head lay right now felt perfect to him.

They couldn't stay all night. Maybe if she had something on below the waist they could get away with remaining just like this until morning. The dew would settle on them, but it was warm enough they wouldn't get cold.

Crazy that he'd willingly sleep in the bed of a pickup when he had a perfectly good house to go home to, but he'd rather be uncomfortable with Bonnie than have all the comforts and luxuries in the world without her.

He'd wake her up eventually and drive her home, but the peace of sleep had settled over her features and he wasn't about to disturb her yet. Besides, who knew when or if they'd ever be in this position again?

Given that uncertainty, Rohn was in no rush to end this moment.

Chapter Nineteen

Bonnie had insisted he take her home instead of to his house, but that was fine with Rohn. As she'd slept, his mind had worked, forming a plan of action.

When he did finally get home, he went right to work. Yes, it had been much too late at night to start such a massive project, but he'd waited long enough already. He wouldn't delay longer.

He figured once he'd finished with his plan, he'd see about wooing Bonnie back into his life full-time. Back where she belonged—in Oklahoma and in his world. If that had to start with getting her into his bed in his house, then so be it. The rest would fall into place later.

The piles of household items around Rohn grew, expanding as if they were a living organism spreading out of control, invading all parts of the house and yard. But unlike a cancer, this growth was a good thing.

He'd finally given in and lain down to sleep at about two in the morning. He was awake again by sunrise, but that was enough rest. He was running on caffeine and adrenaline.

As the morning sun crept higher over the horizon, he took a moment to pause in his perpetual motion and evaluate all he'd done and what was left to do.

After dropping off Bonnie at her place, with the sweet taste of her good-night kiss still fresh on his lips, he'd gone home and headed directly into the living room.

The room had been like a shrine to Lila. In fact, the whole first floor was, except for his office, which had always been his domain, and the kitchen, which had slowly morphed into his personal space, changing to accommodate the way he liked to do things instead of how she'd always done them.

He looked around the stately but unused living room. In the past he'd thought he'd needed all of these things to remain the same in order to remember her. To honor her. To not lose the little details about their lives together to the ravages of time.

It had taken that one comment from Bonnie, that she didn't feel comfortable in his home because Lila was so present there, for Rohn to realize his error.

He would always remember Lila. She lived inside his heart and mind, not inside these dusty items. She was in every fiber of his being and that would never change.

Rohn knew Lila and the kind of woman she'd been, and because of that, he could guess what she'd want him to do now. She had the sweetest most giving soul of anyone he'd ever met. He wasn't honoring her by keeping things exactly the way she'd left them. She wouldn't want him to stop time, freeze everything at the moment of her death like a museum he was honor-bound to live in until the day he died.

She'd want him to live. To do that, he had to let go of the objects from their shared past and move forward.

That's what he'd done, starting last night. Of course, he kept the photos, but there was no need for them to cover every surface of the living room and dining room, not to mention his bedroom and office.

He took his favorite photo of Lila and gave it a place of honor on one of the bookshelves in the living room. The rest, he put in a box for now. He'd get to the store when he had a chance and buy one of those nice leather-bound photo albums. He'd put the photos, which had begun to show the effects of time, safely away. It would preserve them from the sun's rays, while still keeping them at hand so he could look at them whenever he wanted to.

There was furniture in the room he hadn't used in years. There were also items, if truth be told, that he'd never liked very much. He hadn't said anything to Lila because this was her domain—the house, the decor. But now, it was his.

Instead of having the room set up as a formal space with its stiff-backed sofa and fine wood coffee table, it would be a hell of a lot more comfortable—and useful—with casual furnishings.

He'd love to have the boys over to watch a football game on TV once in a while. Or have Bonnie snuggled up next to him on a nice big sofa as they watched a movie—or made out during one.

That idea was what led to the pile of small furnishings, whatever he could move alone, out on the lawn.

It was all decent stuff that could go to the church for someone else to use.

There were some really good items he decided he had to keep. One valuable antique desk that had been handed down from one of Lila's ancestors was completely impractical for the room he was creating so he'd moved that upstairs to the guest room.

It fit nicely in front of the window with the view out over the pastures. If he couldn't convince Bonnie to come and sleep in his bedroom, perhaps sprucing up the guest room would get her to change her mind about sleeping in there.

There was a set of wooden end tables that he knew had been handed down from Lila's grandmother. He didn't feel right just dumping them off at the church for strangers. It felt like they should remain in the family. He could store them in the attic to be handed down, to whom he didn't know.

It wasn't as if he had kids of his own to pass things on to. Tyler had walked into Janie's house, which was fully furnished, so he wouldn't need anything. Maybe Justin or Colton would get married and need some nice tables. These boys were the closest thing he had to sons, anyway.

Even the carpet had come up. He and Lila had bought it the year they'd gotten married, and it showed. The sun hadn't been kind to the fibers. It hadn't been kind to his face, either, so he shouldn't expect the rug to survive any better than his skin had.

He'd rolled that up, debating whether it should go to the dump or the church. By then it was well past midnight and he figured the decision could be made in the morning. Rohn would take a fresh look at the rug later and if it was in good enough condition that it wouldn't insult the pastor, he'd let him decide whether he could use it for the church tag sale or the furniture warehouse for the needy.

It was a good start but Rohn wasn't done yet. He considered ordering new furniture online. Mostly because, all hyped up, he hadn't wanted to wait for the stores to open in the morning. But common sense had prevailed and he realized he'd only have to wait longer for shipping, so he'd held off.

Now that the sun was up and the boys would be here any moment, he could get down to serious work again.

The world was finally waking up, and the businesses in town would open shortly. He'd send the boys to the church and the dump. Then he'd head to the off-price furniture store and see what they had in stock for immediate pickup. He didn't have the patience to order something. He wanted it now, today, so he could ask Bonnie over tonight and surprise her.

Rohn glanced at his watch and wondered where the boys were just before he heard Tyler's truck pulling into the driveway. About time, too. Tyler should be first to arrive. He was only driving from next door.

Now that Ty was here, Rohn could do the rest of what he needed.

Tyler ambled over from his parked truck and frowned. "What the hell?"

"I need your help."

"Obviously. What, did you have a fire or something?" Tyler glanced around at the piles on the lawn.

"Nope. Just redecorating. I need a second set of hands to help me with the big stuff. The sofa has to go first. We can put that right in the truck to go to the church."

"Is something going on I don't know about? Is the church paying top dollar for old stuff or something?"

"No, and I wouldn't take the money even if they were."

"I was joking. Jeez. I'm just saying, first Miss Bonnie and now you." Tyler's eyes widened. "Oh. Never mind. I get it."

Rohn stifled a groan. Thinking he was probably going to hate what came out of Tyler's mouth next, he still asked, "What do you get?"

"You're redecorating to impress Miss Bonnie." Tyler grinned, looking satisfied with himself.

"Yup. You guessed it." Rohn could live with that assumption. It was better than the complete truth. That he was purging the house of his dead wife's things so his new girlfriend would come over and sleep with him.

"Wow. You're going all out for her."

"I guess so." God, was he an asshole for doing this? Was it a betrayal?

He knew he was overtired and he hadn't eaten since early yesterday evening. It was easy to feel overly emotional.

This was the right thing to do. He knew it deep down. He'd always remember Lila, but he didn't have to sit on her sofa to do it.

"When the other guys get here, I'll need you to go up to my bedroom and take out the bed and mattress."

Tyler's brows rose. "You're wanting to impress her in your bedroom, too? Dang, what happened that I don't know about?"

Rohn cocked a brow. "Your ability to carry my twenty-year-old mattress doesn't depend on your knowing my personal shit, so enough with the questions."

"Yes, boss." A cocky smile tipped up Tyler's lips.

Rohn smothered a sigh. "Come on. Let's get that sofa out. Once that's in the truck, the little stuff can get put in around it."

"Yes, sir."

He ignored Tyler's attitude. He knew the kid only called him *sir* when he thought he was acting like an idiot, but at the moment Rohn didn't care. He had to get to the Megamart in town.

One of those big flat-screen televisions hanging above the fireplace would look really cool. It would modernize the room and be perfect for watching sports. Then he could grab something to eat and wait for the furniture store to open. Hopefully they had one of those wraparound sectional sofas. Nice and big in case he and Bonnie decided they didn't want to adjourn to the bedroom for some sport of their own.

Maybe he'd pick up a recliner to supplement the seating. That would be the way to kick back and watch a football game with the guys. A nice wide one so Bonnie could sit in his lap if he was feeling too far away from her.

He was getting way ahead of himself, but he couldn't help it. He hadn't felt this good in years. And it wasn't just because he'd had sex after a five-year dry spell, either. For the first time since Lila had died, Rohn was envisioning a bright and happy future instead of a lonely existence of just getting by.

He'd hopped out of bed before dawn after getting

barely any sleep for a good reason. He was ready to get on with his life.

The sound of crunching gravel as another truck turned into the drive had Rohn glancing past Tyler. "Good. Justin's here."

Tyler scowled. "Damn right it's good he's here. He can help with that sofa."

"It's not that heavy." Rohn shook his head. Tyler was built like a linebacker. He shouldn't worry about lifting half a sofa. "Now, the king-size mattress up in the bedroom, that we might want his help with."

"You didn't say it was king-size."

Rohn laughed when he saw Tyler's eyes pop wide at that information. Redecorating was turning out to be a lot of fun.

Chapter Twenty

Bonnie's house phone rang at ten in the morning. The only person who called the house was Rohn. She ran for the extension, having more energy than she should, given she'd spent the night tossing and turning on the uncomfortable sofa.

Grabbing it, she was out of breath from the sprint when she answered. "Hello?"

"Mmm. Good morning."

She laughed at Rohn's purred greeting. "You sound frisky this morning."

"You're the one who answered the phone breathless. Gives a man ideas, that does."

"I was at the other end of the house cleaning the linen closet. I'm not doing anything that should give you any ideas, believe me." She smiled, even as she chastised him for his vivid imagination.

"I can come over and distract you from your chores if you'd like."

"Like how I used to distract you from your chores?"

"Oh, God, I remember that. You, prancing around in those short-shorts. Damn, I drove around on that tractor for a whole damn summer with a hard-on, thanks to you."

Her cheeks heated. "I wasn't trying to do that. It was a hot summer."

"The hell you weren't. You knew exactly what you did to me."

"No. Well, at least not in the beginning."

She'd never thought that Rohn, Mr. Popular, star football player, would notice her, but he had.

"So what are you doing for the rest of the day, darlin'? Besides giving me ideas, I mean."

"Cleaning out. The usual. What else would I have to do?"

"I'm sorry you have so much work. Can I send the boys over?"

"No. Rohn, you have to stop doing that. They have work to do at your house. Besides, I have to sort through and decide what goes where first. They wouldn't be any help right now, anyway."

"Well, you tell me when you need them again and I'll send them round with the truck."

"Okay. Tyler gave me his cell number, too. In case I need something."

"Yeah, I know. You watch yourself around that young stud." His voice dropped to a low growl.

Bonnie giggled. "Rohn, don't be ridiculous. I'm twice his age."

"And I already told you that you're not."

Bonnie would have fought more, but she knew Rohn was only teasing her about Tyler.

After last night, Rohn should know he had no worries her head would be turned by some young cowboy. Not when an older cowboy had left her with plenty of memories . . . and more. She'd noticed the bite mark on her neck this morning in the mirror. She'd never had a hickey before, not even when they'd been dating. He'd been too afraid then that her father would see any marks on her.

Besides the bruise on her neck, her muscles ached from the hour spent in the truck bed, but it was a good kind of ache. It reminded her of their time together. A time she'd like to repeat.

The damage was already done. After being together, leaving him again would hurt like hell whether they were together once, twice, or a dozen times. As long as she'd done something stupid, she might as well enjoy doing it a few more times.

"What are you doing for the day?" she asked, hoping they'd get to see each other again later.

"*That* is a secret."

She lifted her brow. "A secret?"

"Yup. Wanna know what it is?"

"Yes. As a matter of fact, I do."

"Then be at my place tonight."

"Rohn, is this your way of tricking me into coming over to your house?"

"Bonnie Blue, I don't need to lie to get you here. I can just drive over, throw you in my passenger seat, and bring you here."

"You would not." She acted shocked but deep down that image excited her.

"Oh yeah? Try me. I'd be happy to prove it." Rohn's determination was clear in his tone. "So, my place. Around six, I guess."

"Okay. What should I bring?"

"Nothing. Just yourself. Clothing optional."

Her lips twitched with a smile. "Now, what challenge would that be?"

"Playing hard to get, are we?" he asked.

"Maybe." She loved the playful side of Rohn. It had always been there, even in high school, but now in adulthood his playfulness was extra sexy.

"That's fine. I enjoy a challenge. Now let me go. I've got a week's worth of work to accomplish and only eight hours to get it done before our date tonight."

"Our date? This is a date? I thought it was me coming over to see your big surprise."

"Oh, it is. But why not kill two birds with one stone?"

She couldn't argue. "Okay. See you tonight."

"Definitely." He disconnected the call, leaving her perplexed with the phone still in her hand.

The hours of the day couldn't pass fast enough for Bonnie's liking. She must have looked at the clock a hundred times. When she wasn't doing that, she was checking the house phone to make sure it was working and she hadn't missed any calls from Rohn. But he didn't call again.

He had said he'd be busy with whatever this big secret plan for his day was. She'd know soon, but six o'clock wasn't coming fast enough.

Concentration was futile. So was getting any work done around the house.

She managed to finish the linen closet, at least, so she now had more piles stacked in the living room.

It seemed her life was going to be dominated by piles for the near future.

There was a massive lump on the floor of worn sheets and towels destined for the trash if the local animal shelter didn't want to take them for bedding. Then she had a much neater folded pile of linens—tablecloths and bedspreads—that looked barely used and could be donated to the church.

Inside the linen closet was the bare minimum that she would need while she was there. Just some clean towels, and one set of bed linens she used on the sofa where she'd been sleeping.

She probably should have listened to Rohn's guys and kept one mattress here temporarily, but she couldn't bring herself to do it. Anyway, it was too late now to change her mind. They were already gone. She'd made her bed—or sofa—and now she had to lie in it.

Bonnie glanced at her cell phone and checked the time once more. It was still nearly three hours until she was supposed to be at Rohn's. She needed to shower and get herself ready.

That really didn't leave her enough time to dive into another big project. It did, however, leave her enough time to head to the salon in town and get her nails done.

It was crazy. This wasn't a real date, but she wanted to look pretty for it.

Maybe she had time to go shopping, too. She'd exhausted the limited choices in her suitcase.

Decision made, Bonnie showered quickly. She threw on clean shorts and a tank top that wouldn't embarrass her until she bought something new. She grabbed her purse from the kitchen counter, tossed her phone inside, and opened the door.

The salon might be able to do something with her hair, too. Once she bought something new to wear, and got her hair and nails done, it would be like a total makeover. She had better buy some nice lingerie, too.

As she got into the car, she realized she was acting crazy. Maybe it was about time she did. For too long she'd been acting as if someone had pushed the pause button on her life. She was done living like that.

In town she was impressed again with how much it had changed over the last twenty-five years. There was now a strip mall filled with shops. That was a good thing since she had a lot to do and not much time to do it.

Bonnie ran into the clothing store first. They were having a sale, so she didn't feel guilty picking up two new sundresses. They even had a pair of pretty summer sandals with a cork wedge heel that would match her new dresses. And, luckily for her, they had a small selection of underwear and bras. She picked up a matching set in pink and, feeling the need to be a little bit sexy, a black pair, too.

Feeling lighter than she had in a long time, she paid for her new purchases and headed directly for the salon.

She'd just cleared the door when she heard, "Bonnie Martin? Is that you?"

Bonnie turned to the woman sitting in a chair near the door. It took a moment for her to make the connection and recognize the woman, but when she did, her eyes widened. "Melody? Oh, my God. Hi."

"I can't believe it's you. When did you get back to

town?" Melody asked, standing and coming toward Bonnie.

"Just a few days ago." She accepted the warm hug Melody enveloped her within. "You look great."

Melody pulled back and frowned. "*Pfft.* I'm twenty pounds heavier and twenty-five years older. You're the one who looks great."

"Me?" Bonnie laughed. "I'm here because I'm falling apart. I haven't had a haircut in close to a year and I've been cleaning out the house and I'm afraid it's starting to show."

As proof Bonnie held up her hands, nails out.

"That's nothing. Nails and hair can be fixed easily enough." Melody dismissed her protest with a flick of one wrist. "So tell me. What are you doing now? Are you married? Do you have kids?"

"No." Bonnie shook her head and left it at that. "You?"

"Twenty years married and we've got an eighteen-year-old and a sixteen-year-old."

"Wow. That's amazing. Congratulations. Did you marry anyone I know?"

Melody smiled. "Remember the guy who volunteered in the audiovisual department?"

"Phil?" Bonnie remembered the skinny, geeky guy from the AV department who would come and set up the projector in the classroom.

"Yup. I married him."

"Wow." Bonnie couldn't help the surprise in her tone.

Melody laughed and took out her phone. "He matured late, but he turned out pretty good, I think."

Bonnie looked at a family picture and there was

Phil, smiling with his arm around Melody. She was right. He'd turned into a handsome man. "You two look so happy together."

"Thanks. There's something to be said for marrying a nerd. He's a computer programmer now. He designs networks—heck, I'm not even sure how to describe what he does, but he works from home and makes good money doing it so we are really happy. What do you do?"

"I'm a teacher."

Melody smiled wide. "You always said you wanted to be a teacher. Good for you. I'm glad you made your dreams come true."

"Thanks." Bonnie wasn't sure it was exactly a dream come true but she enjoyed her job.

It was Melody's life that had Bonnie feeling a little green with envy. The way she'd described it, the kids, the husband, all together all the time as one big happy family, it made Bonnie's life feel like an empty shell—it looked okay from the outside, but inside there was nothing.

"So where do you teach? Around here?" Melody asked.

"No. I'm in Phoenix with my mom."

Melody nodded. "Where you got that scholarship to college."

"Yup." Bonnie smiled. "You have a very good memory."

She shrugged. "We were friends. Of course, I'd remember."

They had been friends. Sometimes it was hard for Bonnie to remember that since she'd never invited anyone over after school. She'd always been afraid her father would do or say something horrible to embarrass her.

Bonnie had always felt like a loner, but all those lunch periods together she and Melody had talked and shared their dreams . . . all while Bonnie tried to get a glimpse at Rohn.

Melody smiled. "Remember how many days we sat in the cafeteria and stared at the football players?"

Bonnie let out a burst of a laugh. "I was just thinking the exact same thing. Whatever happened to your dream man, Brian?"

"He married some trophy wife, as I always figured he would. I haven't seen him since the twenty-year reunion." Melody's eyes widened. "You are coming to the twenty-five-year, right?"

"Maybe. If I'm still in town."

"You have to come. You missed the ten-year and the twenty-year." Melody got a devilish gleam in her eyes. "Besides, don't you want to see how Rohn turned out? He's single again, you know. Well, widowed, actually. Poor guy. It was pretty tragic. He wasn't at the twenty-year because that's right about the time his wife died. But that was five years ago. Maybe he's ready to start dating again."

Bonnie felt completely torn between keeping things between Rohn and herself secret, or spilling the truth. Melody didn't even know she'd been secretly dating Rohn that summer. She definitely didn't know how Bonnie had spent her evening last night.

"Um, actually, that's why I'm here hoping to get my hair and nails done. I'm seeing Rohn tonight." It felt good to confide that to someone, even as her cheeks heated with the confession.

Melody reacted about as Bonnie assumed she would. Her eyes popped open wide. "Oh my God. How did that happen?"

"Well, believe it or not, the day I arrived I stopped to grab something to eat and there he was."

"That's amazing."

Bonnie smiled. "Yeah. It is pretty amazing."

"It's fate. Serendipity. You two were meant to be together."

Bonnie rolled her eyes. "I don't know if I believe all that . . ."

"I do believe in it. Trust me. The universe put you two together here and now. Maybe you weren't ready to be together before, but now it's the right time."

It sounded crazy, all this universe stuff, but even so, it made Bonnie feel good inside. Maybe they hadn't been ready to be together twenty-five years ago but they were ready now.

If that were true, then she had a decision to make. If she was going to let herself be with Rohn, she'd have to come clean about the past.

If she did, she could lose him. But if she didn't, she'd lose a part of herself. Keeping a secret that huge from someone she was pretty sure she was falling back into love with wasn't healthy.

Neither was living a life alone, without love.

It was all too much to think about. Bonnie wanted to enjoy today.

"I think the receptionist is trying to get your attention." Melody interrupted Bonnie's internal debate.

She turned to see the smiling receptionist headed her way. Bonnie turned to Melody. "I guess I'd better get this appointment going. It was good talking to you."

"You too, but you're not getting away from me that easily. I want to hear more so call me and we'll get together." Melody grabbed a business card from the holder on the table by the front door and scribbled her number on the back. "I mean it."

Bonnie took the card. "Okay. I will."

This town was starting to feel like home again. She'd stopped by the church to drop off a few bags of clothes that morning, and found the same old pastor still there. And now she'd run into Melody, the one person she'd called friend.

Bonnie had come back feeling like a stranger, oddly out of place in the town she'd spent the first eighteen years of her life in. But every reconnection made her feel more and more like she was still a part of this community. Time and distance hadn't broken the ties, only stretched them a bit.

The receptionist stood nearby. "Is there something we can help you with today?"

Bonnie smiled. "I hope so."

Chapter Twenty-One

Rohn looked around him. It was an amazing transformation. The sectional sofa in dark brown suede would be the perfect place to sit back and snuggle with Bonnie in front of the big flat-screen television that Tyler was currently hooking up to the cable.

An old wooden trunk that had been in the barn collecting dust looked great cleaned up and placed in front of the sofa. Rustic and practical, it was the perfect place for him to kick up his feet or put down his beer. He'd never done either on the glossy surface of the formal coffee table that Lila had in the room.

Colton came into the room. The motion caught Rohn's eye. So did what Colton was carrying—an old clay jug filled with brown spikes.

"What the hell do you have there?" Rohn laughed, knowing full well what it was, but not getting why Colton had it.

"I saw these cattails growing along the creek by the

highway. I thought they'd look cool in here so I went out and cut a few. They match the color of the sofa."

Remote control in hand, Tyler turned from his work on the television to frown at Colton. "Match the color of the sofa? You know, sometimes you really scare me."

Colton screwed up his face. "Aw, shut up. You're the one who was telling us about Rohn's blue shirt that matched his eyes, dickhead."

Justin laughed. "I have to say, between Tyler obsessing about Rohn's shirt and you whipping out your pocket knife to cut cattails along the highway . . . You're both just weird."

Colton scowled. "Jesus, I'm not out there picking flowers and catching butterflies and shit. They're cattails. They're totally manly. Right, Rohn?"

"Yes, they are. Very manly." Rohn grinned.

The cattails actually did match the new sofa. He couldn't say much more because he had been out picking flowers the other day for Bonnie. Hell, if it would make her happy he'd catch butterflies for her, too.

"See? You guys are idiots." Colton frowned and shook his head.

The room was coming together nicely. He'd picked up a throw rug in a colorful Mexican pattern. He'd even bought the one thing he'd always wanted in this room but had never gotten to have—a recliner.

A big fat one that would tilt almost horizontal if he chose to take a nap in it. And the best part was that it had a cup holder in the armrest.

He shook his head, smiling. A cup holder in the

living room chair. Lila would have never gone for that.

Picking out furniture only a man could love was one benefit of bachelor life he should have taken advantage of long ago, but never had. Since he'd been sex-deprived and lonely for five years, at least he could have had a holder for his beer while doing it.

Of course, he hadn't been deprived last night, and he wouldn't be lonely tonight. He glanced at the time on the grandfather clock in the corner.

The old clock had been allowed to stay in the room. It was one of the few things he'd brought to the marriage. It had belonged to his grandparents. He loved that old thing, even if it did tick too loudly and require he wind it every week.

He'd neglected that duty for the last five years, but today, he'd done it. Amazingly, it still worked. Now that the clock was operating again, he found he'd missed the steady *tick-tick-tick* and the hourly chimes. And now the hands on that clock were telling him that Bonnie would be arriving very shortly.

"Okay, you boys about done here?"

Three sets of eyes turned to him.

"Why?" Justin asked.

"Because it's getting late and I figure you'd want to get going home."

Tyler looked a little too interested. "I don't have to be anywhere. In fact, I think we should run out, pick up some beer and pizzas, watch a movie and break in your new room."

He'd never once considered they'd want to stay. Rohn's expression must have reflected that thought.

Tyler broke out in a laugh. "Don't worry. I'm teasing you."

"Jeez, did you see the look on his face? He really thought we were fixin' to stay." Colton shook his head.

Justin moved a step closer and slapped Rohn on the back. "We're going. Don't worry."

"I didn't mean you had to—" Crap, he didn't want them to think he wanted them to go, but he sure as hell didn't want them to stay.

"Rohn, we know you didn't do all this for yourself." Justin grinned. "When a man goes to this kind of trouble, it's got to be for a woman, and I figure the way you keep checking that there clock and your cell phone, that you're expecting her any minute."

"I—"

Justin held up one hand to stop Rohn's protest. "It's okay. You don't have to explain. Just don't do anything I wouldn't do."

"Say hi to Miss Bonnie for us." Colton grinned as he headed out the door with Justin directly behind him.

Rohn could try to deny it, but he knew it was pointless. Justin and Colton had already left and there was no denying what he had planned anyway. He let his chin drop and blew out a breath. Finally, he'd gathered his composure enough to look back and meet Tyler's gaze.

Tyler was sporting a wide grin as he strode across the room toward Rohn. He handed Rohn the remote control for the television and then leaned in closer. "You need any condoms?"

Good Lord, that was the last thing he'd expected to hear from this kid. "No, thanks. I'm good." He somehow managed to keep his voice steady so as to not let the horror he felt over this conversation show.

"A'ight. 'Cause you know, it's always better to be safe than sorry."

"I'll keep that in mind." Rohn nodded, doing his best to keep a straight face while being torn between amusement and embarrassment that this kid, nearly half his age, was lecturing him.

Tyler evaluated Rohn for a few seconds, as if deciding if he could trust him to indeed practice safe sex. As humiliating as this whole conversation was, Rohn held his composure until Tyler finally nodded. "See you in the morning."

"Yup."

"Don't bother getting up early and making us coffee. I'll tell Justin or Colton to pick some up on the way over."

"Now why would you say that?" Rohn's annoyance with Tyler came through in his tone.

Tyler cocked up one brow. "Look around you, boss. This is a damned nice setup you got here. Good chance you might get caught up and not get to sleep until real late. You know, like watching a movie or something."

Rohn didn't miss Tyler's smirk or his insinuation. He hated that Tyler was right, but there was a damn good chance—at least, he hoped there was—that Bonnie would still be here in the morning.

She might not appreciate three cowboys being in the kitchen at the crack of dawn after her first overnight stay in his bed.

Hopefully, the first of many nights.

If everything worked out as he planned, he'd

convince her it was crazy for her to sleep on her father's old, uncomfortable couch.

Once she'd agreed to stay at his place, he'd get her used to the lack of privacy. One hurdle at a time.

Rohn watched the boys' trucks pull out of the driveway and breathed in relief. At least Bonnie wouldn't have to face their teasing and suggestive glances tonight. She might not handle the embarrassment as well as Rohn did.

It turned out the boys had left just in the nick of time. Rohn had just gotten to the kitchen to work on dinner when he spotted Bonnie's car in the drive.

Even just the sight of her damn car put a smile on his face. He had it bad and damned if he didn't love every minute of it. He felt like a teenager, reliving that feeling of falling for Bonnie all over again.

Hopefully this time would end a little better than last time had.

He was a different person than he'd been the first time she'd left him for Arizona. He wasn't letting her get away from him this time.

Unlike twenty-five years ago, he wouldn't hesitate to go after her and convince her, with any means possible, to come back to him.

He strode to the screen door off the back of the kitchen, opened it, and stepped outside into the glare of the sun riding low in the sky as evening fell.

When she got out of the car and saw him, she donned a small, tentative, almost nervous smile and lifted one hand in a wave. She moved closer and cringed. "I didn't have time to stop and pick up anything—"

Rohn didn't wait for her to finish. She looked so pretty in her sundress and heels with her hair falling around her face in soft waves, that he reeled her in with one arm around her waist and kissed her hard.

Bringing one hand up to cup her face, he pulled away just far enough to say, "I don't want or need you to bring anything. You're the only thing I need."

She smiled. "Okay."

He pressed one more hard, quick kiss to her lips and then grabbed her hand. "Come on. I've got something to show you."

"All right." She took quick steps to keep up with him as he pulled her inside. Down the hall, he paused in the doorway of the living room. "Look."

She seemed confused at to what he could be dragging her to see, until she got a look at the room, then her mouth dropped open. "Wow. When did you do all this?"

"Today. And last night."

"That's what your secret errands were about?"

"Yes."

She turned to him, frowning. "Why did you do all this?"

"Because it was long past time I made this house my own. The way I want it. The way I'd use it. Why have a stuffy room I never sit in when I could turn it into a man cave. You know, football, beer, hot wings . . . all the makings of heaven for a guy."

"Yes, I see." Smiling, she turned back. "It's really beautiful."

"Well, I don't know if I'd go that far."

"No, it is. It looks like you. The leather. The wood. You thought of everything. Right down to the cattails."

Rohn had to laugh that she'd noticed them. "Colton gets the credit for those. Poor guy took a hell of a razzing from the other kids when he walked in with them and declared they'd match the sofa perfectly."

She smiled. "I bet he did. He was right, though."

"Yes, he was." Rohn wrapped his arms around her from behind as she stood facing the room. He leaned low, near her ear. "So, do you like it?"

"I love it."

"Wanna take the room for a test drive and watch a movie with me tonight?" He couldn't help but remember how their movie watching had gone in the old days. They'd spend as much time making out in the darkened theater as they did watching the action on the big screen. He could only hope for the same tonight.

"Yeah, I could do that."

"Good." He dropped his hold from around her waist and grabbed her hand again. "Come on. There's more."

"More?"

"Yup." He grinned and led her to the staircase. "I redecorated both my bedroom and the guest bedroom. New beds. New mattresses. And I added a couple of pieces of furniture from downstairs. This is my room."

"Nice." She glanced up at him with uncertainty in her eyes.

He pulled her to the next doorway and watched for her reaction as they moved inside the room next to his. "And this is the guest room."

Her gaze moved from the new bed and bedding he'd bought, to the antique desk he'd moved in. "Wow. It's beautiful."

Excited that she thought so, he forged ahead. "So,

no pressure, but I was thinking you should quit being stubborn and sleeping at your place where there aren't even any beds, and just stay with me."

"Here in the guest room?" She raised her gaze to his.

"Yeah. Or in the master bedroom with me." Rohn shrugged. "Or I was thinking maybe I could sleep in the guest room with you."

She smiled. "But no pressure."

"Nope. Not one bit." But if she said no, he was driving over to her place and sleeping on the damn sofa with her. He'd waited too long for this woman to let her get away.

She turned away from him and looked back at the guest room. He tried to see it as she would. The vase of daisies he'd put on the antique desk. The delicate white lace curtains that would let the morning sunlight in. He'd bought them to replace the heavy ones that had been there for years. There were new sheets, a comforter, and a duvet that he'd purchased, even though until today he'd had no idea what exactly a duvet was.

It was a bright, happy room, and he could see Bonnie being happy in it, waking up to the light of the morning sun rising in the east.

"Okay."

"Okay?" His voice rose in surprise. "You'll stay here?"

"Yes, in the guest room." He waited and wondered until finally Bonnie put him out of his agony and added, "With you."

He laughed and spun her to face him, as gleeful as a kid. "You got it."

Hell, he'd sleep with her in the barn if it meant being able to wake up next to Bonnie in the morning.

The look in her eyes as she gazed up at him made him forget all about dinner and the movie. He wanted nothing more than to break in that new bed.

When she wrapped her arms around him he decided that maybe dinner could wait a little while.

Chapter Twenty-Two

Bonnie woke in the bed in Rohn's guest room and glanced at the empty space next to her. Judging by the bright sun she saw streaming through the window, it was late.

No wonder he'd already gotten up. Work started early on a ranch.

It was also no wonder she'd slept in. They'd both been up late. That they'd made love before dinner hadn't helped them get to sleep any sooner, since they'd done it again later. Twice.

She stretched and felt the stiffness of sore muscles.

It sure had been nice sleeping in a real bed, though.

The air-conditioning kept the room cool. Snuggled down naked beneath the comforter, she'd slept like a baby. Once Rohn had finally let her sleep.

She'd have to bring a bag over so she had clothes and toiletries. As it was, she'd have to do the walk of shame in yesterday's clothes this morning.

The scent of bacon wafting into the room had her

mouth watering and served as inspiration to get up and moving, even with as comfortable as the bed was.

Bonnie hoisted her body off the mattress and felt the plush rug beneath her bare feet. She padded to the dresser where Rohn's shirt from last night lay. That would do for now, at least to get her to the bathroom in the hallway. She couldn't go prancing around the house completely naked, and she felt too lazy to put on her clothes just yet.

The shirt fell past her midthigh. He was tall. She loved that about him. She wasn't petite herself, but she had always felt small next to Rohn and she liked it.

The hardwood floors in the hall felt cool beneath her bare feet as she padded her way to the bathroom.

Inside, she flipped on the wall light and smiled. He'd left a brand-new toothbrush and a tube of toothpaste next to the sink for her to use, along with a bar of soap, washcloth, and towel. He always had been one to think of everything.

Anxious to get downstairs, she brushed her teeth and washed her face fast. She couldn't stay too long. There was more work to be done at her place and she still had to make an appointment to meet with the real estate agent to decide if she should rent or sell the house. And then her meeting with the lawyer to finalize the inheritance was set for tomorrow.

So many details to handle, but she'd make time for breakfast.

Right now, all she wanted to do was go downstairs and kiss Rohn good morning. She almost ran down the stairs, she was so anxious to see him. She wasn't disappointed when she arrived in the kitchen. He stood at the stove, flipping the strips of sizzling meat in the cast-iron skillet and looking like her dream come true.

"Good morning." Her greeting sounded breathless after her sprint down the stairs.

He glanced at her over his shoulder and smiled. She didn't miss his expression of appreciation as he looked her up and down. "Nearly good afternoon."

Bonnie cringed. "Sorry about that."

"Don't apologize. You obviously needed the sleep. And I did keep you up pretty late." He shot her a sexy grin before flipping off the burner and turning to come to her. "You looked so cute sleeping I didn't want to wake you."

"That smell of bacon did it, though." She happily accepted the kiss he pressed to her mouth.

"Yeah, I kind of did that on purpose. The guys will be in for lunch in about an hour. I didn't want you to come downstairs and be surprised by a kitchen full of cowboys. Especially dressed like this." He grinned.

Her eyes widened as she latched on to what he said. "Colton, Tyler, and Justin are here?"

"Yup. It's a normal workday for the rest of the world. We don't all have summers off from our jobs like you teachers do." He tapped her nose with one finger as he teased her.

"But they'll know I spent the night." She had to get dressed and get out before they came in.

"Darlin', that ship has sailed. You think they didn't see your car here when they arrived just after dawn?"

"Oh my God."

"Bonnie. I'm a grown man. You're a grown woman. We're both single and free to do whatever the hell we want."

"But I don't want them to know we're having *sex*." She hissed the last word in a whisper.

Rohn laughed, which only made her frown. "I'm sorry, sweetheart, but they were assuming we were having sex even before they saw your car this morning. Tyler offered me condoms last night, in case I needed them."

"Oh my God." She couldn't look at Rohn. Couldn't stand the thought of them knowing.

Rohn let out a breath and pulled her back to him just as she was trying to get away. "Stop. I won't have you being embarrassed. There's no need."

"But—"

"But nothing. I won't have it. You're moving in here with me." When she opened her mouth to protest he pressed a finger over her lips. "For the duration of your time here. That's all. And if you don't, if you insist on going back to that house, then I'm coming with you. The boys will figure out I'm sleeping at your place soon enough, so why should both of us be uncomfortable there when it is so comfortable here."

Bonnie drew in a deep breath hoping to quell the embarrassment that had her pulse speeding.

"Okay?" he asked.

"Yeah. Okay."

He grinned. "Good. Now grab a seat. The bacon is cooked. I'll throw some eggs in a pan and be done in a jiffy."

"What if the boys come in early?"

"Then they'll see how cute my girlfriend looks in my shirt and be jealous as all hell."

She frowned and pulled the hem of the shirt lower as she sat. "You're awfully flippant about this."

"Darlin', I'm so happy to have you here I'd dance naked down Main Street."

"Just don't expect me to do the same."

"Hell, I'd knock out any man who dared try to see you naked."

Even with as appalled as she was at the whole situation, she couldn't help but smile at that.

"When you go home to work on the house today, make sure you pack up all your things and throw them in the car. Okay?" He glanced at her from behind the refrigerator door before he emerged with a carton of eggs.

"Okay." There was no use fighting him.

He had an answer for everything. He was like a force of nature. It was just easier to go along for the ride rather than try and fight him.

"And you'd better go dress shopping this week because unless you packed something semiformal, you won't have anything to wear when I take you to our reunion."

"Okay. I'll go shopping." She could only see his profile as he cracked eggs into the skillet, but from what she could see, Rohn was smiling.

Yes, he'd won this battle. She'd stay for the reunion.

It would be next to impossible to leave him at the end of the summer and go back to Arizona to work as it was. She'd have to pack every ounce she could into every moment they had together.

After breakfast, work awaited her at the house. It consumed her enough she didn't have too much time to miss Rohn.

The rest of the day moved at a surreal pace as Bonnie anticipated going back to Rohn's with equal excitement and trepidation. Staying with him felt like a huge step. But staying away from him seemed impossible.

Then there was the situation with his ranch hands. She remembered her embarrassment about them knowing she'd spent the night as she drove into the driveway and saw the line of trucks parked by the barn.

One cowboy ambled across the yard toward her. He reached her car just as she parked, and reached out to open her door for her.

"Miss Bonnie." Justin tipped his hat to her as she climbed out of the car. "Nice to see you again."

She might never get used to having men open doors for her. That never happened in Phoenix. "You too, Justin. How are you?"

"Real good. Thanks. You doing okay at your place? You need any help moving anything?"

"I'm still going through all the paperwork. I swear my father must have kept every tax return, receipt, bill, and bank statement he ever got."

"Yeah, my mom's like that, too. A real pack rat, but you gotta love her." His dimples showed as he grinned. He hooked a thumb toward the house. "Rohn's inside."

No surprise, he'd guessed who she was there to see.

"Okay. Thanks." She hesitated.

Her bag was in the trunk, but she didn't want to get it out while Justin was here. It would be obvious she was planning on staying the night.

Nope. She couldn't do it. Couldn't look this young cowboy in the eye while carrying in her luggage to move in with his boss. Rohn could just come out later and get her bag. He was so anxious to have her stop staying at her house and sleep here instead, it would be the least he could do.

"So I'm gonna go on in."

"A'ight. I'm heading out myself."

"Okay. Have a good night."

"Y'all have a good night, too." And there it was, a knowing smirk he tried to hide but didn't.

Another tip of his hat and he was off, headed for his truck and whatever his evening plans were. She watched him walk away. It somehow wasn't fair that she knew nothing about what he was doing but he seemed to know—or at least assume—what she'd be doing.

"Hey. About time you got here." Rohn pinned her between his body and the hood of her car, encasing her with two thick arms. "I missed you."

He leaned in and kissed her, right on the mouth, in broad daylight. Bonnie pulled back. "Rohn. Your guys are still here."

"Yeah. So?"

"So, they'll see."

"And?"

"They'll know."

"I already told you, darlin', that ship has long sailed. But come on. Let's go inside and I'll kiss you in private if it'll make you feel better." Looping one arm around her neck and shoulders, he steered her toward the door. "That'll be better, actually. Dinner won't be ready for a while and we'll have some time to kill. *That* will have to be in private."

Her cheeks warmed as she remembered how they'd killed time before dinner the night before.

Rohn glanced down at her. "Damn, how I love when you blush."

"It that why you make me do it so often?"

"You make it so easy, I don't even have to try." They were inside the kitchen when he turned her to face him, backed her up against the counter, and moved in for another kiss. "When those boys are gone, I think we should christen the kitchen."

"What?" she squeaked at the suggestion.

"You heard me." His mouth covered hers in a kiss that didn't tell her if he was serious or not. With Rohn in this frisky of a mood, he might actually mean what he'd said.

His tongue was warm as he slid it into her mouth. He groaned and stepped closer, pressing against her and letting her feel exactly how serious he was about his suggestion.

She wanted him as much as he obviously wanted her. Being with him all night had only made the need stronger. He moved from her mouth to nuzzle her neck just below her ear. "I loved waking up next to you this morning."

"I wish I could say the same. You were already gone when I woke up."

He laughed. "Sorry. Want me to wake you up at six tomorrow morning when I get up?"

"No. Thank you. I have to get up that early when I'm working. This is my summer break. I'm sleeping in."

"That's fine with me." He drew her earlobe between his teeth and groaned. "Mm, maybe I'll get the boys started and then crawl back into bed with you. How's that sound?"

"It sounds perfect." She turned her face and captured his lips with hers.

Rohn kissed them both breathless and then broke away. He moved to the back door, flipped the lock, and then grabbed her hand. "Come on."

She didn't need to ask where they were headed. She knew. "My suitcase is in the trunk—"

"I'll get it later."

"Okay." Smiling at his urgency, she let him lead her upstairs. She could definitely get used to this schedule.

Upstairs, in the bedroom he'd decorated just for her, Rohn made love to her so sweetly, she had to turn her head and wipe away the tears before he saw them.

How could she possibly leave him?

But how could she stay?

Chapter Twenty-Three

"Hey, boss!"

Rohn turned when Tyler called to him from across the yard. "Yeah?"

Tyler ambled closer. "You know that Justin, Colt, and me are riding Saturday. Right?"

"Yeah." Now that Tyler had brought it up, Rohn remembered them talking about some big competition this weekend. "And?"

"Well, you just told Justin you wanted to start plowing that south field on Saturday. So which is it? We working or can we take off?"

Cussing beneath his breath, Rohn ran a hand over his face. He'd been distracted for days. It was only a matter of time before the guys noticed.

"Right. Sorry. We can start on that field next week. Take Saturday off."

"You sure?" Tyler cocked one dark brow high.

"Yeah. Positive." It would be better if he didn't have a bunch of guys running around the place on Saturday, anyway. Just in case things went bad.

"A'ight." Tyler nodded. "I know you're not bringing any stock for this one, but are you coming to watch the competition? It's close by."

"No. I've got that high school reunion Saturday night."

"That's right. Your big date with Miss Bonnie to the prom."

Rohn rolled his eyes. "It's not the prom."

"No, but it might as well be. You two are acting like teenagers since she moved in."

"She didn't move in. She's just staying here instead of at her place."

"Uh-huh. Gotcha. I gotta go finish up for the day." Cocky as usual, Tyler grinned and spun away to saunter toward the equipment shed.

Rohn let him go. No use fighting the point. He did wish Bonnie's move into his house would be permanent. His guest room had become his bedroom over the past week and he'd gladly make that permanent if she'd agree to stay.

Saturday was the reunion, but tonight, he planned to take the first step in making her presence in his home and in his life permanent.

Nearly a week of her living under his roof, sleeping next to him, making love morning and night, was enough to convince him even the rest of his life wouldn't be long enough to spend with her. But it would have to be, because it was all they had, and he wasn't about to waste another moment of it.

It was risky, asking her to marry him just days before their reunion. If she said no, it would be awkward as all hell. But if she said yes, then she'd be there sporting his ring and he'd be the proudest man on earth as he introduced her to their old classmates as his future wife.

Future wife.

It had been a long time since Rohn had really felt like he had a future. Not since losing Lila. Now, he knew he could, and he hoped it was with Bonnie. Strange how a girl from his past had turned out to be his future.

The ring box in his pocket pressed into his leg. That was another surreal part of his past. The ring.

He'd bought it with his earnings that summer. Saving every paycheck from her father until he had enough to buy a tiny chip of a diamond in a gold band. It was meant to be a promise ring. He was going to give it to her before she left for college to let her know that he loved her. That he wanted her in his future even if they were apart for college. It was to tell her that he'd wait for her and that he'd hoped she'd wait for him.

Things hadn't worked out as he'd planned and he still had no idea of what the hell had happened to them. Why she'd left early without a good-bye. Why she'd acted so odd when he'd called and then avoided all contact after that.

It had hurt like hell, but more than that, it had been so unlike her it was perplexing. It had never felt right. Breaking up was one thing, and he might have been able to handle that if they'd had a fight or if she'd outright dumped him so she could go to college and see other people. That would have hurt, but it would have seemed more normal than her disappearing so completely.

It was something they should talk about if they were going to start a new life together.

Then again, did it really matter?

It was so long ago. They were different people

now. They'd been kids then. They were mature adults now. A whole lifetime had passed for both of them.

A fresh start, that's what they needed. To start from ground zero and build a future. He wanted that future to start now.

Bonnie's car pulled into the driveway just as Rohn made the decision to ask her tonight.

Perfect timing.

He waited by the house for her to park, and then he opened her car door for her.

"Hey, darlin'." He enveloped her in his arms, kissing her right there behind the open door of the car. The guys were still there, but she was his and he didn't care who knew it. She still got embarrassed when he kissed her out in the open. Her blush only made him want to do it more often.

Rohn cupped her face and smiled down at her. "It's about time you came home to me."

"I wanted to finish before I quit for the day."

"Finish? Did you finish?" He asked the question with mixed feelings.

"Almost. I finished cleaning and making piles. I still have to get the piles out of the house but after that, I'm done." She shrugged.

He'd be happy when she wasn't working in that dusty old house pawing through the past any longer. But her finishing the cleanup would mean it would go on the market. Once it was listed with the real estate for either sale or rent, what reason would she have to stay in Oklahoma? He'd have to give her a reason to stay.

"I'll send my guys to you in the morning with the truck to haul it away."

"Rohn, you don't have to—"

"Shh. No arguing. It's done. Now come on inside. I, uh, want to talk to you." He hoped he'd be enough of a reason for her to stay, but the nagging doubt in his mind continued to remind him that he might not be enough.

"Talk to me? About what?" Bonnie asked.

"You'll see." The thought of proposing had his hands shaking. He didn't remember being this nervous asking Lila to marry him all those years ago.

"Okay." She let him lead her inside by the hand.

Once there, he realized he didn't have a plan in place to do this. Hell, he hadn't thought this through at all. Which was funny since proposing had been all he could think of over the past couple of days. He'd just never gotten around to deciding how to actually accomplish it.

No guardian angel was going to swoop down and make this easy for him so he pulled out a kitchen chair for her. "Sit."

"Okay."

The moment she was perched on the edge of the chair, he dug the ring box out of his jeans pocket where it had been for the past two days.

He dropped to one knee, holding the box in front of him.

Bonnie drew in a sharp breath and covered her mouth with her hand. "Oh my God."

He let out a nervous laugh. She knew what was coming and she hadn't run out the door yet. That was a good sign.

"Bonnie Blue, I loved you before. And amazingly, now that you've come back into my life, I've been blessed to be able to love you again. I bought this ring years ago when we were dating. It was to be a promise to you that I wanted a future for us together. I still want that and if you say yes, I swear I'll buy you the biggest and best diamond I can afford, but it seemed right to give this one to you now."

Her eyes brimmed with tears as he opened the box and took out the ring. His hands shook as he held it out to her. "Will you marry me? Will you be my wife?"

He'd hoped her tears were happy tears, but Bonnie shaking her head was his first clue things weren't going well. When she jumped up from the chair and ran out the back door, he was sure.

Squatting on his heels on the kitchen floor, alone, Rohn realized if that wasn't a big old *no*, he didn't know what it was. The embarrassingly small diamond that he'd felt so sentimental about was still in his hands as he cussed aloud to the empty room.

Chapter Twenty-Four

Bonnie got in her car and drove directly to the river. Why? She didn't know. It would hurt like hell to be at the one place that reminded her so strongly of Rohn, but that didn't stop her.

Barely able to see the road through her tears, she hadn't even been aware of where she was headed until she saw the turn for the dirt road. Slowing the car to a crawl, she bounced along the unpaved path toward the site of the memories that spanned decades.

The wild pounding of her heart hadn't slowed during the drive.

He'd proposed.

It should be a dream come true, the man she loved, proposing to her. Loving her enough to want to spend the rest of his life with her. But how could she say yes to a future with Rohn after what she'd done?

All his love and devotion had done was renew Bonnie's guilt, until the secret she'd held inside felt as if it would cripple her.

There was no happy ending in her future. She'd ensured that years ago.

She cut the engine and sat, staring at the river.

It was peaceful. Or it would be if she could quiet her mind. She couldn't stop the voices that yelled at her from inside her own head. She was alone yet she couldn't escape herself.

She wasn't alone for long.

Rohn's truck soon barreled into the dirt road not long after she'd arrived. It skidded to a stop directly behind her car, blocking her in. There was no escape.

He got out of his truck and strode fast to her car, pulling open the door.

She feared his anger, but when she finally dared to look up at his face, she didn't see anger. She did see confusion, and determination, and pain.

"I'm sorry." Her tears started fresh.

He squatted down to be level with her as she sat and took both of her hands in his. "I don't want your apologies. I want you to tell me what you're thinking. What you're feeling. Why you ran away from me."

All she could do was shake her head.

"I know you love me, Bonnie." The intense stare of his blue eyes pinned her, making her unable to lie.

She nodded.

"Then what is it?"

"I lied to you."

A frown furrowed Rohn's forehead. "When? About what?"

"About why I left. Back then." A huge heaving intake of breath cut off any more words.

"Why did you leave?" His words were soft. A plea

for the truth. He continued to hold her hands gently in his.

"I . . ." She couldn't finish.

He stood and tugged her out of the car, wrapping his arms around her. She pressed her face into his chest as the sobs wracked her body. Her tears wet his shirt but he didn't seem to notice.

Rohn ran his hands up and down her back with smooth, slow, calming strokes. "Take your time. You can tell me anything."

Hiding the truth from him hurt so badly, she couldn't stand it anymore. She just wanted it to end. The words came rushing out. "I was pregnant."

He paused his hands in their path up her back. She felt him draw in a big breath and let it out. He squeezed her tighter against him and shook his head.

"God, Bonnie. I'm so sorry you had to go through that alone. Christ. It was my fault. I was careless and got you pregnant. I should have been there for you. Held your hand while you . . ." His words trailed off.

She knew what he'd assumed. He thought she'd run away to Arizona and had an abortion. He didn't understand the full depth of her betrayal.

In hindsight, she probably should have terminated the pregnancy. Then she wouldn't have had to make this next confession that would hurt him even more.

"Rohn, I didn't—"

"Didn't what?"

"I didn't get an abortion." Bonnie felt Rohn's hands still again as he pulled back to stare at her. She dared to glance up at his face and found disbelief in his expression. "I had the baby."

"You what?" he asked again, but this time his tone was not so gentle.

"I gave her up for adoption. I—we had a daughter." That little girl was grown up, living what Bonnie hoped was a happy life. A better life than she could have given her.

He took a step back but his hands remained on her shoulders, squeezing tight. "Why didn't you tell me?"

"I don't know." Her words came out so softly, she was afraid he hadn't heard them.

He drew in another breath, shaking his head. "I gotta go."

"Rohn. Please—" She took a step after him and reached out to touch his arm as he spun to leave.

He pulled his arm from her grasp. "I need some time."

"I'm sorry."

"So am I." The slow, sad sway of his head and the slump of his shoulders as he walked back to his truck broke her. It brought the sadness, the guilt, the horror at herself and her own actions crashing back on her.

She might as well have been that frightened eighteen-year-old again.

That horrible day was as vivid in her mind as if it were yesterday. Her mother had been there with her, through the delivery, during every contraction, every second of the unbearable pain. They'd taken her and Rohn's daughter away the moment the birth was over. Bonnie hadn't even held the baby. The adoption agency had said it would be easier that way.

The paperwork was closed. She'd never know where her daughter went or who raised her. Her daughter would never know the name of her parents.

What else could Bonnie have done?

She should have told Rohn then. He deserved to know, even if she had been firm in her decision about what to do. Now, twenty-five years later, she was going to pay the price for that decision. She'd lost the love of her life, not once but twice.

Given what she'd done, keeping the truth from him that he had a child, she had to think that maybe she deserved it.

Chapter Twenty-Five

All the years Rohn had longed for a son or daughter. All those heartbreaking disappointments he'd lived through with Lila as all hope was yanked from them again and again.

Through all that, he already had a child. A daughter somewhere who didn't even know his name. Hell, he didn't know hers, either.

Rohn slammed a fist against the dashboard. One question resonated through him. Why?

Why would Bonnie run away rather than tell him? How could she keep something so monumental from him?

With him beside her, they could have raised the baby.

His knowing could have changed absolutely everything, or it might have changed nothing at all. The fact remained he should have been at least a part of the decision.

He felt the bulge of the ring box in the pocket of his jeans. Had he been ready for marriage and babies at eighteen? Would that have been the end of his college career? The end of Bonnie's, too?

Chances were good she wouldn't have graduated with a teaching degree if she'd kept that baby. Would he be where he was now if he'd had to get a full-time job straight out of high school rather than getting a college degree? If he'd had to support a wife and a baby on whatever he could earn at whatever job he could have gotten?

Rohn scrubbed both hands over his face.

The anger began to seep out of him, and exhaustion replaced it. He felt bone weary. Physically, it felt as if he could collapse in bed and sleep until morning. Mentally, he knew his spinning thoughts would never let him rest.

He realized all of Bonnie's things were in his guest room. He doubted she'd sleep at his house tonight. Not after how badly he'd reacted to her news, and the overly dramatic exit he'd made afterward. Hell, she probably wouldn't even come get her stuff. She'd sleep at her house on that old sofa and not even have a change of clothes or a toothbrush.

He should go to her. They should do what they hadn't done twenty-five years ago—talk about this.

He'd calmed down considerably.

At least he wasn't still shaking from her revelation. He'd be able to talk to her about this rationally. He was by no means happy about her hiding her decision from him, but he was willing to discuss it.

Keeping communications open was the only hope they had to get past this. As he started his truck, he hoped she felt the same.

Rohn swung by the river first, but she was gone.

He spun the truck around and headed to the only other place he could think of to find her.

He reached her house only to find the driveway empty. Hell, she could have gone to his house and he'd missed her when he was driving around.

Ridiculous as it seemed, he didn't have her cell phone number so he couldn't even call her on it now. He'd been calling her on the house phone the whole time.

That's what he got for being old school. Keeping in that vein, he'd have to leave her a note on the door before he went back to his place to see if she was there or they'd keep missing each other.

He was scrounging through the truck for something to write on, not to mention something to write with, when he saw a man cut across from the neighboring property. Rohn opened the truck door and stepped out onto the drive.

"Evening." Rohn nodded a greeting to the man when he neared.

"Evening." The older man nodded back. "You looking for Bonnie?"

"Yeah, I was, but I don't see her car so I was going to leave her a note." Remembering basic manners, Rohn extended his hand. "Rohn Lerner. I'm a friend of hers."

The man shook his hand. "Andrew. I live next door. And don't bother with the note. She's gone back to Phoenix."

That information was as confusing as it was disturbing. He'd just seen her a little while ago. Barely half an hour. He drew his brows down low. "You sure?"

"Yup. She came knocking, told us she had to get

back to Arizona right away, and asked if we'd give the key to the real estate agent who's coming to look at the property."

"Did she say why she had to get back?" Rohn had his suspicions.

"She said something came up with her job, but didn't say what." The man pursed his lips. "I can tell you she looked upset enough my wife tried to convince her to at least wait until the morning to leave."

"But she wouldn't wait."

"Nope. She said it took her about fourteen hours to get here so we're more than a little worried about her on that long drive. But she promised to call when she got home safe. I can tell her you were looking for her, if you'd like."

Drawing in a breath to quell his roiling emotions, Rohn shook his head. "No, thanks. That's not necessary. Have a good night."

With barely a glance, Rohn ended his conversation with the neighbor and turned for his truck.

Nothing had come up with her job. She was running away from him. Again. Twenty-five years later and nothing had changed. She would still rather run from a conflict than try to work things out.

Could he be with a woman who didn't trust him enough to even talk about things?

A woman in love should choose to turn toward the man in her life when times got tough, not away from him. Bonnie had made the opposite choice twice now.

Two times should be enough to prove to him that she'd never change.

He knew to his very soul if he let her go, she'd

stay gone. Maybe that would be the best thing for both of them.

The morning dawned after a sleepless night and Rohn was not ready to greet a new day without Bonnie in it.

Of course, the boys noticed first thing in the morning.

"Damn, he's cranky again." Colton shot Rohn a glance as he whispered to Justin.

Unfortunately, he hadn't whispered softly enough. Rohn heard every word and all it did was make him more pissed off.

"Maybe if you got to work instead of standing around my kitchen, my piss-poor mood wouldn't offend you so much."

He was in no mood for dealing with anyone today. Not after discovering last night that Bonnie had left him yet again.

Hell, she hadn't just left. She'd all but fled, even abandoning her suitcase and all of her stuff she'd left at his house, just to avoid seeing him again. That was some serious avoidance right there.

"Fine." Colt knocked his hat back a notch and tipped his head toward the door. "I'll give Ty a heads-up it ain't safe around here when he gets in."

Scowling, Rohn could only agree. "Good plan."

Colton paused with one hand on the door, glancing back at Justin. "You coming?"

"Yeah. In a minute."

"A'ight." With a nod, Colton was gone, but Justin remained.

"Something I can do for you?" The tone in Rohn's question didn't invite conversation, but Justin stayed put anyway, leaning against the counter with his arms folded.

"I ever tell you about the last time I spoke with my brother?"

Justin was talking about his older brother who had been killed in action in Afghanistan. Rohn calmed his temper and shook his head. "No. Don't think you ever did."

"We were close, him and me, but there was an age difference and he was always away, so we didn't get to spend much time together. And when he was back, I always kinda felt like he was the big hero and I was the lowly little brother who hadn't been man enough to follow in his footsteps and serve my country."

This was all news to Rohn. Justin was smart, a hell of a horse trainer, and a hard worker. Rohn had never realized he had these issues and insecurities. "I'm sorry to hear that."

Justin shrugged, as if it didn't matter. "No big deal. I chose my path, he chose his. What the folks who did judge me didn't see was what his being gone all the time did to my mamma. If I'd left, too, who would she have? Nobody. My daddy died years ago. Big brother was off fighting a war that ain't ever gonna end. I figured my job was to stay home and take care of things. Be the man of the house."

"That's important." Rohn tipped his head, even though he didn't understand what had prompted this confession from Justin.

"It is, but I always assumed no one else saw my reasoning and thought I was a coward. But I was wrong. That last phone call I got from my brother, right before his Humvee was blown up, was him calling to tell me thanks for taking care of our mother. How he could only be away with a clear conscience because he knew I was there taking care of her."

"I'm glad you got to have that conversation."

"Me too, but that's not the point."

Ah, so there was a point to this. "What is?"

"I didn't want to take the phone call. I watched my cell phone ring and almost didn't answer it. I was going to let it go to voice mail because I was being small, and petty and letting my pride get in the way. It was right after the church had put out a special bulletin like they do around all of the patriotic holidays. They list all the folks serving and there's a special prayer during the service just for them. I always sit there and feel like a piece of shit because I'm safe in that pew rather than riding around in a damn tank getting shot at. But I forced myself to pick up that phone, even though I didn't want to and I'm glad I did."

"I'm glad you did too."

"Here's why I'm telling you this."

Rohn had just about given up hope there was more of a point to this odd conversation, as touching as it was.

Justin continued, "I can't help but notice Miss Bonnie's car isn't here."

"She went back to Arizona." Rohn swallowed away the sick feeling in the back of his throat.

"Without saying good-bye to any of us?" Justin shook his head.

"Yup."

She hadn't said good-bye to Rohn, either, so he didn't have much sympathy for Justin.

"I don't know what happened, but I do know this—you two need to talk."

"She left. She doesn't want to talk."

"I didn't want to talk to my brother that day, either. Thinking about how disappointed my mamma would be if she knew I'd dodged my brother's call guilted me into answering it. It was the nudge I needed. I'm here to give you that nudge. Or a shove, if you need it. Call her. Talk to her. Even if nothing comes of it, you won't be any worse off than you are now, right?"

"I don't know what you think you know about me and Bonnie—"

"I know you're happy when she's here and miserable when she's not. That's all I need to know. All the other details are private. I don't care 'bout them. That's between you two."

"A phone call's not going to cut it." It didn't work twenty-five years ago. Rohn was sure it wouldn't help now. "She left because she doesn't want to talk."

"Then go there in person and make her listen." Justin lifted one shoulder. "Who knows, maybe she ran hoping you'd chase her."

That summer so long ago he hadn't gone after her. Had she wanted him to? Was that what kept them apart? That he'd let her go?

"Jesus." Rohn ran his hand over his face.

Everything in him told him to go after her, but he couldn't just pick up and drive fourteen hours to Arizona on a moment's notice—could he?

He opened his mouth and Justin held up one hand, interrupting him before he even had a chance to talk.

"I can make sure everything is taken care of. Between Colt, Ty, and me, we can hold down the ranch just fine without you. Ty's right next door at Janie's all night, every night. And I'll even feed that old fleabag dog of yours that sleeps out in the barn."

There really was nothing stopping Rohn from going after her, except for his pride. And maybe one other obstacle stood in his way. "I don't know her address."

He supposed he could go to her neighbor's place and see if they knew her address, if they'd even give it to him.

"Did you try a web search?" Justin asked.

"No." Rohn sighed. One day he'd remember he was in a century where anything and everything was available right at his fingertips. "I'll give that a try."

"A'ight. Make a list of anything you want done while you're gone. I'll go tell the boys you'll be away for a couple of days."

"Thanks, Justin."

"Anytime." Justin smiled, as if he knew Rohn was thanking him for far more than just his going out to deliver the message to Tyler and Colton.

Rohn turned toward the office and his computer while Justin headed out the door. He was really going to do this. Drive more than twelve hours chasing a woman who might not want him. Then again, she just might.

One way or another, for better or worse, he'd know soon enough, and the answer would determine his future.

Chapter Twenty-Six

Just after sunrise Bonnie pulled into the driveway lined with cactus and palm trees and cut the engine. She took the keys and her purse, the only things she had with her on her return trip home since she'd abandoned everything else at Rohn's house.

Her feet feeling as heavy as her spirit, she made her way through the back door. She found her mother in the kitchen making breakfast.

"Bonnie. You didn't tell me you were coming home today. You look exhausted."

"I drove all night." She grabbed a bottle of water out of the fridge and plopped down at the kitchen table, so overtired she couldn't move another step. She was lucky she hadn't been in a wreck feeling the way she was and driving all that way.

"Good God. That long drive, alone and in the dark? Why?"

Bonnie scrambled for an explanation other than the truth—that she'd been running away from Rohn. "To avoid the traffic."

"There's traffic on the interstate between Oklahoma and Arizona?"

"Sure. There can be."

Her mother frowned. "I'd get you a cup of coffee but I think you need to go to bed, not have caffeine."

"Yeah, I do." As exhausted as she was, maybe she'd even be able to sleep without reliving that last conversation with Rohn over and over again in her head.

"When you get up later, you can tell me all about the trip."

"We talked every day. What's there to tell?" Thank God she hadn't told her mother about Rohn, since that had imploded, just as she knew it would as soon as she told him the truth.

"Well, for one, you hadn't met with the real estate agent yet the last time we talked. What did they say about selling the house?"

Bonnie had failed on so many levels. She'd ditched the meeting with the real estate agent, instead leaving a message that the neighbors would have the key. She hadn't even finished clearing out the house. It looked much better than it had, but it wasn't empty. She hadn't done any repairs or updates to it, either. That would cost her when—if—any offers came in.

But above all else, her biggest failure had to be how she'd messed up things with Rohn. Again.

She'd hurt him once twenty-five years ago and she'd managed to do it all over again. And this time, he'd surely hate her for it, now that he knew the truth.

It was all too much to deal with. Between lack of sleep, and the overt sadness pressing in around her, she was teetering on the edge of a breakdown. Bonnie pushed up from her seat. "I'm going to bed."

Her mother lifted a brow. "I think that's a very good idea."

At least they agreed on that point. If only Bonnie could hide away in bed forever.

She slept like the dead. It seemed even heartbreak couldn't keep her body awake after she'd pushed herself for twenty-four hours without sleep. The fading light of evening had already given way and night was creeping into her room when the sound of the doorbell broke through her slumber.

Swimming up from unconsciousness, she didn't think much about the noise, besides the fact it had disturbed her. She lay half awake, not inspired to get out from beneath the covers.

Then, she heard the familiar, deep tenor of a voice that had her sitting upright.

Rohn was in her house talking to her mother?

Bonnie flipped back the covers and swung her legs over the edge of the mattress. Her feet hit the carpeted floor. Not bothering with slippers or worrying about changing out of her oversize T-shirt and shorts, Bonnie trotted barefoot out of the bedroom and down the hall, skidding to a stop in the kitchen doorway.

There he stood, tall and strong and looking as amazing as ever. His steely gaze moved to her.

"Hey, Bonnie." He didn't sound angry. He didn't look at her with hatred.

"Rohn." Her heart pounded with hope she feared to feel. "Um, Mom, you remember Rohn Lerner, don't you? From Oklahoma. Dad had hired him that summer . . ."

All these years, she'd kept the identity of the baby's father a secret, even from her mother. Bonnie had never revealed that she'd dated Rohn. As far as her mother knew, Rohn was just the ranch hand.

That might change now though, judging by her mother's interested expression as her focus moved back and forth between Bonnie and Rohn.

"Yes, I do." All her mother's unasked questions hung heavily in the air, but that and all else paled next to the fact that Rohn had come after her.

In spite of what she'd done, he'd still come after her. Could she be that lucky that he'd forgive her?

What she did know was that it was time for complete honesty. As both her mother and Rohn watched, she said, "Mom, I told Rohn about the baby."

Her mother's eyes widened, before she hid the reaction. "Then you two probably want some privacy to talk. I'll leave you alone."

"Thank you, ma'am." Timeless, ageless, Rohn could have been eighteen again, standing in her mother's kitchen with his hat in his hand.

Bonnie's mother walked to her and enveloped her in a hug. When she pulled back, a small smile tipped up her lips. "I probably should have figured that out on my own back then, huh?"

"No. I took great pains to make sure you didn't."

"That makes me feel slightly better that I'm not a complete failure as a mother."

"You're not."

With a small smile, her mother left her alone with Rohn. Bonnie was shaking as she reached for the kitchen chair. "Want to sit?"

"I've been sitting in the truck for the last fourteen

hours so you'd think I'd say no, but I have a feeling I might want to be sitting for this conversation." Rohn pulled out the chair opposite hers and sat.

He was here to talk. She owed him at least that much. "Ask me whatever you want and I'll answer."

His brows rose. "A'ight. Why didn't you tell me you were pregnant?"

"I was going to tell you."

Rohn's skepticism was clear in his expression. He'd believe her soon enough. She swallowed before she could continue.

"That last night we were together by the river I realized I was late. I took a pregnancy test."

"And the test was positive. Obviously." Rohn prompted her to continue as, lost in her memories, she'd paused.

"Yes. I figured in the morning, when you came to work, I'd try to get you alone and tell you. And if I couldn't get to you during the day, then I'd have to wait until we saw each other alone. But I never got the chance to see you again."

"Why not?"

"I hid the used test in the trash can, buried under some other stuff. I thought no one would ever find it. But my father saw me doing it, and he found it."

She should have hid it in her room. Or waited until her father had left to go somewhere and then put it in the neighbors' trash, because against all odds, her father chose that day to look out the window just as she was sneaking it into the trash.

"So he sent you away?"

"I wish that was what happened."

Rohn reached out and took her hand in his. "Tell me."

She forced herself to look at him, tears in her eyes. "I was so scared of what he'd do. Not just to me, but to you if he ever found out."

His nostrils flared. "I could have taken care of myself, Bonnie. You should have told me."

"You didn't know him. You didn't see him that night. He was crazy. He would have killed you. I'm sure of it. I was afraid he'd kill me. He beat me. I was so scared. He was so much stronger than me. I felt so vulnerable." His fingers tightened around hers. She continued, "My mother was afraid he wasn't done. When he left, she put me on a bus to my grand-mother's house that night."

Things were better after Bonnie arrived in Phoenix. Her grandmother was like a fresh breeze in her life. A ray of sunshine cutting through the dark-ness of the past. She didn't judge her or lecture. She talked to her like an adult, and they'd made the decision about what to do together.

Then, amazingly, her mother had gotten herself out, legally. She joined them in Arizona and they lived together, three generations of women. Inde-pendent, with no need for a man in their life. Still, there wasn't a day that Bonnie didn't look over her shoulder, not believing her father would just let them both go. Not convinced, even after decades had passed, that he wouldn't come after her and finish the job he'd started so long ago.

"I do believe you. Christ, Bonnie, I'm so sorry. Why didn't you tell me when you got to your grand-mother's in Arizona, once you were safe? I would have gone over there and—"

"That's why I didn't tell you. I had to protect you."

Rohn let out a sigh. "Bonnie, your trying to protect me tore my heart out."

"I know." She stared at her hand in his, memorizing the feel of it since chances were good he'd pull away and she'd never feel his warmth again.

"And yesterday, you ran away from me again."

"I know. I'm sorry." It was pitiful that she had nothing else to say. Fleeing had become her go-to response after a lifetime of being afraid.

"Why? Your father's gone now. He can't hurt you anymore."

"I figured you hated me for what I did. I thought it would be easier for everyone if I just left."

He shook his head. "There's nothing easy about any of this."

"No, I guess not."

He rubbed his fingers over the top of her hand. "I don't hate you. I didn't then. I don't now."

She nodded and tried to hold the tears in. He didn't hate her, but he hadn't said he still loved her, either.

"Tell me about her. Our daughter."

"There's nothing to tell. They took her away as soon as she was born. I never even held her." That revelation should be the final nail in the coffin of their relationship.

"What about the family who adopted her?"

"I don't know anything about them."

"Nothing?"

She realized it sounded as if she'd handed their baby over to strangers, when that hadn't been the case. "It was a closed adoption. The adopting family is checked out by the agency, but I never knew their names, and they didn't know mine."

He sat quiet for a bit. "Maybe it's better that way."

"Maybe." Bonnie nodded. She braced herself and asked the question uppermost in her mind. The question she wasn't sure she could handle the answer to. "Can you ever forgive me?"

Rohn stood and pulled her into his arms. She held her breath waiting for the answer.

"I already have."

"Really?" She pulled back to look up, and saw the truth in his eyes.

"Yes. With one condition."

"Anything."

"Anything?" He laughed. "Maybe I need to rethink this."

"Rohn." She sighed at his joking.

He grew serious again. "No more running away from me, Bonnie. You stay and we talk it out. No matter what it's about. Promise me that."

"I promise."

"There's something else we have to talk about." He pulled back and dug into his pocket. Pulling out the ring box, he pinned her with his stare. "I want this ring to finally be on your finger. I want you in my life, as my wife."

She looked from the ring to him. "You still want me?"

"Of course, I still want you. I love you. Is that so hard to believe?" Rohn stroked a finger down her cheek. "I see I'll have to work harder to convince you. And I'd like to do it with you as my fiancée. Say yes, Bonnie Blue."

He held the ring up. She laughed through the tears. "Yes."

He wrapped his arms around her and held tight

enough to force the air from her lungs. "You know, we need to talk about how this is going to work."

"Is that why you're squeezing me so tight?"

He laughed and loosened his grip, just a little. "I figured I'd make sure you couldn't run away again this time."

"We agreed, no more running. Remember?"

"Yeah." He hugged her close again. "What would you have done if I'd come after you then? Followed you here and demanded you tell me what was wrong twenty-five years ago?"

She shook her head where it was buried against his chest. "I honestly don't know."

He sighed. "I guess it's time we stop looking backward."

"I agree. We should only look forward from now on."

"So, looking forward . . . what are we going to do? Because as much as I love you, I'm not going to be happy with us living in two different states for very long."

"Um, hi. Not to interrupt, but I might have a solution to that." Her mother's voice broke into the cocoon of Rohn's embrace.

"Mom?" Bonnie turned her head to see her mother hovering in the doorway.

"Sorry. I wasn't eavesdropping, I swear. I was just checking on you."

Bonnie cocked a brow, not believing that. "Uh-huh."

"Go on, Mrs. Martin. If you have an idea, I'd love to hear it." Rohn kept one arm around Bonnie as he turned to address her mother.

"Well, I felt a little nostalgic while Bonnie was gone. I guess I was kind of homesick for Oklahoma, so I started looking up some old friends to see who was still in town. Turns out one of my best friends growing up is now the assistant principal at the school. She says they're looking to hire a middle school teacher." Her mother's gaze moved to Bonnie. "She can set up an interview for you, if you want it."

The idea of moving back to her hometown had Bonnie's heart rate speeding. In the past that reaction had been based on fear of her father. Now it stemmed from hope, thanks to Rohn.

"There is the old house I could move back into," her mother continued.

Rohn nodded. "It's even cleaned out, thanks to all of Bonnie's hard work. Though she gave most of the furniture away, so you'll need to buy new or bring your stuff from here. I can help you move."

He looked very happy with this plan. Bonnie, on the other hand, wasn't quite so convinced this would be as easy as he made it sound. "What if I don't get the job?"

"Then you'll look for another one. Or you could take a little time off. Get used to running the ranch with me." Hope shone through his suggestion.

Waking up every day next to Rohn. Eating breakfast together in his sunny kitchen. His hired hands stopping in for their morning coffee, greeting her with a smile and a *Howdy, Miss Bonnie*. It would be easy to get used to. "I guess I could do that."

Her mother beamed a smile. "So, it's settled then? Should I call my friend and set up an interview?"

Nervousness had her stomach fluttering, but Bonnie said, "Yes."

Smiling and looking as happy as Rohn with the

plan, Bonnie's mother glanced between them. "When should I tell her to schedule it? When do you plan on heading back to Oklahoma?"

"ASAP," Rohn answered.

Bonnie laughed at his enthusiasm. "I'll be back in Oklahoma by Saturday, so I guess ask if she can set it up for next week." She glanced up at Rohn. "I have a hot date for my high school reunion. With my fiancé."

Chapter Twenty-Seven

Rohn laced his fingers through Bonnie's and felt the diamond ring she now wore. Its mere presence on her finger made him want to ditch this reunion and drive them home. There, he'd carry her up the stairs and tumble her into bed.

That would have to wait for later. Right now, they had a reunion to go to. "Ready?"

She glanced from the school, to him. "As ready as I'm going to be."

He smiled at her hesitation. There was nothing to be nervous about, in his opinion. He couldn't wait to show her off to the friends he'd lost touch with over the past few years.

He was sure Bonnie's presence on his arm wouldn't be missed by anyone—particularly not the cliquey girls who'd never given her the time of day. Prom queens came and went, but true goodness and beauty inside and out like the kind Bonnie possessed lasted forever.

"I love you." He bent to press a kiss to her lips.

"I love you, too." Her words made him smile like a

teenager. He wondered how long that reaction would last. How long it would be until he got used to it. He wouldn't mind if he felt like this for the next twenty-five years.

"Come on. Let's go inside." He tugged her toward the entrance.

It was like stepping back in time. Whoever had planned this thing had re-created their prom night twenty-five years ago perfectly. The same venue. The same decorations. The same music. Thank God the dresses were different. There wasn't a giant butt-bow in the room.

Though, if he remembered correctly, Bonnie's prom dress had been perfect. Just like her.

"Hey, Rohn!"

Rohn turned at the sound of his name being called from a distance, and saw Pete grinning and Brian lift his arm in a wave.

As they came toward him, he felt Bonnie hold on to his arm a little tighter. He glanced down at her and smiled in encouragement. Over-the-moon happy to show her off as his, he dropped a kiss on her forehead as his friends drew closer. He saw the interested looks they gave the woman with him.

"Dude, looking good." Pete grabbed Rohn in a hug that forced him to let go of Bonnie so he could reciprocate.

"You too, Pete." Aside from having less hair and more beer gut, Pete looked just as Rohn remembered from the last reunion he'd attended—the ten-year. When Pete pulled back, Brian took his place, slapping Rohn on the back with a one-armed embrace.

"I swear you haven't changed a bit, you son of a gun." Brian turned his attention to Bonnie, looking gorgeous in a dress that matched the blue of her eyes. "Except for this new addition. And who might you be?"

Rohn rolled his eyes. Brian hadn't changed a bit either. He was still an over-the-top flirt. "This is Bonnie Martin, my fiancée. You should remember her. She graduated with us . . . and grew up just down the road from you."

Pete's eyes widened. "Bonnie Martin from our class, and she's your fiancée? Dang, you're full of surprises tonight, Rohn."

Brian let out a laugh. "He sure is. But now I know why he stole that summer job at the Martins' from me the year we graduated. Did you have your eye on her even back then?"

"Yup, I sure did. It just took us a bit of time to find each other, is all." Rohn knew talking about the past had Bonnie on edge. He felt her hold on him grow tighter and decided to change the subject. "So, you know our story. What's up with you guys? You married? Kids?"

He listened to his friends run down the list of who was divorced and who was still married, who had children, and even grandchildren, until he felt Bonnie tap his arm. He leaned in to hear her over the music.

"I see my friend Melody."

"Well, let's go say hello to her." He got a little thrill thinking about Bonnie introducing him to her friend. He turned to Pete and Brian. "We'll catch up with you later."

"Sure thing." Brian looked amused as Bonnie led Rohn away, but Rohn didn't care.

Let them think she led him around. The truth

was, he'd follow her anywhere. Hell, he'd already proven that with a fourteen-hour drive to Arizona.

Bonnie's friend Melody broke into a wide smile the moment she saw Bonnie coming toward her with Rohn in tow.

She wrapped her arms around Bonnie in a hug. "It's so good to see you here. You and your date."

Bonnie smiled. "Melody, you remember Rohn from high school."

"I sure do." Melody extended her hand and Rohn took it, while she shot Bonnie a sly sideways glance. "How could I ever forget?"

"No, I guess you couldn't, could you?" Bonnie laughed. When she saw Rohn raise his brow, she said, "Melody and I used to have the same lunch period as you did senior year."

Melody leaned toward Rohn. "Bonnie had the hugest crush on you in high school."

The information had him grinning. "Oh, really?"

"Melody!" Bonnie squeaked as she shot Rohn a sideways glance. "Melody had a crush, too. On Brian."

"Did she?" Rohn laughed and tipped his head toward where his friends stood on the other side of the room. "I can bring you over to talk to him, if you want. He's single again."

"Oh, good Lord, no. I'm happily married now, but back then . . ." Laughing, Melody fanned herself. "Phew, I had a serious crush."

"We both did." Bonnie hugged Rohn closer, resting her hand on his waist.

Melody's eyes widened as she caught a glimpse of Bonnie's left hand and the diamond ring on her fourth finger. "Is that an engagement ring?"

"Yes." Bonnie glanced up at Rohn, smiling. "We're engaged."

"Oh my God." There was another hug and more squeals and all Rohn could do was watch and smile. "When?"

"Just a couple of days ago, but we're going to wait a bit to get married. My mom has to move back from Arizona. We have to sell the house there."

Rohn watched Bonnie talking—happy, relaxed, laughing—everything she should be on a night like this. She turned to shoot him a smile as she reached for his hand and laced her fingers with his, and he decided something. His number-one goal, from now until the day he died, would be to keep her as happy as she was right at this moment.

His secondary goal was to make sure they didn't wait too long to tie the knot. They'd waited long enough already to be together.

And his immediate goal was to control himself enough to not sneak her out of here and bring her home where he'd strip off that sexy-as-sin dress and do what he'd never get tired of doing with her.

As Melody talked on about something, Rohn caught the heated glance Bonnie shot him, as if she was thinking the same naughty thing he was.

He smiled. Maybe they would be sneaking off to find some privacy, after all.

Hell, he felt eighteen again when he was with her. They might as well act like it.

Read on for an excerpt from Cat Johnson's
next Midnight Cowboys novel,
coming in March!

MIDNIGHT HEAT

USA Today **and** *New York Times* **Bestselling Author
Cat Johnson**

He needs to escape . . .
Justin Skaggs is on the road to anywhere—
as long as it's far from home—
when fate throws a kindred spirit across his path.

She needs to get to Oklahoma . . .
Phoenix Montagno can't believe her luck
when she runs into the hottie from the bar.
He's the key to her getting everything
she's always wanted, but she can't tell him that.
Luckily he's not interested in learning her story
any more than he is in sharing his.

Both have secrets they don't want to share . . .
It's the perfect arrangement.
No personal details. No talking at all.
Just two strangers sharing the cab of a truck
heading in the direction they both need to go . . .
until they decide to share a bed, too.

"The Oklahoma Nights series is a must read."
—Lorelei James

"Well, look who's here. Justin Skaggs, how the hell are ya?"

Justin paused at the sound of his name, his hand still on the door he'd just pushed open. As he moved into the bar and his eyes adjusted to the dim light, he saw the guy who'd greeted him before he'd even had a chance to clear the doorway.

Accepting that there was no way around it, Justin pulled out the bar stool next to the man who'd known his family for decades. "Hey, Ray. How you been?"

"Eh, same old thing. Y'know how it is." The older man, whose clothes reeked of cigarette smoke, hacked out a raspy cough before soothing it with a swallow of his beer.

"Yup." Justin dipped his head, knowing one thing for certain—that Ray should stop smoking. He should probably stop drinking, too, if he wanted to see his grandkids grow up.

As for Ray's statement about everything being the same old thing, Justin could definitely relate. That was exactly the problem in this town—things were always the same. The same people doing the same things in the same places.

In a community that small there was no avoiding running into people he'd known for most of his life. Folks who knew him and his family's past. Even when he wanted to get away from everyone for a little bit, *especially* when he needed to get away, it seemed he couldn't.

All he'd wanted to do tonight was to be alone. His goal was to get shitfaced on some beer—or bourbon, if that's what it took—and then sleep it off in the truck in peaceful oblivion for a few hours. He obviously needed to drive farther to find a watering hole where no one knew him. Possibly across state lines, and even that might not be far enough.

Justin raised one hand to get the bartender's attention. "Bottle of light beer, please."

His original plan to consume massive amounts of the hard stuff wasn't going to play out, so he'd have a light one and then leave. One quick beer, a short good-bye, and then he'd get back in the truck and drive until he was so far away no one knew him.

"How's your momma doing?" Ray's tone was imbued with the same undercurrent of sympathy Justin had gotten used to hearing over the past two years.

"Good. Thanks." Justin hated the question he seemed to be asked everywhere he went. What could he say to answer it?

Certainly not the truth—that his mother, a formerly vibrant woman, was now broken. A complete and utter mess.

His mother was as good as a woman who'd lost

both her husband and her oldest son in the span of less than a decade could be.

Both men had been taken way too young, his father ten years ago by a massive coronary and his brother more recently by war.

Some days she didn't get out of bed. Justin would come home from a full day of work at the Double L Ranch and find her in the same pajamas she'd been in when he'd left that morning. Still sitting in the same spot, either on the sofa in front of the television or, on really bad days, in her bed.

Other days, few and far between, she'd made a small attempt at normalcy. He'd come home and find her cleaning or cooking. But those days had become less and less frequent. More often than not, he'd be the one making dinner when he got home from the ranch at night.

As the man of the house—the only one left—Justin did his best to support his mother. He'd bring her food and coax her to eat when she didn't want to. He'd give her space when she looked like she needed that or an ear to bend when that was what she needed most.

But some days, like today, Justin couldn't deal with his own life, never mind his mother's. Lord help him, because he felt like shit when he did it, but those were the days he'd disappear. Fire up the engine in his brother's old truck and drive.

As the bartender delivered the beer Justin had ordered, the door swung open, letting the light of the afternoon inside the sanctuary-like darkness of the bar.

Justin raised the bottle to his lips and drew in a long swallow of the icy cold brew. It slid down his throat, washing away at least a little bit of his stress. If Ray remained quiet, and the bartender kept the cold ones coming, maybe he could stay and hang here for a bit.

"Hey, is that Jeremy's truck I saw parked outside?" The newcomer's statement was like nails on a chalkboard, erasing whatever calm Justin had managed to achieve.

"You driving Jeremy's truck?" Ray asked Justin.

Justin glanced from the guy who'd just entered—Rod, the old-timer who owned the lumberyard—to Ray.

"I like to run it once in a while." He downed another two gulps of beer, bringing the bottle closer to empty and the time nearer the moment he could leave.

Rod pulled out the bar stool next to Justin. With him on one side and Ray on the other, Justin was penned in. Trapped in polite conversation when all he wanted was to be an antisocial bastard.

"If you're ever looking to sell it, give me a call. I always did like that truck." Ray's offer was the last thing Justin could take.

Jaw clenched, Justin nodded. "I'll keep that in mind."

Jeremy was dead. His truck was one of the last things left on Earth that had mattered to him. He'd loved that damned truck. Justin couldn't sell it any more than he could bring himself to take it over and drive it as his, full-time.

Didn't they understand that?

He said he drove it to keep the engine in shape, but the truth was Justin got in it when he wanted to feel close to his brother. And, truth be told, sometimes when he wished he could chuck it all and join his brother, wherever that might be. Even after going to church his entire life, he wasn't so convinced Heaven existed. At least not exactly in the way the preacher said it did.

One more gulp and the beer was empty. Justin stepped off the bar stool and dug in his pocket for his wallet.

"You going?" Ray asked.

"Yup."

"Put that beer on my tab." Rod directed the statement to the bartender.

"Thanks, but I got it." Justin threw a bill on the bar. "See y'all later."

He didn't wait for change from the bill he'd tossed down, or good-byes from the two men. Instead he yanked the door open and stepped out into the evening air. Only then—outside and away from the oppressive presence of people—did he feel like he could breathe again.

Shit. He wasn't fit for being around any other living thing today. Maybe he should pick up a six-pack, drive to a field somewhere, sit in the truck, and drink it.

It was coming up on two years since Jeremy had died. Justin knew he'd have to be there for his mother on that day. Hell, for the whole month probably. But now, with over a month left to go before that grim anniversary, he'd give himself this time to wallow in his grief.

Justin would let himself get angry, too. At God for letting a good man die too damn young. At the bastards who'd planted that roadside bomb. Even at Jeremy for reenlisting when he could have been home safe instead of in Afghanistan.

He slid into the driver's seat and stared down at the set of keys in his hand. The truck key. The house key. The key to the padlock on the tool shed in the backyard. Some mysterious key that he didn't recognize; he was starting to wonder if even Jeremy had known what it opened.

Justin ran his thumb over the smooth metal of the ring. It was the same key ring Jeremy had carried in his pocket since the day he'd bought the truck. He'd carried it until the fake leather tag on it that read *Chevy* had worn and frayed around the edges. He'd carried it until he'd deployed that final time.

Knocking himself out of the daze he'd slipped into, Justin reached for the radio and hit the power button. The same station that had been playing the last time Jeremy drove the truck before leaving blared to life.

Justin couldn't bring himself to change the station, just like he couldn't throw out the stack of fast-food napkins stuffed in the glove compartment or the two-year-old, half-empty tin of chew Jeremy had left in the console under the dash.

He turned the key in the ignition and the engine fired to life, rumbling beneath him. It would be better to run it more often than the half a dozen or so times a year that he did. That would keep the tires from getting flat spots or worse, dry rot.

He should be pushing it, too. Taking longer trips at highway speeds to get the fluids circulating and blow the carbon out of the engine.

But there were the ghosts of too many memories in this truck. It hurt to drive it. Then again, it hurt when he didn't drive it, so what the hell did it matter?

It would be good for both him and the truck to gun it. Open up the engine and let the mud fly.

Decision made, Justin threw the truck in reverse, backed out of the space and shifted into drive.

He hit the accelerator, peeling out on the gravel of the lot as he turned onto the main road, heading in the direction of the interstate. He would hit the highway for a few miles . . . or fifty. Let the road heal him for a couple of hours.

Escaping, running away from his problems, was no way to deal with them. He knew that. Any psychologist would tell him that. The grief counselor his mother had agreed to go to a couple of times sure as hell would have.

Justin didn't care what the hell the experts said. He had to do what he had to do. If getting out of town or getting drunk—possibly both—was what he needed to do, then that's what he was going to do. The experts be damned.

Getting away for a little while sounded real good. Finding himself a woman wouldn't hurt, either . . .

More from Bestselling Author
JANET DAILEY

Calder Storm	0-8217-7543-X	$7.99US/$10.99CAN
Close to You	1-4201-1714-9	$5.99US/$6.99CAN
Crazy in Love	1-4201-0303-2	$4.99US/$5.99CAN
Dance With Me	1-4201-2213-4	$5.99US/$6.99CAN
Everything	1-4201-2214-2	$5.99US/$6.99CAN
Forever	1-4201-2215-0	$5.99US/$6.99CAN
Green Calder Grass	0-8217-7222-8	$7.99US/$10.99CAN
Heiress	1-4201-0002-5	$6.99US/$7.99CAN
Lone Calder Star	0-8217-7542-1	$7.99US/$10.99CAN
Lover Man	1-4201-0666-X	$4.99US/$5.99CAN
Masquerade	1-4201-0005-X	$6.99US/$8.99CAN
Mistletoe and Molly	1-4201-0041-6	$6.99US/$9.99CAN
Rivals	1-4201-0003-3	$6.99US/$7.99CAN
Santa in a Stetson	1-4201-0664-3	$6.99US/$9.99CAN
Santa in Montana	1-4201-1474-3	$7.99US/$9.99CAN
Searching for Santa	1-4201-0306-7	$6.99US/$9.99CAN
Something More	0-8217-7544-8	$7.99US/$9.99CAN
Stealing Kisses	1-4201-0304-0	$4.99US/$5.99CAN
Tangled Vines	1-4201-0004-1	$6.99US/$8.99CAN
Texas Kiss	1-4201-0665-1	$4.99US/$5.99CAN
That Loving Feeling	1-4201-1713-0	$5.99US/$6.99CAN
To Santa With Love	1-4201-2073-5	$6.99US/$7.99CAN
When You Kiss Me	1-4201-0667-8	$4.99US/$5.99CAN
Yes, I Do	1-4201-0305-9	$4.99US/$5.99CAN

Available Wherever Books Are Sold!

Check out our website at www.kensingtonbooks.com.